The Rogue's Heiress

You are holding a reproduction of an original work that is in the public domain in the United States of America, and possibly other countries. You may freely copy and distribute this work as no entity (individual or corporate) has a copyright on the body of the work. This book may contain prior copyright references, and library stamps (as most of these works were scanned from library copies). These have been scanned and retained as part of the historical artifact.

This book may have occasional imperfections such as missing or blurred pages, poor pictures, errant marks, etc. that were either part of the original artifact, or were introduced by the scanning process. We believe this work is culturally important, and despite the imperfections, have elected to bring it back into print as part of our continuing commitment to the preservation of printed works worldwide. We appreciate your understanding of the imperfections in the preservation process, and hope you enjoy this valuable book.

Gallon
NCW

ANGELICA

The Rogue's Heiress

A NOVEL

BY

TOM GALLON

Author of "Cruise of the Make-Believes," "Tinman," "The Lion,"
"Tatterley," "Meg the Lady," etc.

G. W. DILLINGHAM COMPANY
PUBLISHERS   **NEW YORK**

Copyright, 1910, *By*
G. W. DILLINGHAM COMPANY

THE ROGUE'S HEIRESS

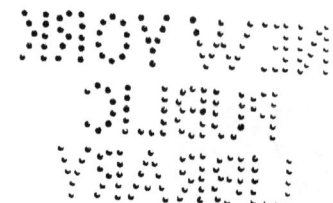

CONTENTS

CHAPTER		PAGE
I.—The Man Without a Penny		7
II.—Half a Million of Money		23
III.—Enter Miss Money-Bags		48
IV.—The Hatching of the Plot		70
V.—The Gathering of the Enemy		93
VI.—Angelica Goes out to Supper		115
VII.—The New Sancho Panza		129
VIII.—The Friend of the Family		151
IX.—Daniel Street Comes to Life		172
X.—The Midnight Oil		191
XI.—The Post-Box		216
XII.—Angelica Says "Yes"		235
XIII.—A Chancery Puzzle		252
XIV.—Angelica Wakes up		265
XV.—"For This Was Love!"		284
XVI.—Joshua Flattery Reads the Stars		301

NEW YORK
PUBLIC
LIBRARY

THE ROGUE'S HEIRESS

CHAPTER I

THE MAN WITHOUT A PENNY

"WHY the devil don't you keep quiet? How can a man sleep with that row going on?"

The tall man jerked his shabby overcoat over his chest, and twisted himself peevishly farther into the corner of the stone seat. The little man in shabby black abruptly ceased a monotonous chanting in which he had been indulging for the last five minutes, started to his feet, and stepped out on to the pavement to look at the man who had spoken. That action was necessary, because there was a seat on either side of the tall statue that upreared itself above them; and the man in the shabby overcoat occupied one of those seats, and himself the other.

"Beg pardon, I'm sure, sir," said the little man, peering nervously at the other. "Wouldn't 'ave upset yer for the world. I was wot yer might call murmurin' a bit of a toon, to cheer meself up a bit."

"That devil's march of yours was enough to make a

man cross the road and pitch himself into the river to get away from it," said the tall man, with an indefinite wave of one hand towards the lights reflected in the river at the other side of the Embankment. "However—the matter is ended," he added, with something of an air. "God knows I bear no ill-will, even towards a man who can make the row you were making. You ought to give it up, my friend, or take lessons."

The little man flogged himself with his arms, though quite without enthusiasm, and stamped his feet on the pavement to warm them. "You're one of those," he said, "that will 'ave 'is little joke. I can see that with just 'alf a eye."

"Now you're dancing," murmured the other fretfully. "You annoy me—and you're not the only one in a damned badly managed world. Don't stand in front of me; go away and be quiet."

The little man made a sort of apologetic dip with his head, and disappeared again to that corner seat from which he had emerged. Singing must have been second nature to the man; for presently he broke out again with his chant; remembered himself hurriedly at the sound of a restless movement on the other side of the statue, and burst out with an apology.

"Sorry again, sir, I give yer my word," he said, striving to peer round the front of the statue. "Bit of a 'abit with me; I fergot meself. W'en a man ain't too well off—an' w'en the thing 'e's sittin' on is precious 'ard, I always feel that a bit of a toon——"

"Good Lord!—when you're not singing, you're dancing, and when you're not performing either of those abominations you're chattering. Come out here; let's have a look at you!"

It was said in such a tone of authority that though, like himself, the man who gave the order was obviously a vagrant, the little man in black obeyed with alacrity. He stepped in front of the lounger on the other seat, and once again gave that dip to his head that seemed his method of salutation. In doing that, and raising himself again, he gave the other man an opportunity to observe him narrowly.

He was considerably below the average height, and he was thin and pinched and starved in appearance. He wore, incongruously enough, a black frock-coat much too long for him; his throat was muffled up in a huge, loose, black wrapper. A bowler-hat was perched upon his head and pulled well down on to his ears; his face was clean-shaven, save for side-whiskers cut off neatly to the line of his mouth. Altogether a shabby, rather mean-looking little creature, with the air of one struggling hopelessly after a disappearing respectability.

"Why—what the devil brings you out to sleep in the streets?" demanded the other man, after his scrutiny. "You look decent enough."

"As things go, sir—yes," answered the little man, rubbing his hand over his chin. "And though not wishin' to rub it in, I would respectfully say that I ain't sleepin' in the streets."

"Nor letting anybody else, if you get the chance," retorted the other. "What are you out for—exercising your voice?"

"You will 'ave your joke again, sir," said the little man,

with a laugh. "Truth to speak, sir, I've on'y just come off work; an' as I'd bin asleep all day, I didn't feel like goin' to bed. So I left my things at my place, an' came out to sniff the air. Late night for me—or early mornin', as you might say, sir; I didn't finish till after three."

"And what are you, most respectable person?" asked the other, though evidently not with any real interest in the answer.

"I'm a waiter, sir—odd waiter."

"Mighty odd, I should say," retorted the tall man. "As you seem a cheery soul, and may be perhaps a little interesting, come and sit down here and talk to me. Sleep refuses to spread her supposedly soft wings over me, and so you shall talk to me instead." He shifted slightly on the seat to make way for the other man, though still retaining the larger part for himself. "That is, of course, always supposing that you have no objection to sitting near me."

"Bless your soul, sir—not me," answered the little man, seating himself delicately on the edge of the stone seat. "Most kind of you to take notice of anybody like me, sir. Most kind indeed."

"I observe—without the least satisfaction—that you address me continually as 'sir,'" said the tall man. "Is that a habit—or a compliment to me?"

"Bit of both, sir, I should say; though if I don't know a gent w'en I see one, after the many I've met, I should surprise meself. Moment ever you spoke to me——"

"My first observation was scarcely gentlemanly," broke in the other, with a short laugh.

"I says to meself—'A gent, if ever there was one, brought low by undeserved misfortune,' I says to meself——"

"You're chattering again," broke in the other peevishly. "If you said that to yourself, you were quite wrong. All the misfortune, my good friend, that has ever fallen upon me has been well deserved, and don't you forget it. I'm not preaching and I'm not whining; I happen to be speaking the bare and brutal truth. Just have a look at the gentleman up above us."

The little man started, and turned, and peered round the statue; got up, and looked at the sky, and then at the seat he had so recently vacated. Then he looked inquiringly at the other man. "The gentleman up above, sir?" he questioned.

"Idiot!—I mean the impressive-looking gentleman carved in stone above us," exclaimed the other. "Get up and read his name. I suppose you can read?"

"We 'ave to in my profession," said the little man.

He got up, and stood in front of the statue, and stared up at it; began to spell the name out with some difficulty. "'Iz—Iz—ambard'—it's a rummy name, sir—ain't it?"

"'Izambard Kingdom Brunel,'" said the man lolling on the seat. "Obviously you can't read half as well as you suggest," he added.

"It's a twister of a name," pleaded the little man. "He must have looked about for it a bit."

"At the time it was given to him he probably was unable to protest," said the other man. "Look at him carefully, my friend—observe Virtue writ large upon him—Determination in the very lift of his chin—Unconquerable Force stamped upon his brow. In his day, Waiter, he did great things, and built great things; and when, in the course of nature, he could build no more, they buried him respectably, and wrote things about him—and stuck up a stone image lest people should forget him. Fine-looking old chap—eh?"

"Did you 'appen to know 'im, sir?" asked the waiter, after a long and msot respectful look at the statue.

"Know him, you fool—how should I? He was before my time. I was led past him once—in his present stony condition—by an impressive parent, who desired to point out to me what I might come to, in the marble sense, if I was only good and worked hard; as I didn't like the look of our friend up above, that was probably the cause of my original downfall. And now, for the Lord's sake, get that twist out of your neck, and let our friend alone, and come and sit down and talk to me. 'Pon my word, I think you're the most original thing I've come across for years."

The little man seated himself again on the very edge of the stone seat, and squeezed his hands, with palms together, between his knees, and looked round critically at the other man. Something in the face attracted him, as it had attracted others before him; he looked again.

The haggard face of a man who might have been thirty, but was more probably thirty-five; a face that would have been handsome, but for a look of restless recklessness that gave an odd twist to the mouth and hardened the features generally. For the rest, he wore his shabby clothes well, and it would have been as incongruous to anyone who happened to notice him as it appeared to his companion that he should be apparently homeless in London in the early hours of the morning.

"It seems to me," said the little man, after a pause, "that it would be a deal more interesting if you was to talk to me than what it'd be if I was to talk to you. I ain't nobody, but jist a odd-job waiter—with not so many odd jobs as I could wish for, and makin' wot you might call a bit of a scratch livin' at it. Whereas, a gentleman like yerself——"

He spread out his hands, and shrugged his shoulders, to suggest that you might expect almost anything from such a man. The other, seemingly a little pleased, laughed softly in his throat; and then suddenly bent towards the other man, and dropped a hand on his shoulder, and spoke in his ear.

"So you might expect almost anything from a—gentleman like me—eh?" he asked, becoming aware of the fact that the little waiter's eyes were twisted round in his direction furtively. "And there you're right, Waiter; there you show a true understanding of the world and of men. Little odd-job man, scraping a scanty living out of your poor game—have you ever been in jail?"

The furtive eyes were turned fully upon him now; they were startled eyes. "N—no, sir," he quavered. "That is to say—more by good luck than anything else, p'r'aps," he added hastily, as a concession to the other man.

"Well, I have," answered the tall man, still keeping his grip of the other's shoulder. "I warned you, you know, that it might not be wise to sit on the same seat with me; now you know why I said it. There's a taint upon me—something that has eaten into the very soul of me, and branded me, and left its mark. I've had three years of it —three hateful, brutal years in hell. And it is written in the scheme of things, as surely as though you saw it written there in the skies above us, that I shall go back—shall drop down into hell again. There is a line somewhere—in Milton, I think—

>Long is the way
>And hard, that out of hell leads up to light,

and it is a way that I am scarcely likely ever to climb."

There was a pause, while the little man sat staring straight in front of him with a troubled face. "P'r'aps," he ventured at last, "p'r'aps you was innercent?"

"Don't cheat yourself; I was very sordidly guilty," said the other. "I had finished up a fine gentlemanly career of utter recklessness, with no hand ever stretched out to stay me, and plenty of hands ready and willing to push me on the path I had chosen; I had finished up all that by appropriating someone's name, and with it a good deal of someone's money. They've an awkward way of calling it forgery."

"Well—there's some of us that gits tempted more than others," said the other, after a pause. "Anybody like me, that goes to places where even the spoons ain't silver, don't git tempted, excep' p'r'aps in the matter of 'alf a bottle of clarit or a few sandwiches. W'ereas, a gent like you——"

Again he made that movement of his hands and shoulders which seemed to excuse in the other man so very much. And again for a time there was silence between them. The little waiter had almost made up his mind to excuse himself, and to get away; and yet was tempted to the mere suggestion of the romantic side of what he had heard to remain, when his companion spoke.

"I've astonished and shocked you," the tall man said. "I've shaken you to the depths of your waiting soul; in all probability you'll dream about me. You brought it on yourself in the first place, you know."

"I ain't complainin'," said the other mildly. "An' I don't suppose I shall dream about you; I ain't given to it. Moment ever my 'ead touches the piller I'm as fast as fast could be till I've 'ad my sleep out. No, sir; I shall say to meself, w'en I thinks about this 'ere, I shall say—'Joshua Flattery, you've 'ad a talk with a real gent, wot's 'ad 'is bit of misfortune, same as might come to the rest of us!' That's what I shall say."

"Is that your name—Joshua Flattery?"

"That's it, sir. Commonly known as 'Josh.'"

"It's as odd and queer as you are," said the other. "However, not to be outdone in courtesy, let me introduce myself. It is not likely that we shall rub shoulders again, Mr. Flattery; you may live to remember who it was you talked with—though God knows that doesn't matter a brass farthing to anyone. My name is Oliver Rackham."

"Glad to know you, sir."

"You're not a bit glad; you're a little frightened," said Rackham, with a laugh. "If you'd known who I was, you'd never have seated yourself here with me; you'd rather have taken your chance with the vagabonds on the seats over there." He jerked his hand towards the other side of the Embankment. "Hadn't you better count over what you have in your pockets," he went on bitterly, "to be certain that I have not robbed you? It's my trade, you know."

"Once doin' of a thing don't make it a trade," urged Flattery, after an uncomfortable pause. "And God knows it's brought you down low enough, sir, if you'll excuse the liberty of the remark."

"There was a time, Mr. Flattery, when I used to sup at one of the big hotels just behind us; I used to choose a table that was in the window, so that I might look out over the river." He spoke almost as if to himself, and now he had drooped forward a little, so that his elbows were on his knees, and his chin propped in his palms. "And fair and dainty women used to sup there with me—best not to talk of them, Flattery."

"Ain't there no goin' back, sir? Spite of that bit o' poetry you mentioned jist now—ain't there no goin' back?"

"My dear Joshua Flattery, I have been trying, for something like a fortnight, to go back," answered Rackham. "I came out of hell into the free light of day; and I was so glad that I swore that never again would I touch any of the old things I had known. I would dig—I would starve in the streets—I would do all things that were noble and fine and honest. But it's a tough job, Joshua Flattery, to do that, when no one wants to help you."

"It's a 'ard world," said the little waiter, after a pause.

"I couldn't dig—because no one wanted a man of my type to dig; the thing was suspicious on the face of it. I didn't like the idea of selling matches; it seemed such an endless business before one got any profit out of it—and it led to nothing. One couldn't take out a patent for selling matches, and get it taken up by somebody, and make a few thousands out of it. So I just—just drifted; and to-night I find myself slipping slowly back on the inevitable road that may lead me down into hell again."

The limited experience of Mr. Joshua Flattery was useless in such a matter as this; it was something at once far above him and far below him. In his humble way he had scrambled on from day to day, glad to think that he had a bed and a certain amount of food—and so was safe. This was a problem he did not understand.

"I made fine resolutions, Flattery, as to what I would do, and how I would begin afresh; and all the resolutions crumble into nothing before the naked fact that I am homeless to-night, and that I haven't a penny in the world. I'm a bigger, stronger man than you, and I have muscles trained in a public school and at the 'Varsity; I might seize hold of you, and shake out of you any stray money you have; and so keep the wolf from off my heels for another few hours. But what would be the good? In the first place, you would probably squeal, and there would arrive the inevitable policeman. And I have a record that would be brought up against me."

"P'liceman or no p'liceman, I don't believe you'd do it," said the other stoutly.

Rackham looked round at him with a queer light in his eyes. "Thank you, Mr. Flattery," he said; "I don't think I should. I should have fallen pretty low to touch a friend."

"Thank *you*, sir," said the little man, sitting more upright.

"You're the cleanest, funniest thing I've met in years, Joshua Flattery—and you've done me good. I, who have tipped a few of your craft with money I'd be glad enough to have to-night, am grateful to you that you have sat beside me, and talked to me, in this damned howling wilderness of London. You're a nice thing, Flattery—and I'm glad to have met you. Good-night."

He got to his feet, and was preparing to move away, when the little man, who had risen also, sidled a little nearer to him. He spoke for a moment almost as one expecting a blow; he shrank a little as he looked up at Oliver Rackham.

"This is a night, sir, as I ain't likely to fergit," he said. "What with the bit o' poetry throwed in as a matter of ordinary conversation, without no effort, as you might say, and what with the givin' of names almost as if I'd bin a gent—the givin' of names from one to the other so free an' natural—it ain't as if I should be likely to fergit it. What I was agoin' to say, sir, was that about this time I generally indulges in a cup of cawfee—an' I thought perhaps——"

Rackham stood with his hands on his hips, looking down at the other man, who was nervously drawing his hand backwards and forwards over his lips. There was a long pause, during which the little delicate matter hung in the balance; then Rackham, with a whimsical bow to the little waiter, held out his hand.

"Mr. Joshua Flattery, you are but part of the mad business; I accept you for what you are. But I am chilled to the bone, and I want something such as I have craved (to my undoing) before this; I want something other than coffee. I'll take you at your word, if you'll be good enough, under the very extraordinary circumstances of the case, to tell me frankly—holding up your hand meanwhile in face of the highly respectable statue of Izambard Kingdom Brunel—exactly what you have in your pocket."

Instantly Mr. Flattery, as though this were quite a solemn rite, raised his hand towards the statue, and answered, "A matter of four shillings—to say nothing of a copper or two over, sir."

"Joshua Flattery, you are a millionaire," said Rackham, with a laugh. "I daresay we can find an early house in the neighborhood of Covent Garden; in any case, it will be easier and more cheerful than this spot. Come along! I wouldn't have missed meeting you for the world."

"I shan't never forget this night—or p'r'aps I might say this mornin'," said Joshua Flattery, highly elated. "I on'y wish I could do summink more for you than a mere matter of 'aving the compliment passed me of takin' a glass with a gentleman like yerself."

Rackham stopped in the street, and faced the other man. "You have four shillings, to say nothing of a matter of a copper or two that seems to be scarcely worth counting," he said. "Answer me a question, and I will tell you if it is possible for you to do me any further service. In the first place, have I done you any harm—morally or intellectually—to-night?"

"If anythink, sir, I think I might almost say you've uplifted me," answered Joshua Flattery.

"Good!" exclaimed the other with great seriousness.

"That is at least something to my credit. Now for another question—and an important one. When this mine of wealth is exhausted, have you any prospect for the future; are there any more odd jobs waiting for you?"

"Lor' bless you, sir, any number," answered the little man. "There ain't nothink fer to-morrer, unless anythink should turn up unexpected; but the night after I've got a job o' waitin' at a dancin' academy. Very good job too, sir, though not anythink to speak of in the way of tips. Been there often, sir; Professor Dorn's Academy—'Amlyn Street, Tottenham Court Road."

"What street?" Rackham asked idly.

"'Amlyn Street—H-a-m-l-y-n, sir. Called by some a mere cheap 'op, sir. But I've seen some good darncin'— though it is on'y eighteenpence single, an' 'alf a dollar for double ticket for ladies an' gents. Refreshments throwed in; but you've got to look slippy not to give 'em too much, an' to watch that they don't come too often."

"Well, regarding the fact that you have money in hand, and that you have a definite engagement at Professor Dorn's Academy in Hamlyn Street, Tottenham Court Road, in a matter of a few hours, comparatively speaking, I think I may venture to suggest that you shall do me a further favor," said Rackham. He carried the thing off with something of an air; yet he spoke with diffidence. "You shall lend me a shilling."

"Sir, you make me a proud man," said the little waiter, diving his hand instantly into his pocket. "Here it is, sir —and I wish it was twenty, if on'y for the sake of the members of my callin' that you 'ave tipped in bygorn days. You are truly welcome, sir."

Oliver Rackham hesitated for a moment, then he took the coin, and spun it in the air, and dropped it into his pocket. It was almost in a shamefaced way that he carried out the rest of his bargain—striding along a little in front of the queer figure of Joshua Flattery, who trotted humbly enough in the rear. And so they came to one of those early houses, the bars of which were crowded already with rough market men—at work before London was well awake.

"Should we meet again, Mr. Flattery, I will repay you," said Rackham, as he drained his glass at one gulp; while Joshua Flattery, for his part, sipped his more delicately, and with eyes of respect upon his companion. "It is quite unlikely, I fear, that we shall meet; but you will have the satisfaction of knowing that for a night at least—perhaps for longer—you have saved a poor devil from the river."

"If I may make so bold, sir—if you would on'y think of that bit of poetry, an' would give up sich thoughts, you might come out on top yet, sir," suggested Joshua.

"You can dismiss any such idea, just as you dismiss any other thought of me, when I leave this place, and we part," said Rackham. "If there was ever anything fine in me it's gone; this thing that I do to-night, even though it be the borrowing of a mere shilling, is but the beginning of the sorry, stupid end. That's nothing to you, and you don't understand."

They came out of the place together, and for a moment stood before its doors, in that light which was neither the light of dawn nor of the lamps that feebly flared through it. Then, with a whimsical raising of his hand to the brim of his hat, and a smile, Oliver Rackham turned and strode away—going, is it were, into a world that must presently, in the imagination of the little waiter, swallow him up.

Remembering that, Mr. Joshua Flattery stood looking after him wistfully, until the corner was turned, and the tall figure was out of sight. Then, with a little sigh, Joshua Flattery turned away, and went off to his lodging.

CHAPTER II

HALF A MILLION OF MONEY

"I WILL not go back!"

That was what Oliver Rackham had told himself, over and over again; and he meant to stick to it. In bitterness of spirit he had fought out his battle with himself; he had determined, as many a stronger man has done before him (and Rackham was by no means a strong man), that he would shut down a gate hard and fast upon that part of his life that was done with, and would begin again. With that resolution he had come out of prison, with the small gratuity in his pockets that decent conduct had earned for him; and it had taken a fortnight to wear the resolution thin until it came to snapping-point.

Now, as he turned the corner of the street in the grey light of the morning, with Joshua Flattery's shilling in his pocket, the resolution that had worn thin was strengthened a little, and might perhaps last for another day. He felt a little light-headed with the drink he had had on an empty stomach; he would get food, and adjust the balance of things.

"I won't go back!"

That was the miserable part of it: that by humbling himself a little he could step back, in some degree, into the easy things of life. There were those who would pity him, even while they tried to hide their contempt for the man who has been found out, and had been held up to public obloquy in a court of law; there were those who might be willing to forget, temporarily at least, what the man had done, and remember what he had suffered. He could go back, and stretch out pleading hands, and get assistance.

But even with that shilling in his pocket he felt that he ought to play the game—felt it in a weak way, as one who has suffered, and is tired, and has been broken a little on the cruel wheel of life. Something might turn up before the twelve pennies were exhausted; out of this great, rich world of London something might stoop to him or rise to him, and help him to help himself.

He got some food, and felt more sure than ever that the resolution he had made could not now change. Moreover, the food was cheap, for he got it in a cheap place; he blushed a little when he left a halfpenny upon the table for the slatternly girl who had waited upon him; it seemed so very little, and yet was much in comparison with the price he had paid for his food. When he came out of the place, and began to move away listlessly through the streets— unconsciously forming one of that great army that forever waits for something to turn up—the greatest craving he had was for tobacco.

On his first day of freedom he had bought a cigar—and then another. After three years they had been wonderful; he had not understood what tobacco meant before. He smoked each of them down to the very last, when they were foul and bitter to the taste; after that he had not dared to afford any more. Now, with the little money in his pocket, he wondered how best he could expend a little of it on that which he craved.

To buy a pipe was out of the question; even the cheapest cigar was prohibitive. It resolved itself at last into a question of a packet of the cheapest cigarettes; and those were gone in no time at all.

The day wore itself away in that miserable wandering, just as other days had done; and night was approaching. The days had always been easy, because one could wander about, and look at the people, and sit on a bench; but the nights were horrible. As darkness fell there began the long line of questioning thoughts as to where one should sleep; whether in this place one would get cleaner company, or whether in this other place one would get no company at all, and might remain blissfully undisturbed. After all, he thought, it might be well if he went back to that place on the Embankment under the statue of Brunel, where he had met Joshua Flattery.

But that would not do; Joshua Flattery might be there. Confound the little fool!—with his talk of jobs, and all his silly chatter. Did he know what he had done, in lending a gentleman money—lending him, perhaps, some extra tip he had got for waiting upon another gentleman? No—a thousand times, no; he could not go back to that resting place again.

Thrift is a rare virtue, and the less money one has the more recklessly is it spent. The remaining coppers in Oliver Rackham's pocket melted away like snow before the sun. Now he was hungry, and more than once he was thirsty; and when it came to a matter of two pennies left he realized that they were practically worthless. Fate, he told himself, had been too strong for him, and would be too strong always. The resolution that had worn out to a very fine thread indeed snapped suddenly.

"I must go back!"

Having said that, and knowing now that it had come to be an inevitable thing, he started off. It was about the time that, under ordinary circumstances, he would have been looking for some place in which to pass the night; now the necessity for that was gone. He doubted, indeed, if he had ever seriously contemplated passing another night in the streets; for, with that weak declaration of the breaking of his resolution, he saw suddenly that his wandering feet had brought him into the very neighbourhood towards which his wandering thoughts had been tending all day.

He was in Westminster, and the great clock-tower loomed huge above him. He had not been in that neighborhood since one memorable night when, coming out of the place towards which he was now going, he had realized, in a dull, half-drunken way, that this was the last night of all, and that by to-morrow the hand of the law would be laid upon him, and the sorry game would be finished. He had laughed then, and had felt that he would play the game like a gentleman to the end; perhaps had even succeeded in doing so. For though, as he had said, the brand and taint of the prison were upon him, they had not quite eradicated something of the fighting spirit in the man that was deeper and better than his weakness.

He hesitated for a little time outside the great building; then pulled himself together with a jerk, and stepped in. For a moment he half decided to climb the stairs; then set his lips a little grimly, and advanced to the lift. The man standing before it looked at him, but made no attempt to move.

"Third floor," said Rackham sharply.

"What name might you be wanting?" demanded the man, with his hand upon the gate.

"Are you usually so suspicious of visitors here?" demanded Rackham, with a sudden savage light in his eyes. "You insolent devil!—for nothing at all I'd open that gate and pitch you down your own lift shaft. I want Mr. Horace Ventoul."

"He's not in," said the man sulkily.

"I presume his man's at home; in any case, I'll wait in his rooms," said Rackham.

The man opened the gate of the lift, and Rackham stepped in. He was aware when they reached the third floor that the man kept the lift there for a moment or two, while the visitor strode down the corridor and set his thumb against the electric bell; he burned with the shame of it. Somebody should pay a price for this in the time that was coming; perhaps it might be Ventoul.

The door was opened, and a stolid-looking man-servant stared out at him. This was a thing to be dealt with promptly; the matter was getting on his nerves. Rackham stepped into the hall, with a nod to the man.

"Ah!—Wood—I hear that Mr. Ventoul is not in. When do you expect him?"

The man did not answer; he simply stared at the visitor aghast. To Rackham it was as though he could see clearly through the placid forehead of the man, and could read what was passing in his mind. He spoke impatiently.

"What the deuce are you staring like that for? Have you lost your wits?" he demanded. "If Mr. Ventoul is likely to be in this evening, I'll wait for him."

He made a movement towards the door of that room he remembered so well; the man-servant barred the way. "I don't think Mr. Ventoul would like——" he began.

Rackham's eyes were dangerous, although he laughed. "Stand out of the way!" he said; and walked straight into the room.

He seated himself in a deep chair, and looked about the room. Nothing was changed; familiar scenes in that place sprang up before him. He had lounged in this very chair, and had talked and played far into the night with various men; there were the cigars, and the decanters and siphons in the same place he remembered. He got up quickly at the sight of them, and opened one of the boxes, and stretched out his hand to take a cigar. Then he drew back, and laughed, and closed the box again. He was half-way back to the chair when, with a frown, he turned and strode back to the sideboard. He took out a cigar, and fiercely bit the end off; lighted it, blowing out the smoke in great clouds. Then he poured out a whiskey and soda, and walked across to the chair again with it in his hand. He seated himself on the arm of the chair, and looked up at a portrait on the wall before him. A portrait of Horace Ventoul.

The portrait was that of an alert, lively looking man of about his own age. That is to say, the face was alert and lively, in the sense of certain deeply cut lines down the cheeks and about the mouth, and in a certain thrusting forward of the face with its rather pointed nose; but the eyes were contradictory, in that they were quiet and almost slumbrous in their expression. One would have said almost that the face was that of a man forever acting a part, and yet never acutely feeling it.

"I wonder what you'll think, my dear and charming Horace, when you come in and find your old friend drinking your whiskey and soda and smoking your Havanas?" said Rackham mockingly to the portrait. "When I think of what you've probably been doing these three years, and what I've been doing—I could throw this glass at the ugly, smiling face of you, you dog! When I think of what you did, in the way of pushing me down that road I was willing enough to travel, I could cut your face in two; I could take you by the throat, and squeeze you, till I saw fear come in those eyes, and could hear you gasp out a prayer that I—I wouldn't spoil your collar! Instead of which, my prosperous one—I drink to you!"

He fitted the action to the word, and drained his glass. He looked at the glass approvingly, and went across the room, with the cigar stuck in the corner of his mouth, and mixed again for himself. The stuff seemed to give him courage for what he had in hand; with a chuckle of satisfaction he began to pour out a third. He was doing that when the door opened, and the man of the portrait came in.

He was so like the portrait, which was just above his head as he stood in the doorway of the room, peering in at his visitor, that the thing struck Oliver Rackham, leaning against the sideboard with the cigar in his mouth and the glass in his hand. He gave a mocking salutation to the man in the doorway.

"Hullo! I'm not drunk—but by the Lord there are two of you! A little more to the left—and I get the light on both your ugly faces at the same time. And you haven't altered a bit, Horace—not the least little bit in the world. I'd swear to you anywhere—and yet I'll warrant they haven't got your measurements, and finger-prints, and the devil knows what, as they have mine. Good health to you, Horace—you can come in!"

Ventoul came quickly round the doorway, and closed the door. He was a shorter, slighter man than Rackham, and he looked shorter and slighter than he was, by reason of the fact that he seemed to crouch a little, as though in fear. He looked at the closed door; he thrust his head forward and peered at the man standing by the sideboard—the man that was shabby and ill-shaven, and not too sober.

"What are you doing here?" demanded Ventoul at last.

Very deliberately Rackham drained his glass—looked at it, to be sure that nothing was left in it—and set it down. Then he gripped his cigar more firmly between his teeth at the corner of his mouth, and thrust his head forward, in mock imitation of the other man, and came at him slowly across the room.

"If you're not civil, you little ugly thing, I'll choke you before your fat man-servant can come in; and I'll go back to jail—just for the love of you," said Rackham. He was walking slowly after Ventoul, who moved away from him backwards round the room, never taking his eyes from him. "I'll spoil your beauty; I'll rumple you, and make a wreck of you, and leave your man—your infernal, respectable, oily man-servant that barred my way when I came in—I'll leave him to sweep up the pieces. Now, have you a word of kindness for a poor forlorn wretch, or haven't you?"

By that time Horace Ventoul was in a corner of the room, with his hands spread out flat against the wall, and his eyes (no longer slumbrous) on Rackham. He faltered out words of apology.

"It's all right, old chap; of course—of course I'm glad to see you," he panted. "I quite expected you'd—you'd look me up."

"And accordingly you must be mighty pleased to see me. Remembering the old days, I've helped myself to what there was, and I've helped myself liberally. (If you dare to look at me in that way again, I'll kill you; because I'm not drunk in the least—I'm only dangerous.) I've got three years to make up; three frightful years, during which they didn't let me have a drink, and they gave me nothing to smoke. Picture yourself chained like that, with nothing to drink, and nothing to smoke, Horace."

"Well—you've forgotten all that," said the other, with a smile. "Sit down, and make yourself at home."

"I've been doing that already," said Rackham, turning away. "I always make myself at home—and it would go hard with anyone who refused me the privilege. And now, as I want to talk to you, and as the sight of your dear, kind, familiar, friendly face has rather overwhelmed me, I'll just have another whiskey and soda, and sit down and hear the news. Also, as I know you like your friends to make themselves at home, and as I feel convivial, and as good tobacco has been rare with me lately, I'll have another cigar. In other words, my dear Horace,—prepare to make a night of it!"

Rackham was, as he had said, in a dangerous mood. The man at the lift had begun it; Wood, the man-servant, had carried the thing a little farther. In a sense, Rackham stood there now, leaning against the sideboard, with a challenge in his eyes and in his speech and in every fibre of his tall frame, not to Horace Ventoul alone, but to the world. He had taken his gruel; he would get back now to something near what he had been before. And the danger of him lay in the fact that he would be better prepared to fight for what he wanted than to beg for it.

Ventoul moved round the room, the better to get the table between himself and the other man. To tell the truth, he did not quite know how to take this shabby creature, who had come back after three years of oblivion; he was more than a little afraid of him. He had cursed his man-servant roundly for ever letting the man in at all; and the man-servant had pleaded, reasonably enough, that he had been helpless in the matter. After a momentary survey of the man leaning against the sideboard, Ventoul pulled out a thin silver cigarette-case, and opened it nervously, and took out a cigarette; lighted it, and looked through the smoke of it at Rackham.

"Of course, you know you're welcome, old Noll," he said jerkily. "We forget a man's faults——"

"Faults!" exclaimed the other. "I want no mercy from you, and no glossing over of what I've done. Only I want to see where I stand with you—and with all the others. Your man, when he let me in to-night, would have barred the way to me, if he hadn't been afraid of what might have happened; you would have turned me out if you had had the pluck. That's not my game at all, Horace Ventoul; I've paid for what I've done, and I've come back. I've slept in the streets, and I haven't a farthing in my pocket; but I don't come to beg. Perhaps that's a distinction without a difference; but you can make what you like of it."

Horace Ventoul laughed a little mirthlessly, and shifted about uneasily on his feet. He glanced at the man standing with folded arms and with the cigar gripped in his teeth; he glanced at the door beyond which lay safety and a man-servant paid to do his bidding; he reckoned up his chances. After all, a man like this could be dealt with by those forces of the law that had dealt with him before; the thing was easy enough. Yet still he hesitated—for there were other matters between them.

"You don't come to beg—and yet you have nothing in your pockets," said Ventoul slowly. "For the life of me I can't see the difference, although perhaps you can. What do you propose to do in the future?"

Rackham shrugged his shoulders. "The world has taken me, and made sport of me—and broken me," he said. "From this time forward I'll make sport of the world. Bit of a one-sided game, no doubt; but that's my affair. I play a lone hand in this, and in a certain devil-may-care fashion I'm beginning to like it. But I want money."

"You've begun the begging part, I observe," said Ventoul, regaining confidence.

Oliver Rackham moved a step away from the sideboard, as though he would advance upon the other man. "I wouldn't say that if I were you," he retorted in a level voice. "How many times in this room have I flung money at you; if I had a tenth part of it now I wouldn't come near you, or look upon your ugly face again. You'll say you won it—and you'd be right. But you were always the lucky one—always the cool one; and I was always the fool that drank too much, and didn't watch the cards, and was only surprised when I realized how much there was to pay."

"You were forever getting into trouble, and losing your money, and wondering how on earth you were going to get any more," said Ventoul, pulling at his cigarette, and watching the other man. "Do you remember that night when you came to me, and confessed you'd forged your uncle's name, and that there wasn't a dog's chance for you —unless——"

"Unless you'd lend me the money to get square again, and cover the thing up," broke in Rackham. "And you wouldn't do it; you were very properly shocked and upset· to think that any friend of yours—driven mad by desperation—had done such a thing. So I paid for it all; and here's the end of it, so far as I'm concerned. There" —he spread out his hands, and let them drop at his sides, and laughed—"I've done with my bullying, but I want to feel that there's some chance for me in the world again. It's a poor sort of world, Horace, when you feel there isn't a place for you anywhere, and when all the backs are turned on you."

"My dear fellow, you're making a great fuss about nothing," said Ventoul, seating himself on the edge of the table, and looking sideways at the other man. "You'll get something to do—or there'll be a chance for you to emigrate, and make a fresh start in another country. To come back here now, and to expect that all sorts of people are going to receive you as though the slate of life could be wiped clean and the writing on it forgotten, is a little absurd. How, for instance, do you suggest that I should help you?"

Rackham stood there staring a little helplessly at the floor. The other man had put the whole matter in a nutshell; had pinned him down, as it were, to one vital question that demanded an answer. He could only shake his head and shrug his shoulders, and by the mere indication of his hands point to his shabby appearance.

"I had a sort of idea that I might climb back again a bit," he said. "I'm not whining, but God knows I want a bit of a chance. I had the knack of doing all sorts of things in the old days; I might pick up one of them and make something out of it. I just want the start."

Horace Ventoul laughed, and took out a fresh cigarette and lighted it. After all, the thing was not so difficult; this shabby outcast was not a man to be reckoned with, save in a manner of sheer brute strength; and even that could be dealt with.

"You had a knack of doing all sorts of things, as you say," he said after a pause. "You could play a little and sing a little; above all, you had an idea that you could write. If you hadn't been a man with money to burn in the first instance you might have written to some purpose, eh?" That alert face was pushed forward, and was a very question mark in itself.

Rackham was not looking at him; there was an amused smile on his face. "Yes—I used to write things—quaint fancies that came into my head from time to time," he said. "But what was the good of it? I never made anything out of it. In the first place, I didn't understand the business side of it, and didn't particularly want to do so. I wonder what became of all the reams of paper I spoilt and left behind me! Three years is a long time—and, after all, they were scarcely worth the keeping, I expect. How I must have bored you and some of the other fellows, when you used, out of goodness of heart, to persuade me to read them to you!"

Horace Ventoul moved restlessly across the room, and flung his cigarette into the fireplace. "Well—what's the good of talking about all that now?" he asked impatiently, standing with his back turned to the other man. "If you're going to make a living, you've got to think of something more practical. You won't make a living by scribbling."

"No—I expect not," said Rackham. "I don't know what made me think of it—except that I was just remembering the mad old days generally. By the way, you used to have a bit of a taste in that direction, didn't you?"

"And never made anything of it," snapped out the other, turning his head sharply towards Rackham. "Look here, Noll, I don't want to be a brute—but it's late, and I —I—want to get to bed."

Rackham laughed, and looked at him; then laughed again. "In other words, you've some game afoot, and you want to get rid of me," he said. "Well—I don't look particularly presentable, I'll admit—but that's not my fault. You might tell me why it is you're so anxious I should go."

"I'm not a bit anxious that you should go, except for the reason stated," said Ventoul, looking at him covertly. "Only you must surely understand that things are changed a bit; you're a man of the world——"

"And my world is not yours—eh?" said Rackham. "All right, my friend, I wouldn't take a sixpence from you under any circumstances—and I'm sorry I came. Good night to you."

He drained his glass and set it down, and moved towards the door. Ventoul's voice recalled him as he had the handle of it actually in his hand.

"Look here—I dare say I can help you to tide over for a bit—if a sovereign or two——"

Oliver Rackham stood thinking about it. Outside were the bitter streets, and no earthly prospect of food or shelter; this man he despised was offering him both, for a time at least. Pride tugged at him, and bade him go without answering; expediency pleaded that he should accept Ventoul's offer. And while he stood, with those two points balancing themselves in his mind, his eye travelled along a row of books set in a book-case at the very edge of the doorway. And suddenly he left the door, and jerked his head sharply forward, to stare at the back of one of the covers.

"You'd better accept my offer," said Ventoul.

Instead of replying, Rackham pulled out the book, and came forward into the room, and very slowly opened it. The title of it he knew well, and the name of the author was set down as "Horace Ventoul."

There was no sound in the room, save the rustling of the leaves as Rackham turned them over. Presently he shut the book, and tossed it on to the table, and looked at Ventoul.

"How much did you get for it?" he demanded sharply.

"What's it matter?" said the other, almost in a whisper.

"The things were knocking about at your place when I came to clear up your papers; I thought there might be something in them, and so I sent them to a publisher."

"And stuck your own beastly name on them," said Rackham. "Upon my word, that's the most unkindest cut of all. You're a thief, and you steal what isn't yours, and what you haven't the power of making for yourself; and then you put your ugly little name on the covers and inside. You might have had the decency even to dedicate them to me; that would have shown something of a sense of humor, at any rate."

"What are you going to do about it?" asked Ventoul, after a pause.

"I'm going to show you up; I'm going to write to the papers about you, and tell them what you've done. I'm going to make such a howling, blazing business of this that you'll wish you'd put the things on the fire directly you found them. They've got 'em up nicely, by the way," he added inconsequently, as he picked up the book again. "What have you made out of it?"

"Not much; I didn't do it for that. I tell you, Noll, it was more a matter—matter of vanity than anything else. I've always had a hankering after that kind of thing, and I just drifted into doing it. You see, I couldn't put your name on them, could I?"

"Why the devil not?" demanded Rackham, staring at him. "It might have been rather a good thing for me—it might have glossed over a few of my sins."

"Well, it's too late now; the thing's done. As I say, I didn't do it for the money; I had enough of that. And it isn't likely that I'm going back now on what I've done, or that I'm going to confess. More than that, I don't see how you can help yourself."

"I shall show you up," said Rackham calmly.

"And I shall deny the whole business. Everyone knows I used to write, and everybody knows what your record is. I'm going to stick to my guns."

"There's the manuscripts; that'll give the game away."

Ventoul laughed disagreeably. "I destroyed them the moment I had corrected the proofs," he said. "Also I destroyed all the other things you'd left behind—odd scraps that were no use. I tell you the thing's done."

Rackham had thrust his hat on the back of his head, and had seated himself on the edge of the table. Ventoul stood like a man at bay, watching him, and wondering what he was going to do. Presently, in the most unexpected fashion, Oliver Rackham began to laugh—gently at first, and then until the thing grew into a roar. Ventoul's face cleared a little, and some of the suspense died out of it. He even ventured to smile himself. And at that Rackham's laugh died away on the instant.

"Look here—you thieving little devil—this is my laugh, and not yours," he said. "I was laughing because the humor of the thing appealed to me—the mere bald fact that I've been rotting in prison for three years, while you've been patted on the back and made much of, no doubt, for the fruit of my brains. I was laughing because I think I was sent into the world to show just how great a fool a man may be. I was laughing to think of how you've been hailed as somebody who could write something, while I've been trotting round the exercise yard, eating my heart out, and wondering how it was going to end. That's what *I've* been laughing about; but, by the Lord! if *you* try the game, I'll choke the life out of you, as I threatened to do just now."

"It's no use threatening me," said Ventoul. "I've only used it—this work of yours, I mean—as a sort of lever; I'm going to write something now on my own account; they're bound to take it."

"That's funny, too," said Rackham. "Even if you do write anything, it's pretty certain to fail, because you never had the proper stuff in you—and yet they'll take it because of what I've done for you. However, there's one matter cleared up, and we'll get that settled now."

"What matter's that?" asked Ventoul.

"I'm no longer pleading with you to help me and give me a start; I'm demanding what is my right," said Rackham, getting down from the table and strolling up towards the other man. "The world and you and Fate and everything else have treated me badly; from this moment my hand is against you all. I'll bleed you—I'll prey upon you—I'll get quits with you. And as you are chief robber in the business, my foxy-faced friend, I'll start with you!"

As Rackham advanced upon him, Ventoul made a swift movement, and pressed his thumb hard against the bell. That action probably sealed the fate of the whole matter; that call for outside assistance was sufficient for Rackham. As the steps of the man-servant were heard outside, Rackham bent over the other man, and spoke sharply—

"He's going to take his orders from me; if you make a fuss, I'll wreck you and him and the place too. You've got a spare room here; it's mine to-night."

By that time the man-servant was in the room, and wait-

"WHATEVER GAME YOU PLAY I'LL PLAY, TOO" Page 41.

ing, with eyes upon his master only, for orders. Ventoul opened his mouth but said nothing; Rackham turned and looked at the man insolently, and spoke.

"Mr. Ventoul is kind enough to offer me his hospitality for to-night," he said. "Just see that things are shipshape in the spare room, will you?—and you might get me some supper. Something cold will do; I'm not particular. And just stir yourself, Wood; I don't want to wait all night."

The astonished man-servant gulped out a "Yes, sir," and vanished. Rackham turned with an ironical bow to Ventoul.

"Now do you understand, little man, what you've let yourself in for?" he said. "I'll stick to you closer than wax; I'll be your shadow; the Old Man of the Sea on the shoulders of Sinbad will be as nothing to me. I've got to fight the world and get something out of it; and you've stolen my chance. I'll use you as a shield; I'll work behind you."

The entrance of Wood, literally trotting with a tray, stopped Ventoul's answer. The man-servant respectfully placed a chair for the guest, and backed out of the room, not without an appealing glance at Ventoul. Rackham seated himself, and shook out a napkin and put it over his shabby knees, and laughed again.

"Whatever game you play, I'll play too; whatever little adroit move is on the board, I'll move with you," he said as he began to eat. "Who knows—you may presently want to write another original book—and I shall be at your shoulder, prompting you how to do it. I've heard of literary ghosts; I'll be a substantial one, I promise you."

"I shan't submit to it; I can set you at defiance; I can point to your record, and say that you are blackmailing me," stammered Ventoul.

Rackham laid down his knife and fork, and got very slowly and deliberately to his feet. "It's a melancholy reflection," he said, with a whimsical shake of his head, "but there are some men who will never learn their lesson, just as there are some boys who won't learn theirs, unless it's caned into them. Perhaps you'll be good enough to repeat what you have just said," he added, moving very stealthily towards the other man.

"Stop! I won't endure it!" cried Ventoul, backing again towards the bell. "The thing is monstrous."

"You're quite right—it is monstrous," said Rackham. "That's what you're paying for now—for your three years of ease and reflected glory, and all the rest of it. If you ring that bell I will first annihilate your man-servant, whose smug respectability puts me on edge, and I will then do the same with you. Now—am I to stop here in peace for to-night, at least, or am I to be annoyed by vulgar personalities?"

"You can stop here—and be——Oh—sit down and eat your supper!" cried Ventoul.

"There is a charming note of cordiality about you that adds sauce to a meal," said the other, as he seated himself again at the table. "Perhaps you'll be good enough just to mix me a whiskey and soda, and you may have one yourself (weaker than mine, of course); and then we shall be really comfortable."

Ventoul walked across to the sideboard; his hand was on the decanter when Rackham's voice arrested him.

"Stop! I don't see why I shouldn't be waited on like a gentleman. That man of yours had suspicions of me when I came in; by the Lord! I'll hustle the fellow. Ring the bell."

Ventoul went across to the bell, and savagely set his thumb against it; he kept it ringing until the man, with a startled face, hurried in. Rackham turned to him in a casual fashion, and jerked his head towards the sideboard.

"Just mix me a whiskey and soda; you ought to remember how I like it," he said. "And hurry a bit; you're getting slow and ponderous in your movements."

Wood almost staggered across to the sideboard; his hand shook as he poured out what was required. He brought it back to the table on a little silver tray; and Rackham, apparently absorbed in his meal, kept him waiting a moment or so before noticing him. There was a devilish light in his eyes as he took the glass and nodded towards Ventoul.

"Good health, old boy!" he exclaimed.

"Will there be anything else you require, sir?" asked the man at his elbow.

"Mr. Ventoul will ring if there is," said Rackham. "Go away—and learn not to breathe so hard; you must be getting asthmatical as well as ponderous."

When the man had gone Ventoul came slowly across to the table; standing at the farther end of it he looked at his tormentor. "How long is this game going to last?" he demanded.

"As it is a game which suits me, and which I like extremely well, it will probably last a long time. This has given a twist to things; it's quite impossible to say what may happen. What you don't understand—but what you will learn in time—is that when a man is shut away from his fellows, and caged like a wild beast, he takes a different view of what the world is and what men are. I shall have quite a lot to teach you, my dear Horace, I can assure you."

He was something like a caged wild beast when presently, his meal finished, he began to stride up and down the room, smoking a cigar, and glancing from time to time at the other man. He seemed to enjoy the situation; and whenever it required pointing in any way, he would take up that book that lay on the table, and flutter the leaves of it, and then throw it down again.

"I thought you were in a hurry to get to bed," he said at last, stopping in his restless walk. "Or does it really happen that there's someone coming to see you—and that I really am in the way? That won't matter now, you know; you can introduce me, and make much of me; I'm much more presentable than I was."

"There's no one coming," snapped the other.

"Then that's so much the more cosy for us—isn't it?" said Rackham. "By the way, what were the press notices like? did they like me—I mean you, of course? Did they say kind things about you? Perhaps they even printed that ugly face of yours in the papers—eh?"

He stopped in the corner of the room before an open desk; began, insolently enough, to move the papers about on it. Ventoul moved quickly towards him, and spoke sharply.

"Let those things alone!"

Rackham snarled round at him, with his head twisted in an ugly fashion over his shoulder. "Be quiet, you dog!" he said. "How do I know what other tricks you've been up to, or whom else you may have been robbing? I've got to watch you; that's part of the new game we're going to play together."

Puffing at his cigar, he calmly tossed over letters and sheets of manuscript idly enough, and merely with the desire to enrage the other man. Presently he picked up a little slip of paper, and raised it to his eyes, and read what was written on it aloud—

"Angelica Susan Brown."

Still with the paper in his hand, he looked around quizzically at Horace Ventoul. "Is that the name of the lady you're expecting?" he asked.

"Haven't I told you I'm not expecting anyone?" said Ventoul. "That's the name of a girl."

"So I very naturally imagine," answered Rackham coolly. "Who is she?"

"I haven't the least idea. I jotted the name down when I heard it, because it seemed quaint. I haven't the ghost of a notion who she is, or where she is."

"Angelica Susan Brown." Rackham murmured the name once or twice to himself, and shook his head over it: "What made you write it down?" he asked at last.

"You're the most inquisitive fellow I've ever come across," exclaimed Ventoul angrily. "If you must know, I jotted it down because it interested me. The girl, whoever she is, is worth half a million of money."

Rackham whistled softly, and raised his eyebrows. "Half a million!" he exclaimed softly. "I'll buy a new suit of clothes to-morrow, and you shall introduce me."

"I tell you I don't know her," retorted Ventoul. "I happened to be talking to a fellow I know, a barrister; he told me of the case. It seems that the child was practically deserted when she was a baby, and has been lost sight of; the money has been thrown into Chancery. They don't advertise these things—at least, not in directions in which people would be likely to discover them; and there the money will probably remain to swell the amount already there. Angelica Susan Brown will probably never hear of her wealth—but the story is an interesting one. Now you know all about it."

He turned away impatienty, and pulled out his watch, and looked at it. Rackham tossed the slip of paper on to the desk, and yawned, and turned away also.

"I suppose you're going to bed," said Ventoul sulkily.

"I suppose I am," Rackham answered. "This has been a very affecting and joyous meeting, my dear Horace, and perhaps the sheer emotion of it has upset me a bit. Nevertheless, I must not allow that very natural emotion to interfere with questions of business. I want some of my profits."

"I'll attend to everything of that sort in the morning," said the other, moving towards the door.

Catlike and swiftly, Rackham went after him, and gripped him suddenly by the shoulder, and turned him round. "On the contrary, my dear Horace, you will attend to the matter to-night," he said. "How am I to know that you will not send your faithful man-servant out in the morning to fetch a policeman—or even two policemen—and so trump up a charge against me, and get rid of me? I will take twenty pounds on account—and I don't want a cheque."

"I haven't got twenty pounds—not here," said the other, after a pause.

"What have you got? I can come again, you know," retorted Rackham.

It came down to a matter of fifteen pounds; and that sum, partly in banknotes and partly in gold, Rackham airily transferred to his pockets. Then, in the most affectionate fashion, and still with that lurking devil in his eyes, he bade his friend good-night, and went off to the room that had been assigned to him. He undressed, and climbed into the pajamas which the thoughtful Wood had spread out for him—cursing the fact that, as they were the property of Horace Ventoul, they were much too small— and was asleep in less than five minutes.

Nor did he wake during the night; and his only dream was that a mysterious person calling herself Angelica Susan Brown, and looking uncommonly like Mr. Horace Ventoul, was counting out an enormous quantity of glittering coins and banknotes into his hands, and that he was quite contentedly receiving them.

CHAPTER III

ENTER MISS MONEY-BAGS

OLIVER RACKHAM woke very early, and with a very confused notion of where he was. The most prominent thing in his mind was the remembrance of having seen someone called Angelica Susan Brown—and yet being unable to recall what she was like. And then he sat up in bed, and remembered suddenly where he was, and what had happened. At the recollection of that he began to chuckle softly to himself.

"I don't believe our dear Horace has slept a wink," he said, with immense satisfaction. "He will have been thinking about all the money that he has lost, and all the other money he's going to lose; he will be seriously upset. I think I'll go and have a look at him."

He appeared like a grim Fate, in a suit of pajamas ridiculously short as to legs and arms, and absurdly tight across the chest, at the bedside of Horace Ventoul. That gentleman having, as Rackham had supposed, passed a very restless night, had fallen into an uneasy slumber some half-hour before, with the bedclothes huddled up so that only the top of his head was showing. Rackham relentlessly jerked the bedclothes away, and sat down on a chair to have a look at the awakened man.

Ventoul sat up with a start, and stared at him; recognised who he was and gave a sort of groan; and lay down again, with the bedclothes hitched up over his shoulders. "What do you want?" he demanded.

"I want to have a look at you," said Rackham, with a smile. "I wanted to see you lying in your dainty loveliness—the very picture of virtue very much rewarded. I've never seen an author half awake before, and even now I dont like the color of your pajamas any more than I like the fit of these I have on. Have you slept well?"

"I haven't slept a wink," growled the other. "Why in the world can't you stop in the bed you forced me to lend you, and leave me alone?"

"Because, for the first moment after quite a long time, I am feeling rather chirpy and happy; and, not being a selfish individual, I wanted someone else to feel chirpy and happy too. I did think of waking up Wood; but he's bad enough when he's up and dressed, and what he'd be like asleep I don't know. Presently I will go and ring all the bells I can get hold of, and make him get up and prepare my bath. I haven't enjoyed many luxuries for a long time; and Wood is a luxury, and I mean to make the most of him."

"Look here," cried Ventoul, sitting up in bed, "how long do you think this is going to last? How long do you imagine I'm going to put up with it?"

"My dear little man," answered Rackham, shaking his head at him, "you made the mistake last night of trying to bully me; don't make the mistake again. I don't want to use absolute violence to you, and I want to forget the wrong you've done me, and keep on a friendly footing with you. We'll let bygones be bygones—under certain conditions already hinted at—if you behave yourself. As a matter of fact I am going out presently to get an outfit, and I may come back—or I may not. Now say 'Good-morning' nicely, and I'll let you alone."

"Good morning," growled Ventoul after a pause.

"That's right; your manners will improve after a time, I've no doubt. Now I'll go and wake up the being I loathe, and see that he gets my bath ready."

Thereafter Mr. Horace Ventoul, lying inwardly raging, heard the ringing of bells, and much banging on a door, and the shouting of Oliver Rackham for the man-servant. That highly respectable being, who was not supposed to get up for at least another three-quarters of an hour, was hurried out in a half-dressed condition, with his hair tousled, to find himself confronted by a scarecrow of the larger sort yelling his name. Fully making up his mind to give notice that very day, he prepared the bath, and then went back and completed his dressing.

"There's a devil growing in me—and I shall have to check it," said Rackham to himself, as he towelled himself vigorously. "I don't want to make the little man's life a misery to him; I only want to pay him back a little for the trick he has served me. He's got to pay for that, only in different coin. I'm afraid he's got an idea that he can do what he likes with me, because of what he knows about me; therefore a sharp lesson was necessary. In any case, I'm afraid he has no great affection for me."

Breakfast was a nightmare to Horace Ventoul, and in another fashion to the man-servant. Rackham really behaved remarkably well, and only broke out once, when the unfortunate Wood was stalking solemnly towards him with a dish, and he shouted at him to hurry. But it was not so much what he did as what he might do; the two eyed him furtively, and fairly jumped when he moved or looked at them.

A little later, when the servant had left the room, Rackham coolly took a cigar and lighted it; then he turned to Ventoul with a smiling face. Ventoul, sulkily regarding him from the farther end of the room, looked venomous.

"My dear Horace, I am going to relieve you of my presence," said Rackham airily. "I've had a bad time for three years, and for something more than a fortnight since that; now I'm going to make up for it. I've been thinking things over, and I've realised that there isn't a ghost of a chance for me, unless a miracle happens, to earn an honest livelihood. More than that, I'm not quite sure that I want to earn a livelihood at all, in a sense of working hard for a poor wage, and for food, and for a roof to cover me; I wasn't brought up to it. I had one poor talent, and perhaps there's a bit of it left in me; but you've done your best to steal that. Well—you're welcome to it; you might even go ahead, with my assistance, and do some more on the same lines. We'll start a partnership for the production of immortal works, and we'll share the profits."

"I want nothing to do with you," said Ventoul, turning away from him.

"I know that, dear old boy—but you've got to have quite a lot to do with me—and whether you like it or not you've got to behave decently to me. If you were not a fool, you'd realise that any poor dog driven into a corner, with sticks and stones flung at him, will bite the first person he can get at; and I'm the poor dog of that fable.

Treat me well, and I may lick your hand; treat me as you were willing to do last night, and by all that's holy I'll bite —and I'll bite deep."

"I think I know that," retorted the other. "When do you purpose coming back again?"

"It is utterly impossible for me to say," replied Rackham, with a laugh. "If, in a new suit of clothes, it should happen that someone takes a fancy to me, and adopts me, I shall cut you dead the first time we meet; or if I picked up a fairly respectable heiress, who might be fascinated by my manners and by my new suit of clothes—then once again I should cut you. Frankly, my dear Horace, I don't like you, but I'm going to make use of you."

"I may find a way of getting out of this tangle, and leaving you in the lurch. What then?"

"You wouldn't go far, my dear Horace," said Rackham grimly. "I should have you, by hook or by crook; and the last state of you would be a devilish sight worse than the first. Make the best of it—and if any bills are sent in to you for goods supplied, make the best of that, and pay."

He got to the door, and came back again. "By the way —I know something of human nature—perhaps a little more than you do," he said. "That man of yours is terribly upset, and it's more than probable that he will seek service in a less disturbing household. If you value his services, I should smooth him down, if I were you, and give him a tip."

"I can manage my own domestic affairs, thank you," retorted Ventoul stiffly.

"As it is obvious you cannot, I will settle them for you,"

said Rackham. And going into the hall, he shouted for Wood.

The man hurried out, and respectfully faced him; Ventoul, from the room, could see what was happening. Rackham thrust a finger and thumb into a pocket of his shabby waistcoat, and drew out a sovereign—one of Ventoul's sovereigns. This he spun carelessly in the air, while he looked at the man before him.

"An unexpected visitor, who demands this, that, and the other at all hours, necessarily causes a good servant—even the best of servants—some additional trouble," he said. "Accept this as a mark of my appreciation—and learn to hurry."

He tossed the coin towards the man, who caught it with something of a scrambling action, opened the door, and went out into the corridor. He was moving towards the stairs, when a remembrance of the lift-man brought him back again; he set his thumb against the lift-bell and kept it there until the lift actually appeared.

"Why the devil is it necessary that I should ring enough to wake the dead to bring a lazy fellow like you up to the doing of his duties?" he demanded. "I'll get my friend Mr. Ventoul, in whose flat I have been staying to-night, to report you if you're not more careful."

He sauntered out into the street; the spring sunshine was beginning to warm the air a little, and it warmed him. Life had taken on another aspect altogether; life held promises. He would be a man again, and take his place among men.

And then suddenly, for some strange reason, there swept over him—well fed, and with money in his pockets, and the sense of renewed power—the cold, chilling blast of the prison. Once again, as he moved along the street, it seemed that he was in the exercise yard, for ever moving, a grey shadow among shadows, round and round—with a man just behind him and another man in front. The thing grew upon him, until at last he was forced, against his will and judgment, to turn his head sharply. And then he saw the man behind.

A slinking, skulking figure—shabbier than he was. A man born to slink and skulk through unhappy days, until at last he slunk and skulked out of the world altogether. And this was the man who, as Fate had willed it, had been the one in the exercise yard always to trot behind him—so that Rackham's furtive eye, turned as it was now, had always caught that glimpse of him. Rackham walked quickly down a side street, conscious that the man was following him; turned suddenly and faced him.

"Well—what's the game?" he demanded, as the man fairly blundered into him, and blundered away again on the rebound.

"No offence, guv'nor," whined the man. "'Ad a sort of idear I saw a pal, and thought I might 'ave a kind word said. You remember me—don't yer?"

"Oh, yes, I remember you," said Rackham. "In that evil den where the rats were kept in cages, and made to go through tricks, you were always the rat just behind me. Remember you! Is it likely I should forget you?"

"I'm glad of that, guv'nor; it puts 'eart into a chap what's down on his luck."

"Don't I look down on my luck?" asked Rackham.

"Don't I look as if I should presently go back again, and fall in with all the other rats—perhaps meet you there; don't I look like that? However, it happens that that's not the case; I've had a little slice of luck. I've got a little money."

"Gorn on the old lay—an' not got copped—eh?" grinned the man, with a glance round about him.

"Something like that, perhaps," said Rackham, with an answering grin. "At any rate, I'll give you a sovereign to go away and to let me alone. I'm off the old lay, as you term it; I've turned honest. I hope not to go inside, and have my hair cut and other unpleasant things done to me, ever again. Now, hook it!"

The man seized the coin—spat upon it—and was gone in a moment; even at his shuffling walk he seemed to vanish.

"At this rate I shall have to trouble our dear Horace sooner than I expected," murmured Rackham to himself as he went on his way. "I would go to his tailors, and get them to send in the bill to him; but unfortunately I can't wait. This has got to be a ready-money affair, and the sooner I set about it the better."

Rackham had lived in places, since his first day of freedom, that had gradually grown more and more mean and sordid as necessity pressed him harder; and that experience was valuable now. He knew where to go to buy cheaply, and yet to buy things that should stamp him, to some extent at least, for what he had been in the beginning of things. So that presently he emerged, as it were, from shabby things, and held his head high—fairly well dressed in ready-made clothes, and knowing that he could pass muster almost anywhere. And still had a fair amount of money left.

His dreams of any possible future were vague in the extreme; for the moment he was merely content to walk abroad in a well-fitting tweed suit and a respectable hat, and to know that he had money enough to carry him on for a little time. And yet deep down in the soul of him was a great and desperate longing for one thing; and it was a longing he knew he ought not to appease.

He wanted a dress-suit! The thing was absurd, of course; he had no right, in the present state of his finances, to think of such a thing. It occurred to him, while he sat in the restaurant eating a moderate luncheon, that he might go now to Horace Ventoul's tailors (he knew the address of them) and bluff the matter out, and endeavor to get something ready-made; but then they were not the ready-made sort of people at all. The thing got on his mind at last to such an extent that he felt he must dive down into some neighborhood where the thing might be possible, and emerge with his prize, even if it took all the money he had left.

In that matter, of course—that mere matter of expense —he showed his ignorance. For, as it happened, he was in the neighborhood of Covent Garden when he made his great resolve; and there presently he found a shop absolutely staring at him, with a legend to the effect that what he coveted was obtainable there—second-hand. Feeling that Providence was really being very good to him, he dived into the place; he proffered his request with some hesitation, and was met with smiling civility; and presently emerged, with a parcel under his arm, and with the knowledge that that parcel had cost him mighty little, as compared with his ideas of former years.

It had all been so simple, and he had been plunging about here, there, and everywhere in his search for cheap things, that the day had slipped away; and he suddenly remembered that he had no lodging. It was obviously impossible for him to seek a lodging burdened with so little luggage as he possessed, unless he paid for it in advance; but that he was prepared to do. He took a clean little room over a coffee-house in an obscure street (arguing to himself that he would not have to go far for very cheap meals), and began to feel that he had at last got a home. He unpacked the dress suit, and shook it out, and looked at it; he had an absurd feeling that, after all, the thing ought to be used as soon as possible. It was a very long time since he had worn a dress-suit.

He put it on, just to see what it looked like, and to make sure again that it fitted him. It had been so cheap that he had gone to the further luxury of a crush hat—also second-hand; he stood up now, arrayed in all his glory.

"I feel good enough to be going out to dinner, or even to a dance," he said to himself, with a chuckle. "I'm not the same man I was a few hours ago; I've come alive! I'm fit for anything. I should just like to be going to a dance to-night—one of the old, sweet times, with a pretty woman in one's arms, and the dear breath of her almost on your cheek——"

He took a turn or two about the little room with that imaginary partner in his arms; then stood still suddenly, and clapped his hands as a thought struck him like lightning.

"By the Lord—I'll go to the 'hop'!" he cried; and burst into a roar of laughter.

He sat down on the side of his bed, and began to wonder if he could remember the address. He went back mentally to that scene on the Embankment, when he had sat under the shadow of the statue of Izambard Kingdom Brunel, and had met Joshua Flattery; he seemed to hear again the little man's voice. And presently the whole thing burst upon him.

"Professor Dorn's Academy, Hamlyn Street, Tottenham Court Road! And it was to-night that he was to be there in his official capacity. I'll look him up; I shall enjoy a dance, even if it is a little mixed."

Still with that feeling that he had more money in his pocket than he had any right to expect, he determined that he would dine out. It would be absurd for him to go down into the coffee-house and dine there in his present raiment; he must go elsewhere. And then he suddenly remembered that he had no overcoat, and that the evening, though fine, was chilly, and not at all the sort of evening on which a man wanders about in a dress-suit without an overcoat. He figured the thing out.

"Even a cheap overcoat would swamp a lot of money; a cab would cost a shilling, or eighteenpence at the most. Therefore a cab is cheaper. I only hope they won't raise my rent downstairs when I go out."

He escaped from the place without being noticed, and made his way into a broader street, where there was a decent restaurant within sight. He dined well, and had a bottle of wine—taking his time over the meal; finally he went out, and hailed a cab, and directed the man to drive to Hamlyn Street, Tottenham Court Road. He thought the man looked a little astonished, and began to wonder what sort of adventure he was in for.

Hamlyn Street proved to be smaller and narrower than he had anticipated; it was a mere cul-de-sac. He found Professor Dorn's Academy easily enough; a few youths and girls were hanging about the entrance, and he could hear within the rather jerky strains of a band. Those about the doorway stared at him a little; and the man to whom he gave his hat, and who was seated amid a melancholy array of bowlers and caps and other articles of headgear, stared still more.

"It's evident that they don't come to hops in war-paint," murmured Oliver Rackham to himself.

By the time he reached the ball-room the spirit of the thing had got into him. He stood in the doorway, and gazed in astonishment at the motley throng before him; he had never seen such dancers in his life. A dancing man himself, he came to realise in a moment or two that the dancing was excellent; it had been taught perhaps in a hard school, but a man or woman would stand a small chance of partners unless he or she knew the business.

There was nothing lackadaisical about it; they had come there to dance, and had paid their money for it, and they were going to have their money's worth to the uttermost farthing. Sitting out was apparently a matter to be very properly scorned; only now and then a perspiring, panting youth or maiden would leave the ball-room for hurried refreshment—to come back again as rapidly as possible.

He remembered the object of his visit, and went off to the refreshment-room himself. There, after a moment or two, he saw Joshua Flattery, looking very different in a waiter's suit, with his hat off, and with a napkin under his arm—hurrying to and fro, and shouting orders to a young woman behind a sort of improvised counter. Rackham seated himself in a corner, and presently attracted Joshua Flattery's attention.

The little man had not the faintest idea who it was that sat before him; he kept casting anxious eyes around to see if he were wanted elsewhere.

"Can I have a whiskey and soda?" asked Rackham.

"You can—but it's extry, because we 'ave to send out for it. And I take the money fust," answered Joshua rapidly.

"All right, Mr. Flattery," Rackham said, with a laugh. "I see that you're still afraid I haven't a penny in my pocket."

Joshua Flattery started violently; then bent and peered at Rackham; rubbed his hand across his forehead with the action of a man suddenly dazed; and then smiled feebly.

"Lor', sir—what a turn you did give me! If it 'adn't bin for the voice," said Joshua Flattery, shaking his head perplexedly, "I should have declared to goodness I'd never seen you before. So the little game the other night, sir— with the bit o' poetry throwed in, and all the rest of it—it was all a bit of a fake—eh?"

"It was nothing of the kind," answered Rackham. "I was a done man then, Joshua Flattery, and I spoke nothing but the truth when I said I hadn't a penny in the world, and hadn't a chance of getting one. Since then, however," —he grinned cheerfully at the recollection—"I have come into money."

"Fitted yerself out, too, pritty neat—'aven't you, sir?" said Joshua critically. "And fancy you rememberin' I should be 'ere, an' comin' to look me up. I'll send for that whiskey and soda in 'alf a jiffy, sir."

"There's no hurry; besides, I've come back to pay you a shilling I owe you," said Rackham. "And I'm going to add a bit to it, for the sake of gratitude."

"You are not, sir," said Joshua stoutly. "It's bin my privilege to sit and talk with a gent, on what you might call almost equal terms; I don't want to be paid for it, sir. If you're so good as to return a little friendly loan—that's neither 'ere nor there; but nothink else, sir, I beg."

"I wouldn't hurt your feelings for the world, Mr. Flattery," said Rackham, as he laid a shilling on the table. "And now perhaps you'll let me know how much the whiskey and soda will be; and perhaps, if I shan't be hurting your feelings by doing so, you'll allow me to have the pleasure of asking you to take one with me."

"You're very kind, sir," said Joshua, as he named the sum required. "It bein' against the rules for me to take refreshment while the 'op is on, I shall 'ave to do mine in secret, in the little room w'ere I change. But I shall do it, and I shall drink to your 'ealth and fortune, sir."

With that the little man hurried away, to dispatch a youth for what was required, and presently hurried back again. The fashion in which he hovered about the table, and, even when engaged on other duties, kept an eye on this wonderful patron of his, was extraordinary. In a moment of leisure, when there were only one or two people in the room, he sidled over to Rackham again.

"I suppose you ain't thinkin' of 'aving a dance, sir—eh?"

he said. "Not quite your class, I expect, sir? Though some of 'em would be mighty proud if they 'ad the charnce of a turn with you, I'll be bound, sir."

"My dear Joshua Flattery—I am out to-night in a new world," said Oliver Rackham. "Life is showing me its possibilities, and I feel like a schoolboy. If I can get hold of a partner, I shall most certainly dance."

"You will 'ave yer joke, sir," said the little man, with a grin. "I feel that proud of 'aving met a gentleman like you, sir, and talked with 'im, and 'ad wot you might call an adventure with 'im, that I can't think of nothink else. An' fancy you comin' down 'ere to pay me back a shillin'—and dressin' for it! It's wonderful—simply wonderful, sir."

"I have paid a matter of eighteenpence for my ticket and I'm going to dance," said Rackham, as he rose to his feet.

Joshua Flattery neglected his duties to the extent of going to the door of the dancing-room and peering in. His mouth was one wide grin, and his eyes were open to their fullest extent, as Rackham, pulling on his white gloves, strolled into the room; the little man wanted to tell everyone that this particular gentleman (who, if the truth be told, was creating very much of a sensation, and had actually stopped the dancing in one or two instances) was known to him. Joshua Flattery wanted to boast about it.

Longing glances were cast at the tall figure; and presently someone, who must have been the redoubtable Professor Dorn himself, approached hurriedly, and asked if he might be allowed to introduce Rackham to a lady.

"I shall be delighted," said Rackham, keeping a steady face with difficulty.

"One of my first, and I might almost say one of my best, patrons, sir," murmured the Professor, as he piloted Rackham across the room. "She sends her friends to me—and she always brings a party—and there's no new dance that comes out, sir, that she don't 'ave both 'er daughters taught it at once. She'll be honored, sir."

The lady was large, and she was clad in blue velvet, with a deep lace collar; she wore silk gloves. She rose with much dignity, and bowed to the mysterious stranger; they started off at once. And the first thing that Rackham discovered was that she could dance extremely well and talk hard at the same time.

"I do so love these things; you're always poppin' up against nice people, and it's fine 'ealthy exercise, to say nothing of it's bein' wot I call sociable. You must reelly, 'ave a turn with my Maud an' my Doris presently; they've both of 'em bin taught since they was tots by the Professor. Wot I always feel is, it does so fit you for any sort of 'igh society you may be called to. An' goodness knows you never know wot may 'appen to you w'en you're in the line."

"The line?" murmured Rackham politely.

"Yes—the public line. My 'usband was wot you might call born in it. It ain't wot it was w'en 'e began, but there's still something to be made out of it, an' you can keep it respectable, say wot they will. You 'ave got a nice step; I 'aven't been bumped into anybody the 'ole time, an' I've gorn round as easy as easy!"

Rackham contrived to get rid of the lady, and to dodge the daughters. He was getting a little tired of it, and felt that it wouldn't be a bad idea if he retired to his modest lodgings. He was just about to do so, and was making for the door, when he saw a girl walk quickly in and look about her.

She was the fairest thing that surely had ever walked into that dingy place. She was rather small; she gave an idea of fineness in all her movements and in the grace of her young figure. She was dressed in a rather shabby black frock; but there was a distinction about the fashion in which it was put on. From the crown of her head to her little worn shoes she was remarkable.

Her brown hair was coiled so that it lay low on her neck; her bright eyes seemed to take in all the room at a glance. Rackham knew that the gloves she was smoothing over her slim fingers were cheap; but they were clean and well-fitting. And the thing that fascinated him most, as he stood watching her, was the bright, alert look of her, as though this was the great occasion of her life—that to which she had been looking forward for a very long time. He changed his mind about going home, and stood back in a recess, watching.

The Professor had seen her at once, and came smilingly forward. In less than a minute she was whirling round the room with a youth who had advanced at the same moment.

The curious thing to Rackham, while he watched her with successive partners, was that it did not seem to matter in the least with whom she danced. She did not seem to know anyone; in the intervals she sat alone, or, if her partner spoke to her, answered quickly and brightly, with a little showing of very white teeth. And the moment the music started she was up and ready, and off again as soon as possible.

But after a time, with that kaleidoscopic business going on before him, he tired of watching her, and went off again in search of Joshua Flattery. He saw from the doorway, however, that Joshua was extremely busy, and so did not trouble him. Instead, in an aimless fashion, he strolled again towards the dancing-room.

There was a sort of dingy lumber-room that formed an *annexe* to the dancing-hall; it was piled up with chairs and a table or two and some music-stands. Rackham had glanced in idly as he was passing; he stopped to watch a little scene that was going on there, and, after watching it for a moment, stood behind a pile of chairs, quite without thinking about the matter; looked and listened.

The girl who had attracted his attention was standing there—erect and defiant, facing a youth who, a moment before, had been rather cumbrously struggling with her in an attempt to kiss her. As Rackham watched, he saw her suddenly flash out a white-gloved hand, and catch the youth a stinging blow on the side of his face.

"You little beast!" she exclaimed in a tense voice. "What do you mean by asking me to come in here, because you had something important to say to me, and then daring to do that? I don't even know your name—and I don't want to. Can't a respectable girl come here to enjoy herself without being insulted by you?"

As Rackham stepped into the room, the youth, with a hand to the side of his face, sulkily replied—"W'ere's the 'arm in it? Not the first time you've been kissed, I lay. Think yerself a fat lot better than other folks—puttin' on airs——"

Rackham might not have interfered, but that the girl, in a moment of sudden abandonment of nervousness and shame and vexation all combined, burst into tears. He stepped forward then, and suddenly took the youth by the collar, and shook him.

"Forgive my interfering," he said quietly. "Has this fellow been annoying you?"

"It—it doesn't matter, thank you," she said hurriedly.

"It matters a great deal, I think; and it might be well if he had a lesson that should teach him not to annoy a lady again," said Rackham, keeping his grip on the youth. "Now, you little viper," he added in a lower tone, "if you dare to squeal I'll knock the breath out of you; as it is, I'm only going to slap you, and kick you out into the street. And when next you show your ugly face here, if ever you do, be careful to behave properly."

"I hope you won't hurt him," said the girl quickly.

"Not for the world," said Rackham, with a smile. "But really people like these require teaching manners."

He took the hapless youth out into the corridor; and there, in the quietest, calmest fashion, boxed his ears, and shook him, and told him a few home truths; finally marched him along the corridor, and pitched him out—a spluttering, foul-mouthed thing—into the street. Then he walked back into that dingy little room where the lumber was, and where the girl stood, now fairly composed, waiting for him.

"I'm very sorry," she said, averting her face from him. "It's the first time such a thing has ever happened. I suppose I ought not to have come here alone; but I've always looked forward to it so much. I didn't care a bit about who I danced with; I'd have danced with a woman. It was just the fun of it—the idea of moving round to the music amongst the people."

She had forgotten her little trouble, and was getting enthusiastic and excited. She laughed a little consciously as she saw the tall man smiling down at her indulgently.

"How did it happen?" he asked. "That fellow was not your type of man at all."

"Oh—I don't mind that; they're all my type of men if it comes to that. I pick out the good dancers if I can— and that fellow could dance splendidly. But somehow or other he got hold of my name—and he thought it gave him a chance to presume a bit. That's really why I came into this room; I thought I'd tell him he'd got to behave himself."

"You certainly showed him he had," said Rackham.

"Well—how would you like to be called 'Angel' before a lot of people you didn't know?" she demanded indignantly. "It just happened that the Professor knew my name, because I come here pretty often; the Professor makes a reduction for me, because he says I dance well and do him credit. But I won't have people calling me by my name, just because they happen to have heard it by accident, without my permission."

"Well—you've got a pretty name, at any rate," said Rackham, highly amused with the girl's indignation. "A very pretty name indeed."

"I shall speak to the Professor about it; I told him at first I didn't want anybody to be getting familiar with me," said the girl, smoothing out her white gloves. "And the Professor was very nice, and he said, in the most gentlemanly way—'Of course, Miss Angelica Brown, I will be most careful.' And he has been."

Rackham stood staring at her—listening to the quick torrent of words, and yet, as it seemed, only hearing that name. Where had he heard it before? Out of what confused memory did it come back to him as a name he had heard, or read of, or dreamed about. Where had he seen someone standing handing out notes and gold to him—someone who bore that name?

"So your name is Miss Angelica Brown," he said at last, stupidly. "And he dared to call you 'Angel'? However, you won't see him again, so don't trouble about him. Are you going back to dance?"

"Yes—I think so," she said, after a moment's hesitation. "And I'm very much obliged to you for your kindness to me—very much obliged indeed." Quite frankly she held out her hand to him.

As he took it, all that business of the previous night was humming again through his mind—that talk of the great fortune in Chancery, and of the girl for whom search might some day be made. What had her name been?

And then suddenly, even in that moment of time while he held her hand, it flashed upon him; it was as though someone had spoken the name in the room.

Angelica Susan Brown!

"You don't happen to have any other names as pretty as that one, Miss Brown, I suppose?" he asked.

She blushed prettily as she withdrew her hand. "Nothing half so pretty," she said. "I'm glad you like that name; I like it myself. The other name isn't nice—at least, I don't think so."

"Might one venture to ask what it is?" he asked.

"My full name," said the girl, smoothing out her gloves, and getting minute creases out of them, and keeping her eyes fixed upon what she was doing—"my complete name is Angelica Susan Brown."

CHAPTER IV

THE HATCHING OF THE PLOT

THE magnitude of his discovery so staggered Rackham for a moment or two that he could do nothing but stare at the girl, standing with her pretty head bent over her gloves, and utterly unconscious of the effect she had produced. When at last she glanced up at him, he had had time to regain his composure; his expression was quiet and grave, although his heart was pounding strangely.

"I think I shall go and dance again," she said; and then stood still and looked at him without the faintest sign of coquetry, and yet with an invitation in her eyes. There was but one obvious thing for him to do: he bowed to her with a smile.

"May I have the pleasure?" he asked.

"I should love it," she said frankly. "I was watching you just now; you dance delightfully."

So once again Oliver Rackham took the floor in that dingy hall, though with a different sort of partner. As they danced his brain was in a whirl; he wondered what the shabby little girl who was his partner would think if he led her suddenly away into a corner, and said with the utmost seriousness—"My child, there is half a million of money waiting for you, and you've only got to prove your title to it, and you can have it. And after that you can dance to such a tune as few people dance to in this world;

and you can set other feet dancing—crowds and crowds of them, that shall be glad to move to any measure you may set!"

He answered absently when she talked to him; he was thinking only of the great discovery he had made. He was going back over it in his mind step by step—that chance meeting on the Embankment with Joshua Flattery, and the lending of the shilling; the reading of that slip of paper in Ventoul's rooms; and then this apparently mad business of the eighteenpenny "hop," with absurd people for partners. It was all like some mad dream; and he wondered if presently he should wake up, and laugh at it all; perhaps even find himself under the shadow of the statue on the Embankment, with the little waiter chanting his melancholy tune.

Their dance ended, she said that she was tired and was going home; after her experience she seemed to dislike the idea of any other chance partners.

"As our friend might be waiting outside, I think I'll walk a little way with you, if I may," said Rackham. "I'll be at the door if you'll get your hat."

There was no sign of the youth outside when they stepped into the street together; nevertheless, Rackham set off to walk with her. She noticed what seemed an omission at once, and glanced at him.

"You've forgotten your overcoat," she said.

"I left it at home," he answered. "I thought it was warmer than I have found it to be. It doesn't matter, I assure you."

What indeed could possibly matter when he thought of the happening of that night? Frankly, and a little brutally, Rackham had made up his mind that he would not lose sight of her; he dared not. Every thought had vanished from his mind except that one all-engrossing one: that this little shabby girl was worth half a million of money, and had not apparently the least idea of the fact.

"Will you ride—or do you prefer to walk?" he asked.

"I prefer to walk; I always walk," she said promptly. "When one spends money on luxuries, as I've done to-night, and as I do very often, one has to look at the pennies before one spends them on 'buses. It isn't very far; but you need not come a step farther if you don't want to. I'm not saying that rudely; I only mean that I shall be quite safe."

"I'll walk a little farther," he said. And then, after a pause—"I suppose you live with your people?"

She shook her head, and laughed. "I haven't any people," she said brightly. "I live all alone and look after myself; there's no one but just me and a canary. I manage to get a living for both of us——"

"And to get quite a lot of fun out of life, I expect," he broke in.

She nodded. "I should think so!" she cried. "Doesn't it seem to you that life's splendid—just to know that you belong to yourself, as it were, and have got a lovely world spread all around you for you to enjoy yourself in. I always think I'm so lucky; you see—I've had such a good time always."

"May a mere casual acquaintance ask what you do for a —a living?" asked Rackham.

"I teach music—piano, you know," she said. "I have a lot of pupils, and I'm running round to them all day long.

You see, they're very cheap—not the sort of people who can afford to pay much. You'd laugh if you knew what sort of terms I get, and how sometimes I have to wait for the money. But I do very well; I've sometimes far more pupils than I know what to do with. Then, of course, when people go away for holidays, and so on, I don't have so many, and that evens things up a bit. May a mere casual acquaintance—" she imitated his tone gravely—"ask what you do for your living?"

"Oh, I'm one of the idle sort; I do nothing."

She drew a quick little sigh. "A gentleman—with nothing to do. That must be nice in a way. I'm not complaining; but it must be lovely not to have to get up in the morning at a certain minute, and then hurry off somewhere and hurry back again. Do you like it?"

"I really couldn't tell you," he said. "There are times when I hate it, and when I loathe myself. Besides"—he thought of his own precarious position at that moment, and had a sudden recollection of Mr. Horace Ventoul—"it may not last. I might lose everything—and then I should be in Queer Street—shouldn't I?"

"But that isn't likely to happen, is it?" she asked, looking up at him quickly. "At the same time, it must be funny, if you've never done any work, to know how to begin. Now, I seem to have worked all my life. My mother—poor sweet dear!—was working when I was a little tiny tot, and could only just remember; and when she died she passed it on to me. In fact, before that I'd begun to help her a little."

They were passing through a very quiet street; Oliver Rackham had a dim idea that they had come to it by way of

Oxford Street, but he was not at all certain. Unconsciously their steps had slackened in that moment of confidence; she dwelt upon the past with this stranger as she probably had few opportunities of dwelling upon it with anyone.

"Did your mother teach music too?" Rackham asked.

The girl clasped her hands suddenly, and looked up at him. "Yes—beautifully!" she exclaimed, in an awed voice. "Ah—she was a musician; she knew all about it. If I lived to be a hundred, and studied hard every day instead of teaching people, I should never come near her. Why—as a baby I used to lie awake just to hear her—with her hands just stealing over the keys—making the divinest music you ever heard. It was a shame she ever had to teach; she was too good for it. With me," she added complacently, "it's different. I haven't got the hands for it, and perhaps I haven't got the brains. I play the things she used to play—but you'd laugh if you heard the difference. She could make a piano talk to you—till you laughed and cried, and felt all sorts of queer feelings down inside you."

"And so she had to teach instead of playing," said Rackham, with a sudden remembrance of that half a million of money tucked away snugly in Chancery, and waiting. "Wasn't there anyone to help her?"

"No one," answered the girl. "Father was dead; he died abroad. Father was a gentleman—so mother always said; I never saw him. He seems to have gone abroad directly after I was born—or perhaps before. Mother used to cry when she talked about him, and when she played over the things he had liked. Everything would have been very different if father had stayed with us, and had not died."

"You didn't know very much about him, then?" hazarded Rackham.

"Mother used to talk about him—when we were alone in the evenings in the firelight. She always believed that there was a lot of money in the family, and that it was coming to us; father had made lots of money, and then lost it. He seems to have been just the sort of man that would have a lot of money; mother and I used to talk about it often and often. When she was dying mother told me that she had always hoped and believed that I should be rich—and it might happen yet. It isn't very likely—is it?"

She turned her bright face up to him, and laughed merrily at the very thought of it, though with the laughter there was almost the sound of tears in her voice at the memories that had been stirred up. And here suddenly, at a street corner, she stopped, and held out her hand.

"I've been chattering away in the most disgraceful fashion," she said. "It's nice to have someone to talk to—and you've been very kind. But you mustn't come any further."

"Why not?" he asked, clinging to her hand for a moment. "Surely I may see you to the door of your house?"

"I haven't got a house—and that's why I don't ask you to see me to the door of it," she answered. "You see, I've only got what you would think a very poor room, up near the stars; and as you're a gentleman, and have been very nice to me, I want you to remember me at my very best. Also I don't want you to know exactly where I live;

you'll think all the better of me if you can imagine me living in some place that's much more splendid than my place really is. Good night—and I do hope you won't catch cold without your overcoat."

She turned and fled down the street, and turned the corner at the end of it into another, and was lost to view. There had been a momentary feeling in Rackham's mind that he would follow her; but he had the decency to check it. He stood there at the corner of the street, staring stupidly in the direction in which she had gone.

"Good Lord!" he suddenly muttered to himself. "She's the funniest little beggar I've come across in years. Angelica Susan Brown! To think that that shabby little teacher of music—counting pennies that she may not spend on 'buses—is worth half a million, and that I'm the only man that knows it! Two nights ago I slept in the streets, and was dependent on the charity of an odd-job waiter; to-night I've danced and walked and talked with half a million of money! Noll, my boy—you'd better get back to your bed at the coffee-house, and pull yourself together with a little sleep, before you give this business serious thought!"

He hailed a cab, and was driven back to his lodging. The proprietor of the coffee-house, who was just closing his establishment, was startled by the apparition of this man in evening dress, and parleyed a little with him before admitting him; and then was slavishly polite to one whom he evidently felt ought to have been charged more for the accommodation. Oliver Rackham went up to bed, and lay there awake for a long time, thinking about his great discovery, and wondering what he should do in regard to the matter of Miss Brown.

All sorts of wild ideas went through his mind during the night, and afterwards while he sat at breakfast in the coffee-house below. The man had been thrown off his balance, in a sense, by all that had happened; to find himself wearing decent clothes again, and with money in his pocket —and to know of all that hidden money, the key to which he alone held; all these things, after his three years of degradation, and his bitter experiences of privation in the streets, had shaken him more than he knew. The world had suddenly become a fairy place, in which anything and everything could happen and was happening; he wondered why he had ever dreaded the future at all. He had touched the very fringe of Romance; he was moving in a world where great things might be done.

It was a bright and sunny day, and he went out into the streets, to think about all that had happened, and to lay quite impossible plans. At first he made up his mind that he would haunt the neighborhood in which he had left her until he met her again; yet, even in coming to that resolution, he was no nearer any definite plan. All that he knew was that this was undoubtedly the girl who was wanted; and to do anything at all he must hand that knowledge on to someone else. For, in the first place, he did not even know how to set about helping her, and incidentally himself.

He was utterly without feeling in the matter; in a sense his experiences had brutalized him, and dulled his sense of right and wrong. Here was a great sum of money lying hidden, and waiting to be laid hold of; how should it be done?

With that indefinite feeling that there was money behind

him the man plunged a little—and more than a little. He knew that the money he had left in his pockets was not sufficient to form the groundwork of any future fortune; it might go, as well as the last two pence he had had out of Joshua Flattery's shilling had gone. Accordingly, he lunched well, and dined well; and then, with something of an instinct of mischief, and more with the feeling that he was now able, in a double sense, to triumph over Horace Ventoul, made his way to that gentleman's room.

There was no difficulty with the lift-man now; and even Wood stepped aside with alacrity, and admitted him. Rackham wore the tweed suit he had bought; that difficulty of the overcoat had to be considered. He handed his hat and stick to Wood, and walked straight into the sitting-room. Horace Ventoul lay back in a chair, smoking a cigarette, and reading a book. Apparently thinking that it was Wood who entered, he did not even look round.

"Don't tell me that you're reading one of your own immortal works!" exclaimed Rackham. And Horace Ventoul jumped up suddenly, and faced him.

"I thought you might be dipping into the book I saw yesterday, in order to improve your style," said Rackham, with a grin. "I'm back earlier than I anticipated; my expenses have been greater than I imagined, and my money is gone. Consequently I've come to the fountain-head, and I ask for a little more on account of my profits. Sit down, my dear Horace; I fear I disturbed you."

Horace Ventoul tossed the book he had been reading on to a table, and came across the room towards Rackham, with his head lowered, and his chin thrust forward. "I've been thinking about you—and about your profits—and about all the rest of it," he said, dropping his words out slowly and with precision. "And I'm not going to have anything to do with you. I'm not afraid of your violence, because there's a way of checking that; and I'm not afraid of your threats, because you can't do anything. The other night you took me by surprise; I wasn't prepared for you. Now I dare you to do your worst, and to talk as much as you like. Tell your story, Mr. Jail-Bird—and I'll tell mine; we'll see who'll be believed."

Rackham's hand shot out, and in a moment he had the other man in his grip. He was feeling stronger and more sure of himself than on the previous occasion; in a deadly, smiling fashion, he swung the other man to and fro, and laughed at his efforts to strike out at him or to free himself. Ventoul shouted feebly for Wood; but apparently that excellent man-servant had had enough of Oliver Rackham and his methods, and was conveniently deaf.

"You're not afraid of my violence—and you'll do this, that, and the other—will you?" exclaimed Rackham, as he swung the other man off his feet, and pushed him back into his chair. "Now, listen to me—and thank your stars that I happen to be in a good temper. You're a stupid fellow; one of these days you'll prompt me to hurt you, and then we shall both be sorry."

Horace Ventoul crouched in the chair, with his eyes blazing, while with nervous, shaking hands he put his disordered dress straight. He was breathing heavily, and was evidently only waiting for an opportunity to rush out and to summon assistance. There was no good opportunity yet; Oliver Rackham loomed huge before him, standing with hands on hips, looking down at him with a contemptuous smile.

"If you had any real brains you'd make the best of the situation, and understand once for all that I'm not to be shaken off," went on Rackham. "You've made money, and a certain amount of fame, out of me; don't be churlish and try and keep it all to yourself. I can't get the fame, but I mean to have some of the money. As for your talk of defiance, and all the rest of it—don't try it. And don't try to run away," he added, as the other made a sudden movement as if to get up, "because that won't help you."

With a wary eye upon his prisoner, he sauntered over to the sideboard, and mixed a whiskey and soda with no light hand. Ventoul's eyes were following his movements round the side of the deep chair; Ventoul understood just what the reckless man intended he should understand—that Rackham intended to make himself drunk, and so prove a more dangerous customer. He got up hurriedly, as the glass was raised to Rackham's lips; he spoke hurriedly.

"Look here—I expect I've got to buy you off; I expect that's the only way. What's your price?"

Rackham drank slowly, with his eyes watching the other man over the edge of the glass; he set down the glass, and laughed. Then he took a cigar from the box on the sideboard, and bit off the end, and lighted it. Finally he came across to where Ventoul was standing, and coolly puffed the smoke into his face, and laughed again.

"A lump sum is no good to me; it would be gone in no time at all," he said. "Besides, I want to see you get on in your new profession, my dear Horace—and you can't do that without me—can you? The only part of it you can manage is to stick your beastly name on the cover. Consequently, I'm not to be got rid of for any price, as you so inelegantly term it. I'll have a little when I want it, and I'll spend it, and I'll come again. And when I want it no longer you'll see no more of me."

"I'll pay you a sum down to get rid of you," said Ventoul doggedly.

Oliver Rackham shook his head and laughed. "When I came here first, you rubbed my misfortunes into me," he said, "and I haven't forgotten it. To-night you called me jail-bird; I shan't forget that. I warned you to be civil, and you've got to be. Besides, I'm coming into money myself soon—a decent little fortune—all on my own account."

"What are you talking about?" demanded the other, looking at him curiously. "Where are you likely to get money from?"

"Ha! ha!—you'd like to know all about that, wouldn't you?" laughed Rackham. "Fate has been good to me, my dear Horace, and has suddenly dropped within my reach the largest golden apple ever tossed to a man yet. One of these days I shall be able to leave you to your little comfortable income, and your stolen ideas, and all the rest of it; I shall go away in a blaze of glory."

Rackham would probably never have said that at all but for the fact that he was unnaturally excited. He had been maddened by the behavior of Ventoul—savage at the thought that this man was snug and well housed, while he lived in any precarious fashion he could, and had no hope for the future. Moreover, he remembered with very real vindictive delight that he had first heard the magic name of Angelica Susan Brown in that very room.

"I suppose you've got hold of some other scheme that'll land you in jail again?" suggested Ventoul.

"Nothing half so sordid, my dear friend," retorted the other. "All romantic and tender and beautiful—bright eyes, and a soft voice, and all the rest of it."

"You're drunk!" exclaimed Ventoul, turning away.

"I'm not—but I hope to be," said Rackham. "And now, as we used to do when we were good little boys at school, I'll give you the barest hint, and see if you're sharp enough to jump at it. Here's the hint: a scrap of paper!"

"A scrap of paper? There's no hint in that."

"Dunderhead! Why, it was in this very room that I saw a scrap of paper, and got a clue."

Horace Ventoul stood looking all about him; he had been so agitated on the occasion of their first meeting that the whole business had gone clean out of his head. He stood looking round; then slowly shook his head, and gazed blankly at Rackham.

"I haven't the least idea what you're talking about," he said at last; and turned away, and threw himself into his chair again. He was impatient to get rid of this fellow, and was casting about in his mind how best to do it.

Oliver Rackham had his glass in his hand; he raised it as if for a toast. "Hint number two! Angelica Susan Brown—God bless her!" He laughed, and drained his glass, and set it down with a bang.

Horace Ventoul started, gripped the arms of his chair, and slowly got to his feet. He came round the table towards the other man, and stared at him incredulously. There was something so confident about Rackham that, despite himself, Ventoul was impressed.

·"You madman! What are you talking about?" he half whispered.

"You're the most complimentary devil I've ever come across," answered Rackham good-temperedly, as he leaned with his back to the sideboard. "When I had the pleasure of meeting you just now it was"—he made a flourish with one arm, and laughed—"Mr. Jail-Bird; now I'm a madman. We'll see what you call me presently, when you know all about it. Meanwhile, as we're dealing with a lady, you shall toast her—and there shall be no heel-taps about the business!"

With a certain sly eagerness about him, Ventoul mixed for them both—mildly as regarded himself, and more generously for his visitor. When they stood with glasses in hand facing each other, Ventoul spoke quickly.

"You know something? You've heard something? What is it?"

"Now I come to think of it, I don't think I'll tell you," said Rackham smilingly. "One doesn't bandy a lady's name carelessly—at least, a gentleman doesn't. Extremely wrong of me to have mentioned the matter. On second thoughts, my dear Horace, I think I'll accept your first invitation, and go away. Here's to you—and good night with it."

He drained his glass, still with an eye upon the other man. Ventoul stood expectant. This might be worth nothing; on the other hand, it might be worth everything. What if this fellow had blundered upon the secret somehow or other; what if his knowledge could be bought? In a sense, he was down to the depths; he could be squeezed.

"Stop a bit, my dear fellow—stop a bit!" urged Ventoul. "I don't want to turn you out. Besides, we haven't drunk the lady's health yet—and your glass is empty. Fill up—and let's drink to Miss Angelica Susan Brown."

"You sly dog! I suppose you think I'll talk better when I'm drunk than when I'm sober—eh?" said Rackham. "Well, I'm willing to humor you; you can mix for me again. And after that I'll tell you all about it—or rather, all about her."

Ventoul mixed and pressed the glass upon his friend; he was all smiles now. "Come," said he, "let's do the thing properly this time. The lady first—a proper toast!"

"I should like to see you—just for once in my life—in the condition to which I am fast approaching," said Rackham. "You're much too careful for that—and much too respectable. I'm neither careful nor respectable—God help me!—and so I fall into the clutches of men like yourself. However, that's neither here nor there. The lady first, by all means. I give you Angelica Susan Brown, and half a million of money!"

He drained his glass, and set it down. Ventoul drank a little of his, and set it down also. Noticing the omission, Rackham pointed to it; and Ventoul, with a smile, drained his glass also.

"And now I suppose you want to know all about it?" suggested Rackham. "If it's a spoof, I suppose you think you'll be able to get virtuously indignant and turn me out; if it's not a spoof, you want to have a hand in it—and to plunge that hand into a matter of half a million of money!"

"My dear fellow, if you have made any discoveries, I want to know all about them, of course," said Ventoul.

"Come and sit down, and let's talk this over. After all, you know, I first gave you the information as to this vast fortune——"

"And I happen to have found the girl, which is rather more important," said Rackham. "I'm not yet drunk enough to forget that fact, and to hold tight to it. I have walked and I have talked with Angelica Susan Brown, and I have convinced myself that she is the person for whom a big fortune is waiting. That being so, I have determined to dip into that fortune, if possible, for myself. If, out of kindness of heart, I let a friend into the game, that friend has got to be properly grateful, and has got to show his gratitude in an appropriate manner. Do you tumble to that?"

"My dear old Noll, if you have found this girl and can produce her, there is something more than a fortune in it," said the other earnestly.

"Your dear old Noll—no longer Jail-bird or madman, mark you!—can produce that girl at any time," answered Rackham, leaning across the table and shaking his head at the other man, "but he isn't going to do it. You talked just now about some beggarly price, to get rid of me; what's your price now for me to stay?"

"Look here, Noll, this is business, and I beg you'll forget any unpleasantness that may have arisen between us," said Ventoul, speaking as though with some difficulty. "Do you know where this girl's to be found?"

"I—I think so."

"You think so?" snapped the other. "You said just now——"

"Don't be in such a devil of a hurry," broke in Rackham. "As a matter of fact, I left the lady last night at a street corner, where she made a somewhat hurried exit—vanished, as a man might say, into the wilds of London. But I don't doubt that I can find her again; in fact, I'm sure of it."

"But are you sure of her name—are you sure that she is the real identical girl that is wanted?" asked the other impatiently.

"My dear fellow, by the merest chance I lighted upon the lady in a place where, of all other places, I should scarcely have expected to find her. In a rather melodramatic fashion I rescued her from a ruffian—sounds rather well, doesn't it?—gained her confidence, and found out all about her. Very romantic; not at all bad-looking; a music-teacher, to be precise, living all alone."

"The half-a-million girl is supposed to be quite alone—deserted in infancy," said Ventoul quickly.

"This girl's father deserted her in infancy, and went abroad. Died abroad. Was always supposed to be connected with money, or to have money coming to him. A perfect gentleman, according to all accounts, though I suspicion the blackguard. Mother a musician, and apparently a lady; died when the girl was able to take on the succession to the music-teaching business. Girl somewhat aristocratic-looking, if better dressed; in other words, quite presentable. There you have everything."

"It's the girl—safe as houses!" cried Ventoul, springing to his feet and clapping his hands. "By Jove, Noll, you're a marvel!"

"Another new name to add to my varied collection; I shall have to keep a list of them, or I shan't know myself," said Rackham, with a laugh, as he got up and faced the other man. "Well, what are we going to do about it?"

Horace Ventoul walked excitedly up and down the room for a moment or two before replying; he seemed to be turning the matter over rapidly in his mind. "I suppose," he said at last, "there's no possibility that the girl guesses?"

"Guesses that she's worth half a million?" asked Rackham. "My dear Horace, she's perfectly contented with her one room, and her canary, and to go on teaching five-finger exercises, and 'The Maiden's Prayer,' and 'The Battle of Prague,' and all the rest of it, as long as she lives. Remember—after all you only heard about it by chance—and I only found her by chance."

"Yes—yes—I quite see that," said Ventoul rapidly. "Now, what we've got to do first of all is to get hold of her, somehow or other, and then we can get to work. Where can you find her?"

"Ah—that's telling," said Rackham. "Do you imagine, my sweet Horace, that I'm going to be fool enough to give the matter into your hands, and let you walk off with her or the fortune, or both? I have made the discovery, and, while I might be prepared to sell it, the probability is that I shall keep it to myself."

"If one man has found her, another can," said Ventoul sharply. "I've got better opportunities than you have, and I can go to work on my own account."

Rackham laughed. "How are you going to begin?" he asked. "Perhaps you'd like to advertise?"

"I might do that; I could get hold of her fast enough that way."

"And, in these days of newspaper enterprise, let all

London, and all the world for the matter of that, know that the young lady is wanted, and probably why she is wanted. Then some enterprising solicitor steps in—finds out all about the fortune—and hands it to her, with a little bit for himself. And where does Mr. Horace Ventoul come in then?"

Horace Ventoul evidently thought about that point rather deeply; he was silent for a few moments. At last he asked—"Well, what's your price for this bit of business—just for handing over all you know to me?"

"I don't think I'll do a deal—at least not with you," said Rackham. "I just thought that I'd like you to know how much your little slip of paper had helped me, and how in a very short time I shall probably be beyond the necessity for appealing to you at all. If you'd behaved nicely I might have gone shares."

"You're the most exasperating brute I've ever come across," exclaimed Ventoul savagely.

"Another pet name; I wonder how many more I shall get. Hadn't you better make some suggestion? I might be disposed to think it over. I'll show my cards to this extent; I'm pretty helpless without money, and you're the only one to whom I feel I have a right to appeal. Mine's not so much an appeal as a demand."

"Now you seem to be coming to your senses," said Ventoul.

"I've never lost them," retorted the other. "Only it's the sport of the game I like—just to keep you dangling at the end of a string, as it were; you make most excellent sport. Now if any unholy hands are to be laid upon this money, I take it that it is essential we get hold of the fair

Angelica, in some way or other, and bind her to us; so that when it is inevitably sprung upon her that this money is hers, and we produce her, we are able to cry—'Shares!' Isn't that the idea?"

"Yes—that's the idea," said Ventoul. "By Jove, Noll, if we can keep this thing to ourselves, and can keep her to ourselves, it won't matter a bit what we spend on the game; the reward will be enough. Why, I might even marry her."

"You might—and then again you might not," retorted Rackham. "You're an ugly little devil, and she mightn't take any violent fancy to you. Besides—where do I come in?"

"I think your little prison record rather disposes of your chances," said the other. "However, we're not going to quarrel over details at present; what we've got to consider is the best way to set about this business—and the best way to secure her. I take it that at the moment she is practically a stranger to you, and knows nothing about you?"

"The Lord be praised!—she knows nothing about me," said Rackham. "As I have told you, I met her by the merest chance; learned her name by the merest chance; and was able to strike up an acquaintance with her."

"She doesn't seem very particular what company she keeps," sneered Ventoul. "Is she a lady? Where did you meet her?"

"That's precisely what I'm not going to tell you," retorted the other. "And I should have to be very drunk indeed to give away that part of the game. It's for you to make the next move."

"Well—suppose I can set some big game afoot—something that shall draw her right into our hands—will you help me, and will you bring her to me?"

Rackham walked across to the sideboard, and took up the decanter; paused in the very act of pouring out the spirit, and set the decanter down. When he came back to the other man his eyes were hard and unsmiling.

"Look here," he said, "I'll be plain with you. In this infernal world I see no earthly chance of getting anything honestly—and I won't starve. I was a fool before, and I made one ghastly blunder, when I robbed an old uncle who had more than he wanted, and who had never done anything to help me, although I was his only sister's son. That's all past and done with; I'm only putting my case before you."

"Well—I'm listening," said the other, watching him steadily.

"There's nothing I can do for a living—it all seems hopeless. Consequently, as life still holds out hands to me, and says, 'Come out into the world, and enjoy yourself!' I've got to get money somehow. This girl doesn't want her half-million; a quarter of it would be more than enough for her wants; consequently, I tell myself that I might as well get something out of my discovery of her. But I want to know what's going to happen to her."

"There's plenty of time to discuss that," said Ventoul.

"The only time to discuss it is now," retorted Rackham. "I've not fallen so low as that—that I could dip into this business, and hurt her. I'll rob her cheerfully—if I can do it safely; but she's a good, hard-working, joyous little thing, and I won't harm her. Is that clear?"

"Oh, I see! you're taking the high moral standard,"

said Ventoul, with a smile. "It comes strangely from you——"

"Drop that!" said Rackham. "I've named my terms, so far as she's concerned, and I go into it—this business of plunder—without any misunderstanding. But I want it understood that if at any time any harm threatens her, I give the whole game away—tell the whole conspiracy—at whatever the penalty. Is that clear?"

"Yes—that's quite clear," answered Ventoul slowly. "I take it we're both in this game for what we can get out of it; the future must decide how we're going to do it. If you'll give me a few hours to think it over, I'll have a plan ready. It ought to be pretty simple."

"Meanwhile—I must have something to go on with," said Rackham.

"Willingly," answered the other, with a laugh. "Shall we say ten pounds?"

"As it's a little like blood-money, and the beginning of what we might call a dirty business, I think we'll call it twenty," said Rackham coolly.

Ventoul shrugged his shoulders, crossed the room to his desk, and unlocked it and took out a cheque-book. He wrote the cheque, and handed it to Rackham.

"I'm taking risks," said Ventoul, "but as I expect a big return I don't mind. Will you come again to-morrow?"

"How pressing you are!" said Rackham, with a grin, as he folded the cheque and put it in his pocket. "No—I won't come to-morrow, because I've got to look for the fair Angelica, and find out whether she can be permanently located. I'll come the next day. Good night!"

He was so ashamed of the business, even then at the very beginning, that when Ventoul held out his hand to him he stood looking at it stupidly for a moment, and then turned away without touching it. Even in the street he stopped for a moment in the darkness, and put his hand on the cheque in his pocket, half-minded to go back, and return it, and be done with the sorry game forever. But it happened that the night was chill, and the few coins in his pocket had come down to a matter of silver; he knew there was no hope for him. So he marched away to his lodgings over the coffee-house, and had soon forgotten any scruples he might have had in a troubled sleep.

CHAPTER V

THE GATHERING OF THE ENEMY

It was only after Oliver Rackham had gone that Mr. Horace Ventoul remembered that he did not know where to find that gentleman, or whether indeed he was ever likely to return. Oliver Rackham with twenty pounds in his pocket, and all London before him, was a disaster in himself; it was impossible to say or to suggest what he might or might not do. And in that estimate of him Ventoul was fairly correct.

For Rackham awoke in the morning with an indistinct notion of what he had promised or what he had arranged, but with a keen perception of the fact that he had in his pocket a cheque for twenty pounds. While he dressed leisurely he tried to think what it was that he had specially arranged—what plot he had hatched with the man he despised, Horace Ventoul.

And then, as might have been expected, there swept over him a wave of contrition. It was disgusting, and it was disgraceful; why should he plot against anyone who was helpless? In a sentimental moment Rackham told himself that this girl was the brightest, sweetest thing that had ever danced into his life; was he to conspire with a man like Ventoul against her? Had she not told him, in her simplest fashion, how she earned money for the support of herself and her canary? (Tears almost sprang to his eyes at the thought of the canary.) Had she not confided to him what her simple, hard-working life was? Perish the thought that he should conspire against her!

With twenty pounds in his pocket London was no longer a city to be viewed with dread; he was the equal of any man. At the best, he was decently clothed, and his time was his own, and he had money in his pocket. At the worst, he might think of this hateful business when the money was gone. That had ever been his way, and should be his way again. All sorts of things might happen before that twenty pounds had gone the way of all other money.

So it came about that the man drifted—just as he had drifted before. If he thought of the girl at all, it was as of someone outside his world—someone who might, in the dim future, hear of her fortune, and take it; someone who, on the other hand, might never hear of it, and might work on contentedly to the end. Life was a game of chances; he would take it hour by hour as it came to him, and make the most of it. For the moment he was in good circumstances; nothing else mattered.

And then, in the most inconsequent fashion, there came upon him a longing to see the girl. It came upon him suddenly, while he sat smoking and idly gazing at the crowd in Hyde Park; it was almost as though she had appeared suddenly before him. He saw her again in that dingy dancing-hall—coming in, alert and eager and upright, with shining eyes, and drawing on her cheap gloves. He remembered her faith in him, and her brave and fearless outlook on life; he thought of that room she had suggested to him, up near the stars, with only herself and the canary. He found himself wondering what she was doing at that moment—beside what cheap piano she was sitting, teaching some urchin to torture future friends and acquaintances.

He decided that he would try to find her. Ventoul was not to be thought of at the moment; Ventoul was a brute, who would trade on anyone; Ventoul should be left severely alone. After all, what had Ventoul to do with this bright young girl, with whom Oliver Rackham, on one mad evening, had danced and walked and talked?

Rackham had bought himself a ready-made overcoat (as being cheaper, in the long run, than innumerable cabs), and he dressed with care, and went again to Hamlyn Street, Tottenham Court Road. He did not intend to dance; he simply meant to wait about the place until he saw her, and, if possible, get into conversation with her again. He paid his eighteenpence for admission, and went in.

But it happened that she was not there. He went and watched the dancers, smilingly telling the eager Professor Dorn, who approached him at once, that he would not dance that night, and meeting indifferently the languishing look of the lady in blue velvet. But no alert little figure stood there to dance with all and sundry. He waited until the last late stragglers had drifted away, and then bethought himself of Joshua Flattery, and went in search of him.

He found Joshua emerging from a sort of cupboard, in which he had evidently been changing his clothes; he carried under his arm the brown-paper parcel which contained his official raiment. He seemed surprised at seeing Rackham again, and deferentially removed his bowler-hat from his bald head.

"I didn't know you was 'ere, sir," he said. "You 'ave take a fancy to these 'ops, sir—'aven't you?"

"Not particularly," answered Rackham. "But I'm an idle man, with but few friends, and so I came to while away an hour or so. If you're going home I'll walk with you."

"Well, sir—I ain't quite the figure to be seen walking with a gentleman like you, sir—but if you don't mind——"

"Oh, that's all right," broke in Rackham. "Where do you live?"

"Neighborhood of Drury Lane, sir," answered Flattery humbly. "Very 'andy, sir, and very cheap—both of which is a consideration."

They walked on in silence for some minues—an awkward silence for Joshua Flattery, who had no conversation equal to the occasion. Oliver Rackham had a question to ask, and was wondering how best to frame it.

"By the way, Joshua," he said at last, "I notice that one of your dancers was not there to-night."

"Bless you, sir, they comes an' they goes," answered the little waiter. "There's some as comes reg'lar, an' some as looks in casual-like. W'ich one was it in partic'lar, sir?"

"A young lady I danced with the other night—name of Brown, I think," answered Rackham.

"Dunno any of their names, sir," said Joshua Flattery, pushing the bowler-hat back from his forehead, the better to scratch his head thoughtfully. "Would it be the little thin one, sir, that comes pretty often—bit better class than some of 'em?"

"That's the one," replied Rackham. "Do you know anything about her?"

"No, sir," answered the waiter. "I can't call to mind that she's ever bin in the refreshment-room, not all the time she's bin there. 'Olds 'erself a bit select, as you might say, sir. She's there most nights, I know, sir."

There was obviously nothing to be got out of Joshua Flattery; and Rackham presently parted from him before they reached Drury Lane, and went off to his own lodging. In view of what had seemed an inexhaustible gold mine, Rackham had left the coffee-house, and had taken a room in a decent hotel near at hand. It was, of course, much more expensive, but that had not seemed to matter at the time.

He lay in bed that night, wide-awake, and seriously disturbed about the girl. His scruples were gone again; he only wondered what was going to happen if, by some chance, she never came near Professor Dorn's Academy again. It would be almost impossible for him to trace her, at all events in any unsuspicious way; all that upon which he had built so carefully would be gone. How could he approach Horace Ventoul again—only to tell that gentleman that the girl had vanished into a maze of streets, and was not to be found?

Five days had gone by since he had left Ventoul's rooms—five days of recklessness. Something must be done, and that, too, within the shortest possible time. True, he had a few pounds left in his pocket; but those few pounds stood between himself and a future that was utterly dark and desolate. Willy-nilly, the plot must be carried through if he would live at all; by his own recklessness the thing had been forced upon him.

That night he went again to the little street opening out

of Tottenham Court Road, and waited with a strange new eagerness, as he saw the various people coming in. And at last she came—just as quickly and eagerly as before, with no thought of him or anyone else, but only with quickening steps as she heard the sorry band begin.

She hurried past without seeing him, and went to take off her hat and coat. She returned in a few minutes; and then he was waiting for her, and holding out his hand with a smile.

"I didn't expect to see you here again," said the girl, as she took his hand. "I thought you had just come once—to see what it was like—and then would never be here again."

"May I dance with you?" he asked. And they set off at once.

She danced more than once with him. She was curiously silent; the bright chatter with which she had been so ready when they had walked together on that previous occasion was markedly absent now. And presently she sat down with him on one of the rout seats against the wall, and laid her clasped hands in her lap, and closed her eyes. She had stopped in the very middle of a dance, and had declared that she was tired.

As they sat there in a corner of the room, the dancers were flying past them—dancers of all sorts and conditions and ages. Rackham found himself looking at the girl closely; at the thin, delicate face with the closed eyes—at the tender lines of the figure—at the little hands clasped together lightly in her lap. It seemed so incongruous that she should be here in this place; incongruous that she should be shabby and tired and alone.

"I thought you were never tired," he said gently.

She opened her eyes, and looked round at him with a smile. "It's a little unusual," she said. "Only to-day has seemed a bad day altogether: pupils were wrong, and one mother wasn't satisfied, and said she wouldn't want me to come again—one of those days when things will go wrong. I came here, thinking I'd shake it off. I think that's what made me glad to see you. I had a horrible feeling this afternoon that life was just a long straight grey road, dotted on each side with pianos, all out of tune; and that I was just stopping at each of the pianos to teach some grubby child; and that there was never going to be anything else but that road, for ever and ever, as long as I live. Life wasn't any more gay and fine; it was just a long monotony."

Almost it was in the man's heart to say to her then: "You need not travel that road any longer; you need not ever teach a grubby child again to fumble out its notes; there's a great fortune waiting for you, and I'll tell you how to get it. And then I'll go away, and starve, and never look into your face again!"

Only of course he did not say that; he hardened his heart, and told himself pleasant sophistries—as, for example, that if she was suddenly put in possession of such a sum of money she must inevitably be preyed upon by harpies and dangerous people of all sorts, and be robbed right and left. Far better leave things as they had been arranged; he would see to it that she was not robbed unduly.

"It might happen," he said, "that you got a chance of stepping off that road for ever—getting out of monotony, and into something sweeter and more wholesome. You'd like that?"

She shrugged her shoulders, and slowly shook her head. "That's never likely to happen to me," she said. "I'm not that sort of person at all. And I'm an ungrateful little brute, to be talking as I have done, without ever thinking for a moment that I'm perfectly happy, and that I've got a tremendous lot to be thankful for."

"Will you dance again?" he asked.

"I don't think so; it wouldn't be like dancing if I danced with anyone else after you," she said quite frankly. "I don't talk to anyone else; they're just here to catch hold of and dance with. I think I shall go home."

"And may a comparative stranger walk a little way with you again?"

"A comparative stranger may—if he will be so very kind," she said, with a little laugh and a bow, as she went off to get her hat.

"You haven't forgotten your overcoat to-night," she said, as they got into the street. "I'm glad of that, because I thought that you might have caught cold the other night, and I should have felt it was my fault. Because, you see, if it hadn't been for me you would probably have taken a cab."

He was in dread lest, when she reached that corner at which she had previously dismissed him, she should do so again; but this time she did not appear to think of it. She walked on quietly, turning corners, and chatting with him on different matters, until at last she stopped dead in front of a house and took out a latch-key. He noted the number, as he had noted the name of the street.

"This is where I live," she said, "and I carry a key, because it saves the landlady from coming up the stairs each time, or down the stairs, as the case may be, to let me in. Good night!"

"Good night!" he said, holding her hand for a moment. "Shall I ever see you again?"

"Perhaps. Who knows?" she said, with the faintest possible touch of coquetry. And then, more earnestly and in a more natural voice, "Yes, I hope so."

She was gone, and he was looking at the blank house. He walked slowly away with that address in his mind. He half thought that he would go and find Ventoul that night, and see what plan that gentleman had evolved and what he purposed doing. But again—as always when the thought of the girl was most strongly upon him—he hesitated, and decided that he would sleep upon the matter.

Morning, and a somewhat extravagant bill for hotel expenses, brought him, as before, hard up against the solid facts of life; he decided to go and see Horace Ventoul. After all, there could be no harm in discussing the matter; a decision was quite another thing.

He found Horace Ventoul looking rather smaller and meaner even than usual in dressing-gown and slippers. The man Wood, holding a tray that clattered at the sight of Rackham, was removing the remains of a late breakfast.

"Have you breakfasted?" asked Ventoul, as he got quickly to his feet at the sight of the other man. And then, as Rackham nodded and signed to Wood to take away the tray, Ventoul went on rapidly, "I've been expecting you for days past. What on earth have you been doing?"

"Wood—I call you to witness that your esteemed master is delighted to see me, and has been quite upset by my absence," said Rackham, detaining the man for a moment with a movement of his hand. "Has Mr. Ventoul eaten with an appetite and slept well while I have been away?"

"That will do, Wood; you can go," broke in Ventoul.

"That will not do, Wood; you can stop!" exclaimed Rackham. And then to Ventoul—"I don't know what there is about you that raises the devil in me always; but I can't help it. Now, Wood, answer my question; I am anxious about your master."

The unfortunate Wood, with an eye upon his master, and holding the tray stiffly in front of him, replied, "So far as I am aware, sir, Mr. Ventoul's 'ealth and appetite 'as bin about normal, sir."

"Wood, you relieve my mind immensely. Now get out," said Rackham. And the man-servant retired in a hurried, perturbed way.

"Well, what have you been doing?" demanded Ventoul, after a pause. "You were to come to me three or four days ago; and here I've been waiting and waiting, and wondering if, by some devil's luck, you'd got drunk and been run over, or fallen into the river, or something of that sort."

"Love like this," said Oliver Rackham, seating himself upon the table and looking round at the walls, "affects me deeply. Did you mourn like this, Horace, during the years that I was playing jail-bird and you were having my immortal works published? I can picture you weeping on the bosom of the respectable Wood every morning, and yearning for my return. It's quite touching."

"You were to come back here, and tell me about this girl; you were to find her, and bring me word of her," cried Ventoul impatiently.

"And I failed to find her——"

"What?" exclaimed Ventoul in dismay.

"Until last night," went on Rackham, with a smile. "Now I know all about her, and where she lives, and I am pledged to meet her again. What do you think of that?"

"Well—what's the address?" asked Ventoul, with an impatient stamp of his foot. "You're the slowest fellow I know."

"You'll find me slower still before you get the address out of me," answered Rackham calmly. "That's my trump card; when I know what your plan is, and when I approve it, I'll produce Miss Angelica Susan Brown. If I gave the game away to you now, you could snap your fingers at me. Come—you've had five or six days to think it all over; I'll warrant you have some idea of what you mean to do."

Ventoul was silent for a few moments; then, sitting in his deep chair, and looking a mere mass of folds upon folds of dressing-gown, with a face peering out above the folds, he said what was in his mind.

"Yes—I've thought of a plan, and a good one. It's a bold scheme; but this is a business that needs boldness. With such a sum involved, it seems to me that we may not stick at trifles. When I first thought of the plan I was a little frightened at the boldness of it; but then nothing was ever carried through in this world that wasn't done boldly. Now, are you listening carefully?"

"I breakfasted early, and I need something to stimulate my wits, when I set them against yours," said Rackham. "Consequently, I'll disgust your fine susceptibilities by taking a drink and a cigar; then I'll listen with deep attention."

Horace Ventoul sat, with an impatiently moving foot, while Rackham leisurely made his preparations; then, when that gentleman was ready, plunged into his scheme.

"The first thing that occurred to me was that this girl, who is quite young, I take it——"

"But little more than a child, I should say," answered Rackham.

"So I thought. Well—it occurred to me that she has pretty much of a struggle of it to make both ends meet at her music teaching; she would welcome anything that offered the prospect of a change and an easier life."

"Curiously enough, she hinted at something of the sort when last I had the pleasure of seeing her," said Rackham.

"That's excellent," exclaimed the other, leaning forward in his chair, and slowly rubbing his hands. "Now, suppose I knew of someone who wanted a companion—or a governess—or something of that sort; someone who was prepared to pay very good wages? Could our young friend be induced to accept such a post, with the prospect that it would be a permanency?"

"What family are you going to get—and where—that will take a girl like this on your recommendation, and pay a big stipend?" asked Rackham slowly.

"My dear old Noll—that question alone suggests your simplicity. In such a case as this, and with such a prize at stake, I provide the family and the establishment and everything. I pay the price—looking for my reward afterwards."

"Where do you propose to start this establishment?" asked Rackham, after a thoughtful pause. "I'm not denying that it sounds well, and looks like treating the girl decently; but where is it to be?"

"In some remote and peaceful place in the country—a place where no questions will be asked about a little governess, or companion, or whatever she may happen to be. Afterwards, when she is well established, I put in an appearance—and the game begins."

"Explain yourself a little more clearly," said Rackham. "In the first place, what do you expect to do when you put in an appearance?"

"That is a matter not yet decided," answered Ventoul coolly. "Suffice it that I, as usual, pay the piper, and I call the tune. The family who are prepared to be so generous to an unknown girl will have their instructions from me, and will be paid by me. Afterwards I shall come in as a stranger—or perhaps even as a friend of theirs; then I shall make the running with the little governess, or companion, or whatever she may chance to be. Anything and everything may happen when once we have the girl, unsuspiciously, in our hands. Well—what do you think of it?"

"It's a beautiful plan; it almost takes my breath away," said Rackham, with a smile beginning to steal over his face. "It's colossal in its audacity, as you suggested—and I don't see how it could fail. There's one particularly weak spot in it which I should like to point out, however."

"Well—what is it?" asked Ventoul, as the other paused.

"I don't quite see where I come in," answered Rackham.

"Oh—of course you're in it; you share with me. You don't imagine for a moment, my dear fellow, that I should leave you out in the cold—do you?"

"My dear Horace—I am absolutely certain that you would, if you got the chance," Rackham said blandly. "Therefore I think we'll drop your little plan, and perhaps I shall think of one on my own account. I may be able to get hold of some money from somewhere; one never knows. But I don't rely on you, my dear Horace, and I'm not taking risks. Moreover, I don't like the idea of this family being scraped up, and arranged, and set down in their particular landscape; and then the girl left to their tender mercies and to yours."

"My dear old Noll—you surely don't think that I mean you to be left outside the picture—do you?" asked Ventoul, as he got to his feet, and came towards the other man. "You must be in it from the beginning; you alone, at the present moment, know the girl, and are in a position to approach her with any such offer as I have suggested. My dear boy—why do you wilfully misunderstand me always?"

"Because I know something of you, my charming Horace, and I've got to look after you. Do you suggest, then, that I am to be a sort of watch-dog in the business? Am I to be one of the family, for instance?"

"You shall go down there in some capacity; that is essential," replied Ventoul. "At the moment I frankly admit that I am in your hands; therefore, even if I wanted to do so, I can't desert you. What do you think of the plan?"

"It's good in its way; but where do you get your family?"

Horace Ventoul laughed. "Curiously enough, that's the easiest part of the whole business," he said. "There's a certain man I know—a worthless, shiftless rascal; I met him by the merest chance. He was a solicitor, and was struck off the rolls some years ago for malpractices. Now he lives by touting for other solicitors, in the getting of clients in criminal cases of the smaller sort, and in giving advice to shady people of all kinds—in fact, in picking up half a crown where and how he can. And the fortunate thing about him is that he is a man of gentlemanly appearance and manner; the further fortunate thing about him is that he has a wife who is almost a lady. Let them dress the part properly, and put them in some little country house, and you'd think they'd belonged to the place for generations."

"We shall be a nice, lively, criminal crew to fight against the girl—shan't we?" said Rackham, with a laugh. "But suppose your broken solicitor-friend gets wind of the business, and is able to make hay while the sun shines on his own account—what then?"

"He won't get wind of it. He will simply be following instructions, at a decent salary, and living on the fat of the land while he's doing it. And the best of the business will be that, as he knows me, and is well paid to be quiet, he won't be asking awkward questions, as any more respectable family man might be."

"And—having got the girl down there, and you having arrived—what happens?"

"I tell you I don't know," retorted Ventoul. "I may make love to her—I may marry her; or, on the other hand, I may go to those who would be naturally interested in the discovery of this girl, and I may say to them—'On payment of so much I can produce the lady.' It's all in the air at the present moment; circumstances must show us what to do."

"And again where do I come in?" demanded Rackham.

"I think you might go down in the capacity of a friend, or a secretary, or something of that kind; you will then be on the spot, and will be able to watch over the girl, as you are evidently so strongly desirous of doing."

"Where can you find this man?" asked Rackham after a long pause, during which he had sat staring frowningly at the carpet.

"I can find him at any time in the private bar of a little public-house in a court leading out of Chancery Lane," answered Ventoul promptly. "There he is generally to be found by such clients as need him; it's the poor wretch's office. I daresay we should find him there to-day if we wanted him."

"Well—I should like to have a look at him," said Rackham, with an air of decision. "And after all I could always keep him quiet, and make him behave, if I was in the same house with him. What's the wife like?"

"Oh—has been rather pretty, and now given to tears and lamentations over her husband's fallen state. She could be made to look quite presentable; for his sake she'd hold her tongue."

"My dear Horace," said Rackham, glancing at the little clock on the mantelpiece—"we will go and see this man at once, and afterwards I will lunch with you at your club or elsewhere—as you like."

"Not at the club—thank you," said Horace Ventoul hastily.

"Ah—of course you don't want to be seen feeding with jail-birds, do you?" said Rackham, with a laugh. "Well, we'll go elsewhere, and the more expensive it is the better I shall like it. Now, get into some clothes, and we'll start."

Horace Ventoul—eager enough now that the business seemed fairly afoot—went off to finish dressing; Oliver Rackham wandered aimlessly about the room, with a visit or two to the sideboard, until such time as the other should be ready. When presently Ventoul returned, they set off together, and drove to Chancery Lane.

Ventoul seemed to know his way well; he dived into a little court, and pushed open a door, and entered the tiny bar of a public-house. There were only two men in it at the moment one, a tall man, of a melancholy cast of countenance, who had an old silk hat perched on the back of his head, and who was leaning with his back against the wall, and with his hands in his pockets. When presently he moved, Rackham saw that there was a mark, at about the height of his shoulders, on the wall, as though suggesting that that was his habitual resting-place. He had a long drooping moustache that had gone to seed from neglect and from much contemplative pulling at it; for the rest he was cleanly shaven, if that term can be applied to a two days' growth of beard.

The man to whom he was talking was of a different character altogether; a little rat-like man, in a check suit that had once been loud but had now faded to a more modest color; he was arguing in a low voice to the tall man, who, with half-closed eyes, seemed to be taking not the faintest notice of him.

"That's our man," whispered Ventoul to Rackham. "He'll look all right when he's dressed."

"He'll take a devil of a lot of dressing," whispered Rackham in reply. "For my part, I should begin by washing him; he'd stand it."

Meanwhile the tall man had noticed Ventoul, and had saluted him by the raising of a couple of fingers to the brim of his hat. At the same time he spoke sharply to the man who had been arguing with him.

"That'll do, Jimmy; you can cut and run. I'll talk to you about it some other time, but so far as I can see at present there's nothing in it."

The man in the check suit shrugged his shoulders, and turned, and went out of the place; the other man remained in his position against the wall, with eyes fixed a little furtively upon Ventoul and his companion.

"Mr. Street," said Ventoul, stepping forward, "is this an hour of the morning when you are prepared to talk of business?"

"All hours are hours of business for me—if I can get it," answered the other, in a voice which, like the man, was as the shadow of some better voice that had gone. "We know each other, Mr. Ventoul, and there is no need for me to say any more. A friend of yours?" he asked, with a nod towards Rackham.

Ventoul performed the necessary introductions; Street looked at Rackham keenly. Rackham, for his part, lounging against the bar, was studying the other man, and fitting him mentally (after a necessary cleansing and clothing process) into the master of a country house; he found the business difficult. Meanwhile, at a summons from Mr. Street, a barmaid had peeped under the wooden screen over the counter, and a process of liquefying the preliminaries was proceeded with. And then Rackham, saying not a word himself, listened while Ventoul, in a low voice, unfolded to Mr. Daniel Street something of the amazing business that was in his mind.

It did not seem in the least amazing to Street, whose eyelids scarcely fluttered over his pale eyes as he listened. Yet it was evident, when he began to go into the matter, that he had taken in every detail, and had got every point clear.

"What you offer, Mr. Ventoul, seems to be rather vague," he said at last. "For how long would this continue?"

"You can call it a summer holiday, if you like; it means money in your pocket, and other things beside. More than that, apart from paying expenses, and providing you with sufficient capital to keep up appearances, there will be a bonus for you at the end of it."

"It will have to be a good bonus," said Street, "seeing that it is a matter of fraud—and pretence——"

Rackham leaned forward suddenly, thrusting Ventoul aside, and flung himself into the business. "Big words, Mr. Street," he said, "and mighty little behind them. The fraud is in pretending to be what you're supposed to be, or what you once were—a gentleman; the pretence is in playing a little game of make-believe, in which I shall be able to assist you. As a matter of fact, Mr. Street, we meet on common ground, if what my friend Ventoul tells me is correct."

"What do you mean?" asked the other, opening his eyes a little, and then letting the heavy lids fall again.

"He means nothing offensive," broke in Ventoul.

"My dear Horace—be quiet!" said Rackham coolly. "I mean just this: that for an indiscretion concerning somebody else's money I have been shut away from the sight of my fellow creatures for a matter of three years. I was given to understand that that had been your case exactly, with this difference—that yours was more deliberate, and was not the impulse of a moment. Now, may we put off high and mighty airs, and talk business? Ventoul, of course, stands out of it; two rogues can go at it together—without flummery."

There was a long pause; and then Daniel Street removed himself slowly from the wall, and rattled his glass on the counter to denote that he wanted it filled. Rackham, with a wave of the hand, declined the mute invitation to join him.

"I suppose there's a certain risk about this?" said Street, after the barmaid had retired.

"There's no risk at all," said Rackham. "It's a little, romantic, fanciful idea on the part of our friend here, who is nothing if not romantic and fanciful. I am given to understand that there is a wife—a certain Mrs. Street— who will be willing to play propriety?"

"I take it that Mrs. Street would do as I wish; I have a sort of notion that she might be glad to get out of

London," answered the man; and for the first time there was almost a note of pathos in his ghostly voice.

"Then what are you hesitating about?" demanded Ventoul impatiently.

The man glanced round about the place—even glanced at that mark upon the wall that was as though he had left his shadow there. "It's a wrench—and a change," he said at last. "I've been used to coming in here—used to meeting the shabby out-at-elbows wretches who, like myself, have been broken and go limping ever afterwards. I shall miss the rooms in a back street at the other side of Waterloo Bridge; but if it means money—and a little peace—I'll do it."

"Then that's settled," said Ventoul. "You shall have sufficient money to dress the part—and to make your wife dress it. You can leave all the rest to me."

"I should like to warn you of one thing," said Daniel Street in his dull voice. "The wife won't have anything to do with it if any harm is meant to this girl."

"Don't you worry, my friend; I'm looking to that part of the business," said Rackham, with a glance at Ventoul. "The lady will be in my keeping."

"As a matter of fact," said Ventoul, "there's no reason for you to tell Mrs. Street anything about it. I take it she knows very little of the way in which you get your living; isn't it possible that you might come into money, or something of that sort?"

"No—I shall tell her," replied the man. "That's about the only decent thing I've ever done—to be straight with her. It will be all right; she's got rather a womanlike capacity for following blindly."

It was arranged that Daniel Street and his wife were to go that evening to see Mr. Horace Ventoul, and to settle final details; Oliver Rackham was to seek out Angelica. So much, at least, he promised, when with Horace Ventoul he stood again on the pavement of Chancery Lane. And by that time a few golden coins had passed between Ventoul and himself; he jingled them in his pocket now as he watched Ventoul climbing into a cab.

"Broken—and limping ever after!" he quoted from Mr. Street, as he turned away. "Shall I limp for ever—or is there some way out for me? I wonder!"

CHAPTER VI

ANGELICA GOES OUT TO SUPPER

WE may conveniently leave Mr. Horace Ventoul, discussing details with a Mr. Daniel Street smoking an unaccustomed cigar, and with a Mrs. Daniel Street (a little, fat dumpling of a woman, somewhat afraid of life as it had been presented to her, and still more afraid that Daniel might again come within the clutches of that law of which he had once been an ornament), and may follow Oliver Rackham in a quest for the heiress.

At the outset he congratulated himself on the fact that he had the easier task. Let Ventoul push his foxy face into that matter of details with the other rogue, Daniel Street; to Rackham was left that delving of the girl out of London, and the breaking to her of what was to be, if it could be managed, her immediate future. In a mood that was half reluctant and half one of sheer devilry at the task before him, he set about to accomplish it.

This was to be no night of evening dress; he walked abroad in simplicity. Moreover, he determined that the precious hours should not be wasted in that dingy dancing-hall in which he had first met her; he would secure her before she had time even to reach it. Judging that she must leave her lodging at a certain hour in order to reach Professor Dorn's Academy at its opening, he presented himself in that little street of dreary houses a good half hour before she could possibly need to start, and waited, with his back against the lamp-post on the opposite side of the street.

"Here I stand," he said to himself whimsically—" a man come out to capture a maid. And I can't even do that properly, because I'm going to capture her for someone else. That seems to be my fate; I've written things for another man to publish. And now, because I haven't a penny to bless myself with, I must lure this girl's feet into the net, so that another man may draw the strings of the net tight, and get hold of her. If I had the courage to turn burglar, or to knock some inoffensive citizen on the head for the sake of his purse, or his watch and chain, I wouldn't be standing here now; but having no courage for such deeds, I'm out to capture Angelica Brown—not to mention the Susan!"

He had to wait a long time—more than an hour, in fact. More than once he thought that he would cross the road, and ring the bell, and demand to see her, but the voice of caution restrained him. And at last the door opened—long after it was possible that she could have started for Professor Dorn's Academy—and she came out. He was across the road in a moment, bowing before her, hat in hand.

"Why, what are you doing here?" she asked; and there was a little pleased flush on her cheeks as she looked at him. "You've not been waiting?"

"For an hour that has seemed like a minute," he answered gallantly. "As a matter of fact, I felt that I wanted to see my little friend with the light feet again, and so I came up here on the chance that those light feet might carry her outside the house. And, you see, I'm in luck."

"But you've waited an hour!" she said, in deep commiseration. "I suppose you didn't like to ring the bell?"

"I thought of the landlady who has to come upstairs or downstairs whenever the bell is rung, and so I hesitated," he declared, with a laugh. "You're not dancing to-night?"

"Not to-night," she said. "I'm just going out—to get my supper."

"You seem a very extravagant young person," he said. "Where do you sup?"

"Oh, I didn't mean that at all," she said, with a laugh. "I go to a place where they sell cooked things, and I buy—oh—ever so little. You see, I reckoned it out; if I didn't go to the dance, I could afford something extra for supper, and still save."

"May I suggest that I am a very hungry man, and that I have had no supper?" he said. "And would you please come and have supper with me?"

"Oh, I couldn't!" she exclaimed, drawing back a little. "You're only doing it just to please me; I expect you've dined in some great place not so very long ago, and don't want anything to eat at all."

"I would call your attention to the fact that I am not in dining dress, and that I have waited rather more than an hour (which still seemed something like a minute) to ask you to come out to supper," he said. "There isn't any harm in it, or I wouldn't ask you to do it."

"Of course there isn't any harm in it," she said. "I don't think you're the sort of person to ask me to do anything that there's any harm in," she added, with those frank eyes of hers upturned to him. "And as I've never been out to supper in my life, I'd love to come—please."

Somehow the eyes—so like those of a child—disturbed him a little. Half he made up his mind just to have this meal with her, and then to drop that further business altogether. Half he made up his mind that, for some indefinite time, to be measured carefully by the coins he had in his pocket, he would meet her like this, and talk with her; and then would suddenly disappear, leaving her to the life in which she had so bravely fought. At all events, the matter need not be decided on the instant; which was always to Oliver Rackham's undoing.

They went off at once. She was so excited about the business that she scarcely hesitated when he put her into a cab, and directed the driver to take them to a certain little restaurant in the neighborhood of Soho; she simply sat and looked out at the streets and the people—and her eyes were shining, and her lips were parted a little. Rackham more than ever made up his mind to go and see Ventoul, and, if possible, pick a quarrel with the estimable Wood; and so go out of the place and of the plan luridly, leaving a sort of wreckage behind him. But that, too, could be thought out a little later.

The restaurant was a very ordinary one, and rather noisy —with a continuous calling in foreign tongues for various dishes down a species of trap in one wall, and much hurrying to and fro of waiters. Three years ago Rackham might perhaps have dined at such a place as a new experience; for the most part he would have sought something a great deal better.

But Angelica, peeling off her gloves, and settling herself in her chair, was a radiant little being, looking about her with shining eyes. As a matter of fact, she took no notice of Rackham at all; she was watching everything that was going on—from the entry of a new customer to the hurried flight of a waiter with a dish. And even when the first dish was set down before her she could scarcely eat, because there was so much to look at in this new world she had not seen before.

"You're not eating anything," he reminded her.

"I beg your pardon; there's such a lot to see," she replied, with a little start and a smile. "Are there people who dine and sup like this just as often as they like?"

"I'm afraid so," he answered gravely. "You see, everyone doesn't work as hard as you do, Miss Brown; quite a number of the other people have money to burn. Don't you find yourself wishing sometimes that you didn't have to work so hard?"

"Ah—you're thinking about what I said the other night—and I'm sorry for that," she replied. "I want you to think of me as being very much in love with life—and very happy; the other night was just what you might call a wicked night, when I was discontented, and was dreaming impossible dreams. And that's not good for hard work—is it?"

"Perhaps not; but suppose some of the dreams that seem to be impossible should come true—what then?"

"I don't want to think about anything to-night but just this wonderful supper—and you, who are kind to me, that's all," she said complacently. "I'll pretend, if you like, that I haven't got any work to do—and that I'm rich—just for an hour."

He was silent again, watching her; he did not quite know how to broach the business—in fact, he did not want to broach it at all. But his hand was set to the plough, and he knew he could not look back. Besides, he argued, if he turned aside from the business now, it would only be to leave the girl and her fortune in the hands of Ventoul. Rackham had set his feet on a path on which he could not turn, and on which he must perforce walk blindly.

She was sipping her wine when at last he plunged straight into the business. "Suppose a good fairy should come along, and should say to you: 'You can give up all this business of dreary music-teaching; you can have a settled income, and only a little work to do; and you can live in the country, where the trees and the flowers and the birds are'—what would you say to that?"

"But no good fairy ever will say that," she said, setting down her glass, "so what's the use of talking? You're spoiling my dream instead of making me believe in it."

"I wouldn't spoil any dream of yours for the world; but I can make one come true," he said. "I'm quite serious, I assure you."

She leaned across to him, studying his face intently; he could see that she was a little startled—frightened almost. He went on rapidly, before she could answer.

"Some friends of mine are going down into the country to take a big house there," he said, studying the table-cloth intently, for her eyes were disconcerting. "Just a friend and his wife—and they want a companion for the lady. You'd be treated as one of the family; you'd have a good salary; you'd have a rest. What do you think of the prospect?"

"But they don't even know me!" she gasped.

"But I do—and they would accept my recommendation."

"But you don't know anything about me—except just my name," she faltered. "And why should you do all this for me?"

"Why does one do anything in this world to help a fellow-creature?" he answered evasively. "Put the case to yourself; I find a young girl, struggling along cheerfully and happily, and making the best of the very hard business of life. I am introduced to her by that strangest of all masters of the ceremonies—Chance; and I find myself interested in that girl. Then one day my country friends—most charming people, I assure you—mention to me that they want to find a young lady—refined and nice, and above all cheerful—as companion. What more natural than that I should think of you?"

"But you take my breath away," said Angelica, after a pause. "To think of you waiting in the street for an hour, to bring me to this lovely place to supper—just to make me this offer! You must be the kindest man in the world!"

"I wouldn't believe that, if I were you," he said. "And by all means think over it a bit; it doesn't do to jump suddenly in these matters," he added, with a feeling that perhaps, after all, she might refuse, and so lift the growing burden of villainy from his shoulders.

"But that wouldn't be fair to you," she said. "It wouldn't be treating you in a generous way at all. Only I'm sure you understand," she went on, with her hands clasped, and leaning eagerly across the table towards him—"I'm quite certain that you must understand that this would be such a big step for me to take. It would mean giving up my pupils—which is a certainty; it would mean taking something that might only last a little time. You see, these friends of yours might not like me."

"There's not the faintest doubt about that," he said. "On that point you may put yourself entirely at ease; if I recommended anyone to them it would be all right. In other words, Miss Brown, if you accept now, you may regard the matter as settled."

"I don't know what to say," she replied.

"Then think over it," he said. "At the present moment think about something else—and do please finish your supper. I am turning your beautiful evening into a species of nightmare."

He chanced at that moment to turn his head in the direction of the door; in a moment he stiffened in his chair. Mr. Horace Ventoul had pushed his way through, and was glancing about for a table. Rackham leant one elbow on the table, and shielded his face with his hand; but that face was distorted for a moment with laughter. This was the sort of situation he enjoyed, and for the moment all thought of the girl or of the problem that was then singing through her brain was effaced. He meant to stretch Horace Ventoul on the rack, and was simply devising the best way of setting about it.

Ventoul had evidently left his interview with Daniel Street and Mrs. Daniel Street the worse for the encounter. As a matter of fact, Daniel, with his former legal knowledge to aid him, had driven a harder bargain than Ventoul liked. He had come out to walk it off; had ended by driving to a restaurant in which, on one solitary occasion years before, he had dined with Oliver Rackham. That was a fact which Oliver Rackham had forgotten.

As luck would have it, Horace Ventoul seated himself at a table immediately behind that at which Rackham sat with the girl. Rackham could see him in the mirror immediately behind Angelica; that is to say, he could see the back of his head as he bent for a moment over the menu a waiter had handed to him. Then, in his rather throaty voice, he gave his order, and the waiter vanished. Horace Ventoul dropped his forehead into his hands, and sat with his elbows leaning on the table. Rackham, within a foot of him, had hard work to control his face.

"Is anything the matter?" was Angelica's startling question.

"I beg your pardon," said Rackham, speaking more loudly than he meant. "Something suddenly amused me."

Glancing again in the mirror, he saw that Ventoul had suddenly raised his head, and was listening. Moreover, he, on his side, was watching the mirror before which he sat —peering at it that he might get a view both of Rackham and his companion.

From mirror to mirror Rackham grinned at him cordially, meeting the amazed look in Ventoul's eyes calmly. He saw that Ventoul was twisting and turning about, the better to get a clear view; he knew that Ventoul was straining his ears to catch whatever might be said. And in the meantime Angelica, quite unconscious of all that was happening about her, was thinking over her problem. At last Ventoul determined on a bold move. He twisted about in his chair, and suddenly spoke Rackham's name with an air of the most extraordinary surprise.

"My dear old Noll—the idea of finding you here!" he exclaimed, getting up and coming to the side of the other table.

"Staggering—isn't it?" said Rackham, as he shook hands with him. "It's wonderful how one runs against people in London. Have you only just come in?"

"This instant," replied Ventoul, watching the girl intently, and yet speaking to Rackham. "I think I'll come and sit at this next table."

"Do, my dear fellow—by all means," exclaimed Rackham heartily. "And may I present"—he hesitated, and waved a hand towards Angelica—"Miss Brown. This is Mr. Horace Ventoul," he said to the girl, in the most impressive manner at his command—"a very celebrated author. You're sure to have heard of him."

Horace Ventoul would in all probability have made some neat deprecatory speech, but for the fact that he was so taken up with Angelica. He did not seem to be able to get his eyes away from her; even during the business of arranging with the waiter to put him at the other table he kept glancing at her and watching her every movement. And, so far as Angelica was concerned, this was, of course, the very crowning point of a great occasion. She kept glancing at Ventoul with looks of awe, and then hastily averting her eyes.

Ventoul seated himself at the next table and began his meal; but he found it impossible to eat. He talked commonplaces with Angelica and with Rackham; he gave contradictory orders to the waiter; and all the time kept turning furtive glances on the girl.

"Mr. Ventoul," said Rackham presently, "is one of those authors, Miss Brown, who writes but rarely, but always writes well. Like the immortal Shakespeare, he does not hesitate to lift a good idea when he finds it; but that's neither here nor there. He's a great man; he has had his portrait in the papers, in just the same fashion in which they insert those of criminals or prize-fighters or other celebrities. And he rather likes it."

"I'm afraid he's teasing you, Mr. Ventoul," said Angelica, with a dubious glance at Rackham.

"Oh, it's only his fun," replied Ventoul, a little venomously. "Rackham doesn't really mean it."

"Is that your name?" asked Angelica, in a lower tone across the table. But it was a tone that Ventoul caught.

"You have it at last," said Rackham whimsically. "'Noll' stands for Oliver—and the other name you've just heard. Oliver Rackham—yours to command."

"Didn't you know his name before, Miss Brown?" stammered the amazed Ventoul.

"I didn't ask him; I never thought of it," said the blushing Angelica. "Of course we've been friends a long time—or it seems a long time; but his name didn't seem to matter."

Rackham, with an immovable face, turned and signed to the waiter to approach; paid the bill, and rose from his chair; Angelica rose also.

"We'll leave you to finish your supper, my dear Horace," said Rackham. "I wish you had come in a little earlier; we might all have supped together."

"But I've had all I want; I couldn't possibly eat any more," said Ventoul hurriedly, as he began to scramble out of his seat.

Angelica had moved towards the door, after bowing to him; Rackham suddenly dropped a heavy hand on Ventoul's shoulder, forcing him back into his seat. "You haven't had half enough, my dear Horace," he said, in a fierce whisper. "Do you imagine for a moment that you're going to follow us, and spy upon me—eh? You are lucky to have set eyes upon the lady; don't spoil it. You will linger in her mind as a pleasant memory. Good night!"

As he followed Angelica out of the restaurant, Rackham, glancing back, saw Horace Ventoul still standing there agape, staring after them. He joined Angelica outside, and walked gravely away with her.

"It must be nice to know people like that," said Angelica.

"It is—sometimes," retorted Rackham.

"Isn't it curious that I had never thought about your name before, Mr. Rackham?" said Angelica after a pause.

"Well—you see—mine is not an important name," said Rackham. "There's nothing celebrated or wonderful about me. But for an accident, you might have gone on to the end of the chapter, just thinking about me as having no name at all. Which might, after all, have been better," he added softly.

"Will you think me ungrateful," she asked suddenly, after they had gone on some little distance, "if I ask you to let me wait a few hours, and then write to you? I can't tell you how very grateful I really am; you're the first person that's ever gone out of his way to be good to me, or to think of me; and if I spoke to you now about it, I should probably say—'Yes.' But I want to feel quite— quite sure."

"Oh—yes—you'd better write," he said. "I'll just write down the name of the hotel I'm stopping at."

They stood together in the street, while he pulled out his pocket-book, and scribbled on a leaf of it his name and the name of the hotel. As he gave it to her, she looked up at him wistfully, with those eyes that were always so disconcerting; her lips were quivering a little.

"You're sure you don't mind?" And then, as he shook his head—"You shall have a letter to-morrow."

They walked on almost in silence until they reached her lodging; there, with a simple "good night," they parted. Rackham walked back to his hotel—stopping once in the street to laugh aloud at the thought of Horace Ventoul in the restaurant; smoked a long time before finally retiring; and went to bed at last, wondering what Angelica's answer would be.

The answer was brought to him at about noon on the

following day. In a rather scrawling, girlish handwriting he read—

"*Dear Mr. Rackham,*
 "*If you please, the answer is yes. And I am more grateful to you than I can ever tell you. Yours very truly,*
"*ANGELICA BROWN.*"

CHAPTER VII

THE NEW SANCHO PANZA

With the showing of that note to Horace Ventoul by Rackham came the sealing of the matter; things began to move from that very day.

"I give you my word, my dear Noll," said Ventoul, with a little awkward laugh, "that until last night I had a suspicion that you were getting money out of me on false pretences, and that there was no Miss Brown at all."

"Thank you, my dear Horace; I guessed as much," retorted Rackham cheerfully. "You see, you were so greedy over the half-million that you didn't mind speculating a bit—and the speculation has turned out well. By the way—what did you think of the lady?"

"Not bad; rather interesting, I should think," said Ventoul, with a yawn. "It was funny, lighting on you like that, in the restaurant. You seemed very chummy, the pair of you, by the way."

"We are certainly rather friendly," answered Rackham. "And didn't little Horace think he was going then and there to step in, and make a party of three of it, and begin the game right away!" he added, with a laugh.

"I can't for the life of me see why you should have shut me out," said Ventoul viciously. "I'm paying the money."

"And for the present I am calling the tune," broke in Rackham. "However, we don't want to quarrel about it; you know now that the lady is willing to take up her new position with our highly respectable friends the Streets; you can go ahead as fast as you like. You can find your country house, and put your tame, respectable people in it —and there you are. It'll cost you a bit, friend Horace, and you never did like parting with money; but you'll reap your reward afterwards."

"I want the girl's address, to begin with," said Ventoul aggressively.

"And you won't get it," answered Rackham. "You see, my dear Ventoul, you're not a person quite to be trusted, and so I've got to look after you—and after her. At the present moment youth and purity, and all that's nice, has its little habitation somewhere up near the stars —and that's nothing to do with you. When the right moment comes, Miss Angelica Susan Brown will take her flight from London into what I believe are the safe arms of Mrs. Street; then you can make your plans after that."

To that resolution he held strongly, and neither threats nor persuasion would move him. There was nothing for it but for Horace Ventoul to go on with his part of the plot (which he did with the more swiftness, now that he knew that the girl actually existed) and to leave Oliver Rackham to carry out his part in due course.

It was a fluttering and an anxious time for that gloomy wreck Daniel Street, and for the patient, anxious woman who bore his name. Daniel Street, for his part, had dwelt in shady places so long that he was used to them, and almost liked them; he would have been suspicious of anything was too blatantly straightforward. He knew, of course, in his own mind, that there was something shady about a transaction in which he was called upon to play a chief part; but that did not trouble him. He was a man who had long since given up hope of ever re-establishing himself with his fellows; it was clearly mapped out that his destiny should be to go on for ever in those dubious ways into which he had been forced. And, after all, this might prove a little oasis in the desert wherein his occupation had been the getting of stray half-crowns from time to time; he would have money to play with, and much might happen in such a scheme as this new and amazing one that had been opened out before him.

There were other conferences than those which took place between Ventoul and the Streets. There were nights when Mrs. Daniel Street lay awake, thinking over phrases and arguments by which she might persuade him in the morning to give up this idea; for indeed she was afraid of it. She seemed to see Daniel Street again in the dock, and again sentenced, as he had been sentenced before. Once again she drew a mental picture of herself waiting outside prison gates on a dreary morning for a man who came out at last, and walked off with her in a grim silence.

Yet to all the arguments and all the pleadings Daniel Street retorted that it would be all right. He was being paid for looking after somebody's house, and for playing the gentleman for a time; that was all that need concern them. And so at last the woman—secretly pleased, if the truth be told, that she was to have new clothes, and to get out of the sordid riot of London streets for a time—yielded, and said no more.

To Horace Ventoul, with that golden fortune for ever dangling before his eyes, and with the memory of the girl —sweet and demure and altogether presentable, as he had seen her—the carrying out of the mere business of taking a house was not difficult. He discovered what he wanted— a modest, old-fashioned, country residence, set in pretty gardens on the outskirts of a village known as Pentney Hill, in the county of Sussex. It was the sort of place to which a highly respectable person, such as Daniel Street appeared to be, would be likely to retire; there were shady lawns and a wide verandah, and the place was looking its best with the near approach of summer. More than that, as Pentney Hill is a little inconvenient in the matter of train service, the rent was extremely moderate.

Angelica Susan Brown, going round to her daily pupils, and dropping hints here and there that they must soon know her no more, and dreaming her dreams about what this wonderful new life was to be, might have been astounded could she have seen the doings of those she was so soon to know intimately, or could she have heard some of their conversations. There was comedy as well as pathos about the business, although Mr. Horace Ventoul, intent upon keeping down expenses, was not the man to see either.

There was comedy in Daniel Street struggling between a desire for frock-coats and silk hats and a yearning for the clothes proper to a country gentleman; there was pathos in Mrs. Daniel Street trying to wring a little more money out of Horace Ventoul, the better to dress herself properly to her supposed station in life. And there was comedy again (could anyone but Horace Ventoul have known it) in that gentleman's frantic anxiety concerning what would probably be done by Oliver Rackham, at any moment, or under any circumstances.

For Rackham was an unknown quantity; it was quite impossible to know what he would do. Horace Ventoul was juggling with vague and intangible things; and behind him always stood Rackham, who might upset his best trick at any moment. Now, for instance, while all these negotiations and preparations were in progress, the fellow had utterly disappeared.

After the agreement for the house was actually signed, and while the lodgings of Daniel Street and his wife were being besieged day by day with parcels delivered by tradesmen's vans, Oliver Rackham took it into his head to appear, at about one o'clock in the morning, at Ventoul's chambers, and to declare solemnly that he was done with the whole business. He had been thinking about it, and he had come to the conclusion that Ventoul was a man not to be trusted; Rackham was sorry he had ever had anything to do with it. And, as he was in one of those moods that Ventoul had come to regard as dangerous, that unfortunate gentleman had to set to work to placate him.

At something after three in the morning Oliver Rackham went out of the place with an unsteady gait, and with fresh money in his pocket; pausing on his way to deliver a little lecture to the scandalised Wood, who had been kept up by his master as a precautionary measure.

"There was a time, my good fellow," said Rackham benignantly, "when I loathed the sight of you; but I've decided to forget and forgive. I thought you were just a placid nonenity—which is not a bad phrase for half-past three in the morning, is it? But now I've come to the conclusion that having lived so long with my friend Mr. Horace Ventoul has had a degrading effect upon a mind originally pure and good. There is evil in your eye— and there is inherent wickedness in the turn of your mouth. I shall have to look after you; you're a naturally bad lot, unless you're checked. Good night to you!"

He had left behind him Angelica's address—with threats of violence against Horace Ventoul if that gentleman even dared to go within a hundred yards of it. It had been settled that Mrs. Daniel Street, so soon as she should be actually in the house, should write to Angelica, and should state that her dear friend Mr. Oliver Rackham had recommended the girl to her as a companion, and what date would be convenient for Miss Brown to come down to Pentney Hill? That letter had been actually composed by Rackham himself, and a fair copy written out; Ventoul was to see that it was properly sent off by Mrs. Street.

But all these delays had not improved Horace Ventoul's temper. True, he had to be careful; for Oliver Rackham was a difficult being to deal with, and might, as he had threatened to-night, throw up the whole business, and leave them all in the lurch. Now, however, Ventoul had got the long-coveted address, and that half-drunken madman, as he termed Oliver Rackham, might well be left out of the matter.

As the house was to be a modest establishment, Ventoul had insisted that only two servants were to be engaged; another should be obtained later on, if necessary. The Streets, having nothing practically to move except themselves, had settled down quickly enough; it now only remained for Mrs. Street to write that letter to Angelica, which was the very crux of the whole situation.

Previously to that, however, it had become necessary to establish a modest banking account for Daniel Street, in order that he might pay necessary expenses, and might, above all, send a cheque to Angelica in advance of her salary. That had been grudgingly enough done by Horace Ventoul; and Daniel Street had seen immense possibilities for the future in being able to write his name again on a cheque.

Mr. Daniel Street sat beside a window, looking out over the grounds, and placidly smoking a cigarette which, from old economical habits, he had just rolled for himself; Mrs. Street sat at a diminutive but very lady-like desk, and copied out the letter which Horace Ventoul had given her.

"Dear Miss Brown,

"My old and respected friend Mr. Oliver Rackham has mentioned your name to me as being a lady who might care to take up the position of companion to me. If you knew the trouble I have had to secure someone who would be a real comfort to one who is not, I honestly believe, difficult to get on with, you would sincerely pity me."

Here the lady turned round to her husband, and addressed him a little nervously. She was still plump and rather pretty, although her blue eyes showed signs of rather feeble weeping that had grown almost into a habit. She spoke gently, but in a voice that had grown habitually tremulous and appealing.

"It don't seem quite fair to say that, Dan, does it," she said. "I mean that bit about the difficulties I've had in getting somebody to suit."

"My dear Daisy," said Daniel Street, turning his head a little in her direction, "we're here to obey orders, and whatever you say won't matter in the least, one way or the other. Ventoul knows his business, even if the other fellow doesn't. Copy it out, and be quick, or you'll lose the post."

Mrs. Street went on with her copying, shaking her head now and then over sentences as she wrote them.

"I have been trying to find someone of a cheerful disposition, who could be really a friend to me, and I am glad to hear from my dear old friend Mr. Rackham that you are willing to give me a trial. I put it in that way, because it seems so good of you to fall in with my wishes, and to come to a little country place like this, after the many delights and gaieties of London. But I will try and make you happy.

"My husband (who is most conscientious in all money matters) . . ."

(Here Mrs. Street furtively glanced at the man by the window, and as furtively sighed, and dabbed her eyes with her handkerchief.)

". . . insists that I shall enclose you a cheque for the first quarter's salary we propose to pay you, and which I hope you will think sufficient. I would make it more, but it is honestly all that we can afford. Mr. Rackham suggested that he thought you would be content to accept fifty

pounds per annum, at all events at the beginning. My husband thought that you would probably have things to buy, and the money might be useful.

"*If you will let me know what date you will arrive, and the train, I will see that you are met at the station. And, my dear, I do hope that we shall get on well together.*

"*Believe me to be, dear Miss Brown,*

"*Yours very sincerely,*

"DAISY STREET."

That was the letter that was delivered to Angelica on the following morning; the letter she read with tears in her eyes—tears of gratitude that this wonderful thing should have happened. Fifty pounds a year—and a beautiful house, and food and friends—and the country!

There could be no more trudging the streets on bitter winter days (she remembered that there had been bitter winter days now, for the first time), no more counting up of shillings, no more loneliness. And with this wonderful money that had come into her hands she would go out, and visit certain shops of which she had only known the outside, and buy things of which she had only dreamed.

Angelica replied at once, in words that were a little hysterical; she thought the salary more than sufficient, and if Mrs. Street could wait so long, she would come down in a week. There were things to be settled up, and things to buy, and (though Angelica did not say that) farewells to make to the London she was leaving behind.

Ventoul was duly informed of the date Angelica had decided upon, and, while inwardly cursing the delay, was glad to know that the thing was at last settled. He wrote a long letter to the Streets, giving them minute instructions as to what they were to do and what not to do.

Oliver Rackham, going to Ventoul about the middle of that week, when there was a lull in the proceedings, discovered Ventoul mildly jubilant. Indeed, he was even disposed to be a little facetious with Rackham over his part in the affair.

"Well—my dear Noll—so all the scruples have vanished now, I suppose?" he said slyly.

"What—about the girl?" Rackham asked carelessly.

"My dear Horace—will you never understand that I gave up having scruples at about the time I discovered they stood in the way of my ever making any money—or getting any money? If I have wavered at all, it has been from the feeling that I didn't like helping you—and I still don't like that part of the business. How's our friend Daniel Street getting on?"

"The whole business is costing me a great deal more than I ever thought it would," said Horace peevishly. "And now even the girl must keep us waiting a week, instead of going down at once."

"Splendid!" exclaimed Rackham boisterously. "Poor dear Horace having to pay out money for something he's by no means sure about yet! I know it must hurt dreadfully. And the fair Angelica keeping you all waiting, while, I suppose, she runs about, and buys pretty things, and all the rest of it. It's quite comical, Horace."

Ventoul winced. "Well, at any rate, she goes down in three days now," he said. And then added sharply—"By the way, what are your plans?"

"I haven't made any," retorted the other coolly. "I don't like making plans. I might go down with the lady—or soon after—or before; I might not go down at all. I'm going to keep you dangling again, Horace; you shan't know when to expect me, nor what I'm going to do."

"You'll come back soon enough when you want money, I expect," Ventoul answered. "Now that the girl has made up her mind about this, you'd better not try my patience too far; I've no further need of you, you know."

Oliver Rackham looked at him for a moment or two in silence; then he picked up his hat, and adjusted it at a careful angle, and moved to the door.

"Where are you going?" demanded Ventoul, in some alarm.

"I am going," said Rackham deliberately, "to the fair Angelica; and am going to expound to her the whole infernal plot from beginning to end. Then, if she likes to go off, and take her money for herself, she may. I warned you what would happen if you threatened me."

"Now, my dear Noll—I most humbly apologise," exclaimed Ventoul, getting quickly between Rackham and the door. "Only just now I'm driven almost to distraction with one thing and another, and I sometimes wish I'd never taken the thing up at all. Be reasonable."

"Be civil, you dog!" exclaimed Rackham, with an ugly look in his eyes, as he took off his hat and tossed it on to a couch. "Now—what's your part of the programme?"

"I shall probably go down to Pentney Hill within a few

days, and put up at the inn there—do the thing in style, you know, and take Wood with me."

"It'll be devilish amusing," said Rackham. "And shan't I be astounded to see my dear friend, the celebrated writer —Horace Ventoul!"

"That was a clever stroke of yours the other night," said Ventoul. "She was interested at once."

"Wasn't she?" retorted Rackham. "And how much more interested she'd have been if she'd known who wrote the book, and under what circumstances it was stolen."

"While you were shut up with other jail-birds," said Ventoul viciously.

"We are getting much too complimentary to each other; I think I'll leave," said Rackham, with a smile.

Thereafter we are to imagine him disappearing vaguely, and wandering, perhaps a little unhappily, about the streets —purposeless, vacillating, changeful as ever. That had ever been the way with him; he had had no purpose in life, save perhaps a freakish one of mischief, or of the mere killing of time. And so it was with no very definite purpose that he found himself one afternoon in that dull little street in which Angelica lodged, and from which he had remembered she had gone, or was going, that day.

The door of the house was open, and a cab stood before it. "I'm in luck," said Rackham to himself—"unless some other lodger is also flitting."

A trunk was brought out—carried between the cabman and a servant-maid of a grubby type; and then Angelica stepped forth, carrying a bag in one hand, and a bird-cage, carefully covered over save for the top in brown paper, in the other. She did not notice Rackham, who astonishingly enough stood holding the cab door open. She carefully deposited the bag and the bird-cage on the front seat of the four-wheeler; she turned round, to thank the little servant-maid and to bid her farewell; and then she saw Rackham.

"Oh!" cried Angelica softly.

"Please may I come and see you off?" asked Rackham, humbly standing hat in hand.

"Of course you may—and it's wonderful of you," said Angelica. "But have you been waiting for an hour again?" she asked in distress.

"I came up this very moment; if I'd been a minute later I should have been too late to see you at all," he replied. "Are you ready?"

"In a moment," said Angelica, and dashed into the house again, to seize and hug an elderly woman who was weeping softly at the parting. Rackham rightly conjectured that this was the landlady, and that Angelica had been something more than a model lodger.

She came out again breathless, and got into the cab. Rackham got in also, and they drove off together. Mindful of the fact that Angelica's eyes were brimming with tears, and that she found it necessary to stare hard out of the other window, he tactfully said nothing for a while, and peeped in through the brown paper at the canary, cheerfully hopping on its perch.

"It's a little hard—just leaving everything," said Angelica, in a strangled voice, presently. "But it's a lot better, having someone you know and—like—with you. It was sweet of you to come."

"He's a jolly little chap," said Rackham, referring to the canary.

"Oh, I wanted to ask you," she exclaimed hastily. "Do you think they'll mind—mind having him, I mean?"

"Of course not. They've got to like him," he replied.

"You see—I thought he could be kept in my room, and then they wouldn't hear him if he sang too much," she said.

"My dear Miss Brown, they positively adore canaries," said Rackham. "I don't know whether they have any themselves, but it's been the dream of their lives to have one in the house."

"That's very nice," said Angelica, with a little sigh of relief. "I had thought of writing and asking them; but then I thought that if I took them by surprise they might like him at once, and that would save all the bother. And really there wasn't time to write; I have had such a busy week."

"Tell me about it," he pleaded.

"Well, first of all I had to go round to all my pupils, and to say 'good-bye' to them. There were pupils that I had simply hated; and yet it was hard work telling them that I couldn't come to them ever again; I found they were much nicer than I had ever thought possible. And then I had to buy things. Mrs. Street very thoughtfully sent me part of my salary in advance."

"That was kind of her," murmured Rackham. "And I suppose all the things—or most of them—are in the trunk on the roof?"

"All except the things I've got on," answered Angelica.

"It was delightful going about and buying things; it's been the most lovely week I ever spent in all my life. Will you please tell me: do I look all right?"

He looked at her gravely; he saw the change in her. She was still as simply dressed as ever—but the shabbiness was gone. Everything was in perfect taste. "Yes—I think you look all right," he said.

"Of course, there were lots and lots of things that I wanted to get, but I said to myself, 'No, my dear; remember your place. You've got to be a companion, and you mustn't look as if you were a fashionable lady, just because you've suddenly got some money in your pocket.' So I was most careful."

When they came to the station Rackham very naturally made for the booking office to get her ticket; but her quick hand on his arm arrested him. "Oh—please!" she whispered. "I know exactly how much it is, because I looked it up in the time-table; and I've got the money ready," she said hastily.

He understood in a moment, and held out his hand for the money. She laid it in his palm, and whispered quickly, "Third class, please."

There was only a matter of five minutes to spare, and Rackham stood at the door of the carriage looking at the girl seated in the corner. Her eyes were soft as she looked at him; once or twice she bit her lips quickly, as though she found it difficult to keep them from trembling; and at those moments Rackham looked away. He could not think then—refused to remember what he had done, or what share he had had in the whole amazing plot. And when at last the whistle sounded, and the train began to move, she gripped his hand that lay on the carriage window, and said words that were to haunt him long afterwards—

"Oh, you have been good to me!" she whispered.

Lounging about London, and sitting, in sunny weather, in the parks, and idly watching the people; sleeping in a small hotel bedroom; and waking again to other idle days; through it all he carried that phrase. A little resentfully, if the truth be told, because, he argued, he had been dragged into this thing without being able to help himself. And the exasperating part of it was that her eyes, as she had looked at him out of the window of the railway carriage at that last moment of parting, refused to be driven away from his mental vision.

"She can take care of herself," he said more than once. "In any case, no one's going to kill the goose that lays the golden eggs—or even harm it. She'll have a better time than she's ever had in her life before; why should I worry?"

Nevertheless, it was sheer cowardice that kept him in London. He would go down to-morrow—or perhaps the day after; or he might not go at all. At any rate, there was time to think about it.

And then one night, on an impulse, he went off to Ventoul's rooms. He marched to the lift; but the lift-man, now very respectful, touched his cap, and told him that Mr. Ventoul was away.

"When's he coming back?" demanded Rackham quickly.

"Couldn't say, sir. Took his servant with 'im, sir. Went away yesterday."

Rackham came out of the building slowly. It was evident that Ventoul was not letting the grass grow under his feet; he had already started for Pentney Hill.

"Well—it's nothing to do with me," said Oliver Rackham. "I can't do anything. Horace has got the money, and the house, and the Streets—and he's got the girl. I'm out of it, as far as I can see. Besides, if she ever found out——"

He stopped at that point, and strode away through the streets. There was still money in his pockets—enough for some days at least; the matter could be left to-night. If only that haunting memory of the girl's face and that other haunting memory of the phrase she had used would leave him!

He set about to get rid of both. He was a lonely man, with not even a chance acquaintance to turn to; all the chance acquaintances he had ever had, to say nothing of friends, had dropped away in that matter of three years. Therefore, in a savage, brutal fashion that had no thought of any morrow in it, he started on a solitary debauch.

He came at last out of a place that seemed filled with the noise of many tongues, and the reek of tobacco smoke, and the glare of lights, into a quiet street near the river—a street that sloped exasperatingly downhill, and made his feet more unsteady even than they were at that time. He thrust his hat back from his head, and let the night air blow upon his hot face; he tried to steady the twinkling lights that fringed the edge of the river. He knew where he was now; he was on the Embankment. Far back in the ages, as it seemed, he had walked in this place, in a different dress, and had sat somewhere and talked with someone. Yes—he remembered now; it was a little freak of an odd-job waiter, who had annoyed him, to begin with, and afterwards had lent him a shilling. He ought to have paid that shilling back long before this; he must remember to do so.

And so it happened that he came to that statue, with the seat on either side of it, and sat down there. It was cool here, and if no one disturbed him he might sleep for a little while before going back to the hotel. He only wished that the lights wouldn't gyrate so.

He had fallen into a doze, when he became aware of some noise quite close to him; he started fully awake, with the fancy that it was the noise of someone singing. He remembered now; that infernal little odd-job waiter had awakened him once before in just that way. He got to his feet and peered round the statue.

There, with his hat on the back of his head, sat Joshua Flattery—so exactly in the attitude in which he had been on that other memorable night that he might never have moved at all. And Oliver Rackham, with some of the mists clearing out of his brain, stared at Flattery, just as Flattery, with his tune dying away on his lips, stared back at Rackham.

"'Ullo, guv'nor!" said Flattery, a little limply.

"You've not been here ever since, have you?" asked Rackham.

"Ever since wot, guv'nor?" asked Flattery again.

"No—no—of course I'm wrong," said Rackham, sinking on the seat beside the little waiter. "It doesn't matter; everything is wrong to-night—everything has been wrong for a long time. Don't look at me like that, man," he added, turning away his head.

"No offence, guv'nor," said Joshua Flattery gently. "Bless you, sir, a gent may do lots of things that another man can't do—p'r'aps can't afford to do."

"You're a merciful little devil," said Rackham, dropping a hand upon his shoulder. "Do you remember the first time you found me here—not so long ago?"

"You was a bit low down, guv'nor; things 'ad gorn very wrong with you. Then you got up—an' you came out on top, as one might say—didn't you?"

"My dear Joshua Flattery, I'm a bit lower to-night than I was then," said Oliver Rackham, with a smothered laugh. "There's something in me, little waiter-man, that won't let me up—something low and mean that comes out always and asserts itself."

"Don't you believe it, guv'nor," said Joshua Flattery confidently. "You was made to come up; you've got the right stuff in you, sir. Why—think wot you've done already. 'Ere was you, in a manner of speakin', without a penny in the world, an' doin' me the honor of borrowin' a shillin' from me, an' payin' it back 'andsome——"

"I'm glad I paid you back; I'd almost forgotten," said the other slowly.

"And then comin' out in evenin' dress, an' causin' wot you might call a bit of a sensation at the Academy 'op. You're not down, sir—you're jist gittin' up!"

"You're a cheerful little devil as well as a merciful one," said Rackham, turning to look at him. "But why are you sitting here to-night—singing to yourself as you were when I came up?"

"Well, sir, if the honest truth must be told, I was feelin' a bit low meself," answered Flattery, pushing his hat forward over his forehead by way of change. "Jobs ain't bin too frequent, an' I seem to be losin' 'eart a bit. I'd give somethin' jist to 'ave a bit of a rest an' a change—jist to be sure of w'ere I was, an' wot was goin' to 'appen to me."

"It's a very common malady, Joshua Flattery," said Oliver Rackham, with a little sigh. "It's exactly my case at the present time; I scarcely know where I am or what I'm going to do. That's why, as you probably have observed, I've been drowning some of my sorrow to-night—which is a bad beginning, but one that comes easily."

"Pull yourself up, guv'nor; think of the 'appy time you've 'ad, and the other 'appy times you're goin' to have. Why, when I saw you last you was askin' me about a young lady that used to come to the Academy; I saw you darncin' with 'er once. There was brightness; there was 'appiness, sir, if you like!"

"Stop it!" exclaimed Rackham hoarsely, with his hands over his ears. "Who sent you here to-night to torture me? You don't know what you're talking about."

"No offence, guv'nor," said the little man, edging away from him a little. "I on'y thought it might 'ave 'appened that you'd seen the young lady; I thought if I reminded you——"

"Reminded me! As though I wanted reminding. And yet"—he sat up, and stared straight before him—"surely I've found you to-night to some purpose. Graceless dog that I am—God knows I wanted a reminder. Just as

"YOU SHALL HAVE ADVENTURES SUCH AS YOU HAVE NEVER HAD IN ALL YOUR WAITING LIFE BEFORE."

Page 149.

we sat here at the beginning of things, so we're here again to-night; there's a Fate in it!"

"I don't unnerstand wot you mean, guv'nor," whispered Flattery.

"I mean that I've been asleep—I mean that I've let things slip past me when I might have grasped them," said Rackham. "But it's not too late; I can do something yet. And you shall help me."

"Me, sir?" Joshua Flattery's eyes were wide, and he edged a little farther away from the other man.

"You simple little waiter-man—out of your mouth I've heard truth; bless you for it! I'm not quite sober yet—but I will be sober for the future. I'm starting off to-morrow to rescue somebody that's in captivity—a hapless maiden, I think they'd call her in the old romances. I'll be a very Don Quixote—even if I tilt at windmills; and you shall come with me, my Sancho Panza, to help me."

"Me, sir?" whispered the little man again.

Rackham turned, and took him by the shoulders, and rocked him playfully to and fro. "Yes," he said. "You're out of a job—aren't you? Well—I'll give you one—and it shall be a good one. If Mr. Horace Ventoul can take that placid-faced, muddle-headed scoundrel Wood with him, then—by the Lord!—I'll take my man too. No more waiting for you, Joshua Flattery; I'll give you a better billet than that. You shall come with me into the country, Sancho Panza; you shall live on the fat of the land; you shall have adventures such as you've never had in all your waiting life before. We'll cut a dash, Sancho Panza. Will you do it?"

"Is there money in it, sir?" asked Joshua Flattery, after a moment's hesitation.

"Money?" Oliver Rackham shook him to and fro, and fairly laughed in his startled face. "There's half a million!"

CHAPTER VIII

THE FRIEND OF THE FAMILY

It is extremely doubtful if Joshua Flattery believed for a single moment that astounding statement made by Rackham. True, he had known as astounding things to happen to this man whom he had found a penniless outcast, and who had been able to cast off his shabby clothes, and flutter it with the best in gorgeous raiment, and with money in his pocket. Nevertheless, as was his custom, he heard the statement respectfully, and with politely raised eyebrows of wonder.

"You don't say so, sir!" he said.

"But I do say so, Joshua Flattery," exclaimed Oliver Rackham boisterously. "You mustn't breathe a word about it to a soul, of course—because it's a dead secret; but in a little time I shall be plunging my hands into more money than you've ever dreamed of. Keep it dark, waiterman—keep it dark!"

"I wouldn't breathe a word—not for the world, I wouldn't," said Flattery impressively.

"It's a plot," said Rackham, nodding his head at the other man, and speaking somewhat sleepily. "It's an infernal plot, with an infernal scoundrel behind it. But we shall be one too many for him—or two too many for him, if it comes to that, Sancho Panza—shan't we?"

"Not a doubt of it, sir," said Flattery stoutly, wondering a little what it was all about.

"When I call you Sancho Panza, I want you to understand clearly, my dear waiter-man, that I intend no insult," said Rackham. "It has sometimes happened that a humble individual like yourself may fairly be said to represent some great historical or fictional character; and that is how you appeal to me."

"Something in the poetry line again, sir?" asked Joshua. "I ain't never forgot how you once quoted a bit o' poetry to me, in this very spot, an' 'ow proud I was to think that you should 'ave selected me for wot I might call that honor."

"Sancho Panza was not connected with poetry—but with romance," said Rackham slowly. "He lives for all time—and he was the faithful follower of a wonderful man—just as you shall be. I am going forth into the world—and you shall follow after me. And now, my dear Sancho Panza—I think I'll go home to bed."

"P'r'aps I might walk a bit with you, sir," suggested Joshua, as the other stood, swaying a little. "And then to-morrow I might take the liberty, sir, of looking you up, and seein', sir, if all we've 'ad the pleasure of talkin' about to-night 'as got wot I might call anythink be'ind it."

"My dear Joshua Flattery—you distrust me," said Rackham, looking at him with mock sternness. "Don't attempt to deny it, because I can see hesitation in your manner and doubt and uncertainty in your eye. You don't believe in me, because you think—and you are quite right in thinking it—that I'm drunk. I was—but I'm not so any longer. With fair ladies to be taken into consideration, a man must be very sober indeed. And that, little waiter-man, shall be your future task; you've got to look after me."

"Let's make a beginnin', sir," said Flattery. "If you'll tell me where you live, sir, we'll be 'ome in no time at all."

It happened that the hotel was comparatively close at hand; Rackham dragged the name of it with some difficulty out of the depths of his memory, and the two set off together. It was a sight to see them going along—Oliver Rackham with great dignity, and with long strides, which he found more convenient than shorter ones; Joshua Flattery trotting beside him, with his ridiculous little bowler-hat stuck on the back of his head, and the long tails of his frock-coat flapping in the breeze. So they came to the hotel; and there Joshua would have left him at the very door.

But Rackham would not allow that for a moment. In the lordliest fashion he marched in, with Flattery meekly and apologetically following him; and together they went into one of the public rooms. There Rackham rang the bell, and summoned a servant.

"This, my dear Flattery," he said, "is a great occasion. We must celebrate it. I have already been celebrating it—but I cannot let the occasion pass——"

"You was good enough to say, sir," whispered the little man, with a nervous glance at the servant who was waiting—"you was kind enough to mention that in the future I was to take the liberty of lookin' after you, sir. We can't begin too soon, sir; wot about a little move towards bed?"

Oliver Rackham looked at him for a moment or two in a sort of amazed silence; then burst out laughing. "You're a capital chap," he said; I'll take your advice." Then, turning to the servant, he demanded fiercely, "And what the devil, sir, are you standing staring at? Go away; I don't like the look of you."

The man hastily withdrew, and the incongruous pair were left alone together. And presently it happened that Oliver Rackham, having been at last convinced that it would be better for him to retire, went slowly up the staircase, with an arm affectionately round the shoulders of Joshua Flattery. Nor would he let the little man go until, safely in bed, he addressed a final word or two to him.

"We're going to do great things, my little friend," he said—"very great things. We're going to have adventures—vice shall be confounded and virtue made triumphant. Jolly lucky thing for everybody that I found you—or you found me—which was it?—to-night. Come and see me in the morning, Sancho Panza—and everything shall be settled. Great things are going to happen—enormous things."

He said no more, and the little waiter, leaning over him, discovered him to be asleep. Very softly Joshua Flattery tiptoed to the door, and switched off the electric light; murmured "Good night, sir," and closed the door, and went down the stairs into the streets; bowing a little apologetically to anyone he passed on the way.

It was high noon when Oliver Rackham awoke, with but a hazy notion of the happenings of the previous night. He dressed, and went downstairs in search of a belated breakfast—and there discovered Joshua Flattery seated in the hall, with his bowler-hat between his knees—a humble, patient figure, waiting for him. Instantly something of what had happened the night before swept through his mind; he turned in wrath to the hall-porter of the hotel.

"How the devil long has my friend been waiting here?" he demanded.

"It don't matter in the least, sir," pleaded Joshua, alarmed at having public attention called to himself in this way.

"We didn't know, sir——" stammered the man.

"You don't know anything; you're a benighted idiot, unfit even to open doors," said Rackham. "You've no discrimination—and no manners."

He took the protesting Joshua Flattery by the arm, and led him into the coffee-room. Without a word he seated himself at a table, and ordered his breakfast, and demanded to know what Joshua Flattery would have.

"I've 'ad my breakfast, sir—howers an' howers ago," whispered Joshua, quailing under the eye of the waiter.

"Then have lunch; it's about time for it," said Rackham. "Bring lunch for this gentleman at once. I shall breakfast at this side of the table, and my friend will lunch at his side. You don't often see that done, waiter; it'll be a new experience for you."

Joshua Flattery, seated on the extreme edge of his chair, and eating uneasily, was a sight to inspire pity. Rackham ate his breakfast calmly, without a word to the little man at the other side of the table. When the respective meals were finished, he leaned across, and looked at Flattery; there was a curious whimsical expression on his face, and in those eyes that always seemed tired.

"This is an occasion, my dear Flattery, not to be repeated," he said. "Last night you discovered me in a condition easily to be excused by you, but inexcusable from my point of view. Let's forget it. From to-day we have work to do; from this moment the tilting at windmills begins. I'm a sorry sort of fellow for any poor devil to follow—but you've been a sort of mascot to me, and I believe in you. You're an odd-job waiter, living as best you can; I'm an odd-job waiter—on Fortune, and I live as best I can. Do you follow me, as I suggested last night? There may be money in it."

The little waiter gulped, and glanced round the room. This was a moment in his life—the first great moment he had ever had to face. But he had tasted life in the company of this mysterious man; he would taste it again. With lips that trembled a little, and in a voice that shook, he answered solemnly—

"I will, sir."

"Good!" exclaimed Rackham. "We start to-day. If there are any little additions to your wardrobe necessary for an extensive stay in the country, you shall have money to make them. We will start this afternoon; we will arrive on the scene of operations this evening. As you are my friend for the moment—lunching with me—I won't insult you by giving you money here; that shall be done in the street. Now we will consult a time-table, and arrange where to meet this afternoon."

The time-table was fetched, and the train decided upon; Joshua Flattery was to be at the station with all that he possessed, and Rackham would meet him. As a matter of fact, Joshua had been completely swept off his feet by this man; his head was in a whirl; and it is probable that if Rackham had told him to take a header into the river he would have been in a mood to do it. Anything that had ever happened to him was as nothing compared with this.

Oliver Rackham, arriving at the terminus with his few possessions in a newly purchased second-hand travelling-bag, was aware of Joshua Flattery, with a very new and very shiny and very cheap suit-case (the sort of suit-case that seemed to shout out the amazingly low price that had once been chalked upon it), being hustled and jostled in various directions by railway porters and impatient passengers. Rackham rescued him, and presented him with a third-class ticket.

"You will get out at Pentney Hill, and you will look for me," said Rackham. "As befits my station, I am going first-class; there is money for both of us at the other end. Don't look so frightened; and remember that I lead and you follow."

"I'm gittin' used to the idea of it, sir," said the little man faintly.

They alighted in due course at the little country station —an amazing couple. There Joshua Flattery gave himself up to the sheer delight of it—to that strange business of finding himself in a place of trees and country roads and general rusticity. He stumbled out on to the platform, with his little bowler-hat on the back of his head, and the little second-hand suit-case tripping him up as he walked, and looked about for his patron. That patron had already secured the one fly in the station-yard, and was preparing to drive down to the house. Joshua Flattery, in sheer ignorance of the situation, would have followed him into the interior of the vehicle.

"Sancho Panza," breathed Rackham in a fierce whisper, "your place is on the box."

Meekly the little waiter climbed up there, and they set off. To tell the strict truth, Rackham was alternately in fits of silent laughter at the thought of what he was doing, and in tremors as to what the result might be; for he was going into an unknown country. This might happen—or that; he might touch comedy or he might touch disaster. Sure of his powers in one direction at least, he knew that he was capable of tackling Mr. Horace Ventoul, and perhaps even of beating him on his own ground; but then it was never possible to predict what that gentleman might have done. So that it was in a very whirl of suspicion and doubt and audacity that he drove up at last to the house, and waited until Joshua Flattery should descend from the box to open the door and let him out.

A neat little maid-servant opened the door of the house, and stood waiting. Rackham paid the driver, and stalked into the house, leaving Flattery to see to the luggage. He had to put on a bold front; he could not possibly know how he would be received, or by whom. That matter was set at rest almost immediately by the appearance of Mr. Daniel Street in the little old-fashioned hall.

Mr. Street was, of course, equally at a loss. In this vague business of pretence he did not know whom he had to welcome or whom reject; yet a glance showed him that this man had been in the original plot, and must therefore be welcomed. He stepped forward, with a hand tentatively outstretched.

"Ah—my dear old friend," exclaimed Rackham, "this is most delightful. I thought I'd take you by surprise in your country retreat. And how is Mrs. Street—after all this long time?"

Rackham had raised his voice, because it was quite possible that Angelica might be within hearing; and the game had to be played. He was conscious that Daniel Street was watching him a little uneasily; also that Joshua Flattery, with his luggage, was immediately behind him, and was standing bowing vaguely, with his ridiculous hat in his hand. And he came to a sudden recollection of the fact that he had not met the mysterious Mrs. Street.

"It's delightful of you to come down," Daniel Street said at a venture. "My wife will be charmed, I'm sure. I suppose you intend"—he glanced at the luggage—"to stay?"

"Why, of course, my dear Daniel; what else did you expect? Having nothing better to do in town, I decided to come down, and have a look at you. My man here will look after my things; I suppose someone can show him where my room is, and where he is to sleep?"

This was a fresh phase of the game for Daniel Street; but it had been a strange game from the first, and he was prepared to play it properly now. He moved off in search of a bell that he might ring.

Rackham went quickly after him, and gripped him by the arm; Joshua Flattery was still standing with the luggage, hat in hand, gazing about him. "You understand, of course," said Rackham, in a low voice, "that I am a guest here, and that I shall probably be stopping for some time. It's all right; this is part of the great game we are all playing. You will also please understand that

Mrs. Street is an old personal friend of mine—just as you are."

Daniel Street shrugged his shoulders, and glanced at the man who had whispered to him; the matter did not seem to trouble him. He led the way into a room opening out of the hall, and rang a bell; in the interval of waiting for the servant to appear he turned, and asked a vital question—

"By the way, I forget your name?"

"My name is Oliver Rackham—old friend of the family; get it safely into your mind. My man's name is Flattery; get that into your mind also. And explain to your charming wife that it is necessary that she should know me quite intimately, in order that we may not give the game away before Miss Brown. By the way—I trust Miss Brown is well?"

"So far as I know, she's very well," answered Daniel Street; and at that moment the servant entered the room, and was sent in search of her mistress.

Mrs. Daniel Street—for ever in a state of alarm as to what might happen—came in nervously. Oliver Rackham summed her up at once, and was, if the truth be told, a little sorry for her. She bore her new honors meekly, and looked always for inspiration to that husband who had failed her once, and who would, in all probability, fail her many times more.

"My dear Daisy—this is Mr. Oliver Rackham," said Street, in his toneless voice. "You have not met him before; nevertheless he is an old friend whom you have known for many years. Will you please remember that?"

"I've got to remember such a lot of things, Dan," said Mrs. Street timidly. "It's one thing—and then it's another; my poor head is fairly buzzing with it all. None the less I'm pleased to meet you, Mr. Rackham, and I do hope I shall remember that we've known each other for years, and shan't make any mistakes."

"That's not likely, Mrs. Street," said Rackham. "And I'm more than sorry that you should have any trouble over this business. I only wanted to be quite sure where we all stood—to begin with. Will you be good enough to let someone show me my room?"

"Your room?" Mrs. Street glanced from him to her husband and back again. "Oh, yes, of course," she added hurriedly. "And there's someone else in the hall; is he going to stop also?"

"Yes, that's my man," said Rackham amiably. "He'll want a room too."

Mrs. Street went out of the room with a hand to her forehead. In the hall she stood for a few moments gazing at Joshua Flattery as though not quite knowing what to do with him, while he looked equally unhappily at her. Then finally she begged him to follow her, and, with Joshua carrying the luggage, they went upstairs.

Meanwhile, in the room she had left, Daniel Street fidgeted and eyed Rackham a little uneasily, and tried to whistle. Rackham rather enjoyed the man's discomfiture, and meant to prolong it as much as possible. At last, however, he asked sharply—

"Well—how have you been getting on?"

"The house is very comfortable, and the surrounding country pretty," answered Daniel Street, without looking at him.

"Damn the house, and the country too, for that matter,"

retorted Rackham. "Don't try your lawyer's caution with me. I asked a question, and I want as straight an answer as you can give. Remember, I'm in this, too."

Daniel Street meditated on what answer to give, while he looked at Rackham out of half-closed eyes. "If you mean—is anything happening?—no," he said at last. "If you come to that, I don't know what's supposed to happen. Ventoul is down here."

"So I guessed. And the young lady?"

"At the present moment is writing in her room," answered Street.

"Where is Ventoul stopping?" demanded Rackham.

"At the inn in the village. He dines here to-night."

"Then we shall be quite a party—shan't we?" said Rackham. "Kind of you to invite me—devilish kind."

"It pleases you to be sarcastic, Mr. Rackham," retorted the other. "It occurs to me, however, that Mr. Ventoul may have a word or two to say about this visit of yours."

"Bless you, my good man, he'll welcome me with open arms—just as you have done. I'm the friend of his boyhood, and I know that he's been positively longing for me to come down here. And don't forget, my dear Daniel Street," he added, in a different tone, "that I am down here at your invitation—dear old friend!"

Mrs. Street, returning, asked that he would go and see his room; he went off at once. He found he had a large cheerful room at the front of the house; he began to tell himself that he might stay here for a very considerable time, and take quite a holiday. And then, as he unstrapped his bag, he fell to chuckling to himself at the thought of Horace Ventoul coming to dinner that night.

"He'll feel perfectly certain that he's got the field to himself, and can do as he likes," he said. "Staying at the village inn—the noted author in search of quiet! Well—here's his collaborateur in that—and other things—come down in search of quiet also. We shall be a merry party! By the way, I wonder where they've put Flattery?"

He went in search of him. A maid-servant whom he met on the stairs, and to whom he put the question, directed him up another flight; he opened a door, and looked in, to see the man on his knees beside that cheap new suit-case of his, tenderly and carefully lifting out his precious waiter's suit, with the air of one who felt that it might, if roughly handled, fall to pieces.

"What are you going to do with that?" demanded Rackham, when he had closed the door.

"I was thinkin' of puttin' it on, sir," answered the little man.

"You'll do nothing of the sort. Do you imagine you're going to wait at table?" asked his patron.

"I 'ad 'oped to do so, sir," said Joshua. "Not bein' used to this, I don't quite know what my dooties are, sir."

"Your duties are to wait on me, and see that I have all I want; and when I don't want you you'll have to walk about the country, and admire the scenery, and kill time generally. At the present moment you ought to be in my room, laying out my clothes."

"I'm sorry, sir—I'll come at once. You won't mind me askin' now and then, sir," he pleaded, "if I don't quite understand what I ought to be doin'—will you, sir?"

"My dear Flattery, your duties for the most part will be

extremely light, unless something special happens," said Rackham. "You're a sort of make-weight to myself. Come along now, and I'll show you my room, so that you can find me when you want me, or when I want you."

Joshua Flattery obediently followed him. He was in a dazed condition, not knowing in reality what was going to happen to him in the hands of this extraordinary man, and in this strange house.

"You needn't stop now; I can look after myself," said Rackham. "And don't forget that that little habit of yours of singing, or moaning, or whatever it is, has got to be dropped; you mustn't sing here. You were at it when I opened the door just now."

"Sorry, sir; I was feelin' a bit lonely, and was jist cheerin' myself up," said the man apologetically.

"There'll be quite enough to cheer you up in this house, without any singing," said Rackham, with a laugh. "Now, be off with you."

It being now seven o'clock, Rackham proceeded to dress for dinner. There was a devilish feeling in his mind that this evening he was going to enjoy himself; in a sense, he felt that he was master of the situation. Daniel Street could not turn him out, and Horace Ventoul dared not; because, to all intents and purposes, Horace Ventoul was supposed to have nothing to do with the house. Just as, in London, he had squeezed money out of Ventoul, and had done practically what he liked with him, so here, in the country, he would pursue the same tactics.

He strolled downstairs in due course, and found his way to what appeared to be the drawing-room. There was no one there, and he stood for a little time staring out of the window. And then suddenly the door was opened, and someone, lightly humming a tune, flashed into the room. That is the only expression possible to suggest exactly how Angelica came in, and closed the door, and then stood staring at him in amazement.

"Mr. Rackham!"

He came towards her, and took her outstretched hands; he looked down into those eyes that were so like the eyes of a child; he had a little pleased feeling stirring through him that she was glad to see him.

"My old friends, the Streets, have been asking me—begging me, in fact—to come down for a long time. So I thought that I'd accept," he said.

"I can't tell you how glad I am to see you," she said, releasing her hands, and speaking a little shyly. "I've thought about you often and often, and wondered what you were doing up in London.'

"And wished that you were up in London, too?" he suggested.

She shook her head, and laughed. "I haven't got tired of the country yet," she said. "I didn't know, you see, what it was like—except from pictures, and from what people told me. And everybody is so kind to me. I'm a sham—a fraud—because really I have nothing to do, except to talk or read to Mrs. Street! I'm really the laziest person in the world."

"And you're not getting bored?" he asked.

"Not in the least," she answered. "London seems years and years away—back in the ages; it doesn't seem possible I ever lived there. I won't say 'thank you' to you again—because I know you don't like it; but I put you in a little, special, tiny prayer every night."

"Have you seen anyone you know—met any friends, I mean?" he asked hurriedly, without looking at her.

"Yes—that gentleman you introduced me to that night we had supper together—Mr. Ventoul," she exclaimed eagerly. "He came down here a day or two ago——"

"In search of rest and quiet," broke in Rackham, with a twitching of his lips.

"Yes—that was exactly what he said," she went on innocently. "And isn't it funny?—he knows Mr. Street quite well. The inn's not very comfortable—I mean the inn in the village, where he is staying; and so he comes over here to dine. I expect he'll be here to-night."

"That's most delightful," said Rackham. "It will be nice to meet him again."

Daniel Street came in at that moment, clad in the frock-coat which was a compromise with him for evening dress. Mrs. Street followed immediately afterwards, in a dress that was a little youthful for her, and of which she was obviously proud. Both were a little at a loss to know what to do or to say; but Rackham put them at their ease.

"I'm delighted to hear that Miss Brown is so comfortable, and is having such a good time," he said gaily. "I was quite sure from the first, my dear Mrs. Street, that you would like her, and would get on well with her. I understood the tastes of my old friend," he added rallyingly; "I knew precisely the sort of lady she wanted."

Poor Mrs. Street glanced at her husband, and then smiled nervously at Rackham; finally sat down with her hands folded in her lap, and waited. Rackham heard a bell ring, and a sharp and confident voice speaking to the servant; then the door opened, and Horace Ventoul, in evening dress, and very sure of himself, walked in.

Rackham, standing leaning against the window-frame, watched the little comedy. In the first place, the somewhat careless fashion in which Ventoul touched Mrs. Street's hand, and her frightened glance at him; the greeting between Ventoul and Daniel Street; then the smile and the outstretched hand for Angelica. And it was while Ventoul was actually holding Angelica's hand that he became aware of Rackham, standing there, with his hands in his pockets, and with a mocking smile on his face.

So astounded was Ventoul that he almost gave the game away then, by blurting out something that would have set suspicion afloat. He stood there, holding Angelica's hand, and staring open-mouthed at Rackham.

"My dear old boy," said Rackham, lazily coming forward, "this is indeed an unexpected pleasure. Fancy your knowing my old friends, the Streets! Well—well—it's a mighty small world—isn't it?"

"I'm glad to see you," faltered Ventoul, with a vindictive glance at Daniel Street.

"I knew you would be," retorted Rackham. "And when these dear people had been worrying me, in the most delightful fashion, for weeks past, to come down and see them, and stop as long as I liked—that was the expression, wasn't it, Dan?"

"I believe so," said Street.

"Of course I couldn't resist the temptation any longer. So down I came, with my man and all, and here I shall stop until dear old Dan absolutely takes me by the shoulders and turns me out."

"You've brought your—man with you?" asked Horace Ventoul, almost forgetting everything in his amazement.

"Yes—I decided recently I'd have a man; I wanted someone to look after me and my things. He's a good old chap—a bit slow, but he'll improve. And I hear that you're staying down at the inn with *your* man."

"Yes," said Ventoul sulkily, "I came down here a couple of days ago——"

"For rest and change," supplemented Rackham, with a nod. "You must need it; any man who uses his brain as you do must need frequent rest and change."

"It must be a very wearing life," said Angelica, with a sympathetic glance at Ventoul.

Ventoul did not answer. He turned and strode across the room to Mrs. Street, who had nervously risen, and was watching him. "What the devil is the delay about dinner?" he demanded in a fierce whisper.

The unfortunate lady hurried out of the room, and Ventoul, with a glance at Rackham, sat down beside Angelica. There was an uncomfortable pause, while Rackham stood by the window, and strove to catch Ventoul's eye, that he might enjoy its expression to the full. But Ventoul simply sat, with his hands pressed together between his knees, and stared at the carpet. And then, mercifully, the door was opened, and the servant announced dinner.

Everything favored Oliver Rackham that evening. It became obvious, when they went into the dining-room, that on previous evenings, while Mr. and Mrs. Street naturally sat at opposite ends of the table, Ventoul and Angelica had faced each other at opposite sides. The servant, however, in laying the extra place, had, of course, put the new guest next to Angelica, leaving Ventoul in his usual place at the right hand of Mrs. Street. So that now Ventoul fumed alone on his side of the table, while Rackham and Angelica chattered away together on theirs. Moreover, Rackham, noticing presently the brooding face of Ventoul, began in sheer devilry to gird at him, in a subtle fashion that only he should understand.

"Look at our friend over there," he murmured to Angelica, in a tone just loud enough for Ventoul to hear. "He's thinking out plots. There's one plot he's got in his mind at the present time that he simply can't get away from; he's told me that it's with him night and day. Never take up writing, Miss Brown; it's awful work. It makes you unsociable to your neighbors; it makes you apparently morose, when in reality you're nothing of the sort; it's not worth the fame you get out of it. Now, my poor friend Ventoul curses the day he ever published that book of his; he would be a far happier man if he'd never done it. I can assure you, Miss Brown, from personal knowledge of the dear fellow——"

"For God's sake, change the subject, Rackham!" cried Ventoul violently.

"My dear old boy, I didn't know you could hear," said Rackham. "Miss Brown is naturally interested in anyone so famous as yourself; but I ought to have remembered your modest, shrinking nature. Forgive me, dear old boy —I wouldn't have pained you for the world. By the way, has Miss Brown seen the book?"

"I'm not in the habit of talking about my work," said Ventoul sharply.

"No; that's where you make a mistake," urged Rackham remorselessly. "You try and persuade him, Miss Brown, to let you read that book. I've read it—in fact, I may say I know it by heart almost."

"I hope you will lend it to me, Mr. Ventoul," said Angelica. "I've often wanted to ask you."

"You wouldn't care for it; it's a poor thing," said Ventoul, with a glance at Rackham.

"Well—I like that," said Oliver Rackham, with a laugh. "The idea of running down your own work like that! But that's just like him, Miss Brown," he went on. "I assure you that the very first time I discovered, by the merest chance, that he'd had a book published, with his name in nice gold letters outside, he tried to prevent me from reading it—positively didn't want me to know what was inside the covers. Isn't that beautiful?"

Ventoul sat there writhing. Even when Mrs. Street ventured to speak to him he snapped out a reply that caused Angelica to raise her eyebrows, and look at him in some wonder. To him the dinner seemed endless; he sat there fuming, and inwardly cursing the servants, and the whole business from end to end.

But at last the time came for Mrs. Street and Angelica to retire. Rackham held the door open for them, and bowed them out with due solemnity; closed the door again, and set his back to it; and looked with dancing eyes at Ventoul, who was sitting at the opposite side of the table.

"Charming dinner party!" exclaimed Rackham.

Ventoul, forgetful of everything, sprang to his feet.

"You bully—you jail-bird—you thing out of the streets—I tell you I won't stand it," he almost screamed. "Get out of this house!"

At any other time Rackham would probably have retorted in characteristic fashion; now, however, he was so sure of himself—momentarily, at least—that he merely laughed, and came across to the table, and sat down at his ease.

"Get out of the house, indeed!" he exclaimed. "I'm too fond of you for that, my dear Horace—too much interested in you and your career. I'm here, and I'm going to stop; I like the country, and the house seems comfortable. Sit down, Horace; sit down, little man, and let's talk over matters!"

CHAPTER IX

DANIEL STREET COMES TO LIFE

HORACE VENTOUL, striding up and down the room, with his hands locked behind him and his chin thrust forward, might have been to anyone else a man to be feared; Horace Ventoul, on the very horns of a dilemma, and with Oliver Rackham to be reckoned with, was a poor thing indeed. He turned now to the only person on whom he could vent his spite—the man he had bought—Daniel Street.

"This is nothing to do with you," he said savagely. "Go away; get out of the room; wait anywhere you like until I want you."

Daniel Street, with a covert glance from one to the other, walked towards the door. And once again that exasperating Rackham took the business into his own hands. He airily waved a hand towards the retreating Daniel Street, and called out to him—

"So sorry, dear old Dan; but we'll meet presently. Charming of you to have asked me down; you won't get rid of me in a hurry. Do have another glass of wine before you go."

With another glance back at them, Street went out, closing the door softly behind him. A moment afterwards Horace Ventoul stole on tip-toe to the door, and, turning the handle quickly, flung it open; but there was no one there.

"Suspicious as ever!" murmured Rackham, pouring out a glass of wine, and drinking it off. "But that's ever the way of a rogue; he goes along, with his chin turned over his shoulder, looking for the trouble that he knows is just behind him—or he thinks it is, at least." And then, in an ordinary tone, as he leaned forward, with his arms folded on the table—"So you stole a march on me—did you?"

"I'm paying for this house—and I'm paying for everything in it," said the other, keeping always the table between them. "You said you didn't know whether you were coming down or not; I put you aside altogether."

"Wherein you were wrong, my dear Horace," answered Rackham. "I had a sudden pricking of conscience—a sudden distrust of you. I told myself that I had been wrong in allowing you so much latitude—in letting you take so much into your own hands. Consequently, I came down at once—with my man."

"Who is this man?" demanded Ventoul. "Do you think I'm going to support him, as well as you?"

"Of course you are. You have no sense of proportion in these things, my dear Horace; you are going after half a million of money as though it were a beggarly legacy of a hundred pounds. I am a gentleman, I trust—or I am supposed to be; one must do things in style. Consequently, I travel with my man. As to his credentials; he is a most delightful fellow—a little, out-of-work, odd-job waiter I picked up in London, and have, in a sense, adopted. You'll like him when you know him; and as he is particularly sensitive, don't upset him. Remember that he is a protege of mine, and in consequence must be duly respected."

"Curse your proteges—and curse you!" exclaimed Ventoul, from the other side of the table.

"My dear Horace, if you use bad language to me again I will take you up by the scruff of your neck, and carry you in before the ladies, and there beat you," said Rackham calmly, with his eyes upon the ceiling. "How many times am I to plead with you to be reasonable; how many times am I to urge you to remember the difficulties that beset your path, and to beg that, instead of making an enemy of me, you will make an ally and friend of me? You can't shake me off; I'm going to stop here, to see fair play in the coming fight."

"You will get no money out of me!" exclaimed Horace Ventoul. "Not a penny!"

"One does not require much money in the country," said Rackham, still with his eyes on the ceiling. "And if I run short I can always take some of the more valuable things in the house, and run over to the nearest town, and pawn or sell them. Pray don't let a little thing like that worry you, dear old boy."

Ventoul raged up and down the room for a few minutes longer; now and then he stopped, as though making up his mind to speak; and then went on again. At last he stopped at the other side of the table, and shook a fist across at Rackham, seated smoking.

"Street shall turn you and your man out; it's ostensibly his house, and he's supposed to be able to do what he likes in it," he said.

"Mr. Daniel Street is an old, personal friend of mine—and the fair Daisy loves me like a brother," said Rackham. "You forget that I introduced Miss Brown to my old and valued friends, the Streets, and that she is grateful to me for having done so. Try again, Horace."

Again much walking about the room; and once again Ventoul stopped before him. "What do you intend to do down here?" he demanded.

"Really I couldn't tell you," answered Rackham. "I am a little jaded with London; I'm going to rest, and look at the scenery, and generally play the guest at a country house. You see, you're an outsider; you don't know the Streets as well as I do, and so you have to put up at the village inn—with your man. By the way, how is the brute?"

"We're not discussing servants," snapped Ventoul.

"I was about to observe that *I* am privileged, in being able to put up at the house here—with *my* man. That makes a bit of a difference—doesn't it?"

At that moment Daniel Street opened the door, and came in. He hesitated for a moment, with the door in his hand; then, as he was not repulsed, came into the room, and closed the door.

"The ladies will be expecting that we should join them," said Street, in his hollow voice. And then, as neither man spoke, he looked at Ventoul, and asked a question. "Does he go—or stay?"

"I stay, friend Daniel," Rackham answered instantly. "And don't forget that you're delighted to have me here, and that our dear Horace and I have lingered over our wine, because we've had so many pleasant things to say to each other. By the way, Daniel, I think you said this was Liberty Hall, and that one smoked all over the place—didn't you? You may have forgotten it, but I think that was what you said."

"He must do as he likes," said Ventoul, in an undertone to Street. "And now, I suppose we've got to go in and face the women, and put the best aspect we can on the whole business—and listen to music and drivelling talk, as usual. You'd better lead the way, Rackham."

"I'm rather afraid that if I did you might be tempted to do me an injury from behind," said Rackham, with a grin. "Therefore, I think it will be safer, and look better, if we go in arm-in-arm, with our dear host following. Smile, my dear Horace—smile, you little devil—as though you'd just heard a good story. Are you ready? Then, march!"

They walked into the drawing-room in that order; Rackham with a firm grip on the reluctant Ventoul's arm, and his head bent as though whispering to his shorter companion; Daniel Street, with an inscrutable face, following behind. They found Mrs. Street, obviously very nervous and anxious, sitting bolt upright in a chair in which she should properly have lounged; they found Angelica evidently eagerly awaiting their arrival.

"My dear," said Daniel Street, "I have told our guests that this is Liberty Hall, and that we smoke everywhere. I trust you don't object?"

"Not in the least, Dan," faltered Mrs. Street. "For my part, I like the smell of it."

Rackham seated himself beside Angelica; she glanced round at him shyly, and again he felt how disconcerting her eyes could be. She was so obviously glad to see him that that was disconcerting, too. After a moment or two, the better to get away from that matter of the eyes, he asked her somewhat abruptly if she would not sing.

"I expect you know, Mrs. Street," he said, "that Miss

Brown is a musician. Knowing how very fond you were of music, I selected Miss Brown chiefly for that very reason. She plays divinely, and she has the voice of an angel."

"You're laughing at me, Mr. Rackham," said Angelica. "I didn't tell you I sang."

"I guessed it," said Oliver Rackham. "Besides, I want my friend Ventoul to hear you; surely you have not sat with closed lips on those other evenings when he has been here? Ventoul, with his poetic soul, appreciates music as few people can do."

Mr. Horace Ventoul, as a matter of fact, was at that moment staring moodily out of the window, with his hands behind his back; he was meditating what he should do in the present crisis to get rid of Oliver Rackham. Mrs. Street had seated herself near her husband, and was looking at him apprehensively; and of course the only utterly unconscious person in the room was Angelica.

"If Mrs. Street would like——" Angelica began.

Mrs. Street glanced round quickly, and then, with a half-smile, waved a hand towards the piano. "If you would, my dear——" she murmured.

Rackham sat back with folded arms, and eyes half closed, as he listened to the girl softly touching the notes and singing. She had a clear, little, flute-like voice; it seemed almost that she sang to him only. That was disconcerting again, and he turned his head away, and watched Ventoul's back, as that gentleman still stood looking out through the window. Ventoul's back was more of an inspiration to Rackham's present mood; therefore he watched that, and listened to the song.

The song ended, Ventoul turned suddenly, and spoke. "Thank you, Miss Brown; that is the sort of melody that stirs me tremendously," he said.

"Ever poetic—how wonderful it must be to have a mind and a soul like that!" murmured Rackham.

"If Mrs. Street can spare you, won't you come for a walk round the grounds?" said Ventoul abruptly. "It's a lovely night, and this room seems oppressive."

Angelica looked round a little nervously at Mrs. Street and at Daniel; glanced at Rackham. But Rackham, apparently absorbed, leaned with folded arms back in his chair, with his eyes closed. Angelica crossed the room slowly, with another apologetic look at Mrs. Street, and approached Ventoul.

"I shall be pleased," said Angelica.

The two went out together through the open French windows. For a moment or two Rackham sat with his eyes closed, while Daniel Street and his wife watched him. Rackham had a cigar in his mouth, and was lazily puffing it; Street had rolled one of his eternal cigarettes, taking the tobacco for it from a paper packet; Mrs. Street was nervously clasping and unclasping her hands. So they sat in silence as the others walked away through the grounds.

Meanwhile, Angelica was to make a discovery. As they paced slowly along, with Horace Ventoul occasionally making some grave remark about Angelica's voice, or the beauty of the night, they heard in the distance someone moving towards them, singing. It was a curious sort of singing—something between a moan and a chant; and it proceeded from Joshua Flattery, who, tired of the house and of having nothing to do, had, after supping discreetly with the maid-servants, come out to take the air. Joshua had begun to tell himself that he rather liked the peace of the country, when he came face to face with Angelica and Ventoul. And of course quite naturally stopped, and drew back, and took off his absurd bowler-hat.

Ventoul, again forgetting himself, addressed this vague figure sharply. "Who the deuce are you?" he demanded.

"No offence, sir," said Joshua humbly. "Name of Flattery, sir; I came down with Mr. Rackham—Mr. Rackham being so kind as to take what you might call a interest in me, and thinkin' I might like a look at the country. Joshua Flattery, sir—at your service; I'm Mr. Rackham's man, sir."

Angelica had hurriedly stepped across to where the little man stood, bare-headed, in the moonlight. "Why— I've seen you before," she said. "I've seen you very often. You were the waiter at the Professor's dances, weren't you?"

"Yes, miss; and many's the time I've seen you there, miss," said Joshua quickly. "Lor', miss—ain't it a small world? I was sayin' to Mr. Rackham on'y yesterday that I wondered wot had become of you, miss. And to find you down 'ere . . . well—ain't it surprisin'?"

"Do you know this man?" asked Ventoul.

"Why—yes," said Angelica, with a smile. "He used to look after the refreshments at a—a sort of dance I used to go to in London. Don't you see it all, Mr. Ventoul? Mr. Rackham, who went out of his way to be kind to me, and to send me down here to Mrs. Street, has found this man—not too well off, I'm afraid—in London, and has taken care of him. Oh, Mr. Ventoul—isn't that wonderful of him?"

"You may well say that, miss," broke in Joshua Flattery hastily. "'I'll make your fortune,' says Mr. Rackham to me, 'an' your dooties shall be light,' 'e says. Jist to come down 'ere, miss, an' look after 'im, an' lay out 'is clothes. Anybody'd be proud to serve Mr. Rackham, misc."

"I'm sure they would," said Angelica. "And I hope you'll be very comfortable."

"Thank you, miss," said Flattery; "and if one may say, so, it's a pleasure to set eyes on your bright face again."

They left him standing there, hat in hand; they walked on together slowly. Ventoul was inwardly raging; this constant praise of Rackham was getting on his nerves. Here was the fellow posing as a philanthropist, and bringing a sorry, seedy follower down to this place at Ventoul's expense. The thing was intolerable; Ventoul bitterly fumed at his inability to do anything to prevent it.

As they went back to the house they heard again the sound of music. Angelica left her escort abruptly, and walked in through the French windows; and there was Oliver Rackham, seated at the piano, and playing. Moreover, Angelica recognized that the man was playing music that was greater than any she knew, and was playing it with a touch that seemed to call back to her that mother who had been a musician and not a mere teacher of music. Angelica stood with hands clasped, drinking in the music —her bosom rising and falling, and her lips parted, and her eyes shining.

Rackham let his fingers glide over the keys into a final chord, and got up, with a little awkward laugh on his lips. "I've been trying to reduce our friend Mrs. Street to a state of proper despondency," he said; "and it would appear that I have succeeded."

Indeed, Mrs. Street was weeping without concealment—dabbing at her eyes and sniffing audibly. As for Angelica, she came forward into the room with eyes only for Rackham.

"It was beautiful!" she exclaimed softly. "It seemed to me for a moment something like what I had heard my mother play when I was a child, and when I sat in the firelight and listened to her. Won't you play again?—that is, if it won't make Mrs. Street cry too much."

"Rackham has a knack of doing different things fairly well," said Ventoul from behind her.

"And nothing very well—eh, Horace?" said Rackham. "Whereas, you see"—he turned for a moment to Angelica, with that malicious smile upon his face—"our friend, Mr. Ventoul, does one thing superbly, and is noted for it. No—I won't play again; I'll give Mrs. Street an opportunity to dry her tears."

"I'm sure I'm most sorry, Mr. Rackham," said Mrs. Street, smiling and dabbing at her eyes; "but I haven't been so moved—not for years. There's music that you can hear, and let it run through your head and forget all about it—and there's other music that seems to call up all the things you might have done, and all the things you've been sorry for—and perhaps some of the blessed things that are coming to you in the future. And that's just what yours did to me."

"I would give anything and everything to be able to play like that," said Angelica, with a sigh.

The time came when it was obviously impossible for Horace Ventoul to wait any longer; he must perforce return to the inn in the village. He had waited far longer than he should have done, as it was; and he had had to sit and talk platitudes with Daniel Street, while Oliver Rackham, turning glibly over certain sheets of music that had been left in the house, spoke of this, that, and the other to the girl—with now and then a little passage played or hummed, or now and then something explained. And all this was something in which Ventoul could not take part.

And then—the other side of the picture—the vindictive side. For suddenly it seemed to Rackham that he must go further yet than he had done—must show that cloven hoof that could be brought out so readily. He glanced at a clock on the mantelshelf, and spoke rallyingly to Daniel Street.

"Poor old Horace has got to go back through the village to the inn—a lonely road, Horace," said Rackham. "I think I'll walk back with you—and we'll have something just to fortify us before we go. May I ring the bell?"

He rang the bell without permission, and the servant appeared. Daniel Street, with a glance at Ventoul, told her to bring in the decanters and a siphon and glasses—gave the order with some eagerness. For, if the truth be told, Daniel had been strictly limited in his potations since his stay in the country; all that was wanted was in the house, but Ventoul had kept a strict eye upon it. Ventoul beat a foot softly on the carpet now, as the servant returned with a tray.

"May I mix for you, Horace?" asked Rackham.

"Thank you—no," answered Ventoul shortly. "And I don't think I want anyone to walk back with me; I can go alone."

"I'm going to give you a little one, friend Horace, to put Dutch courage into you for going past dark corners; and I'm not going to leave you until I've seen you safely in your own room in the inn," said Rackham, with mock affection. "I should never forgive myself if anything happened to you, dear old boy. And I'm also going to mix one for my old friend Dan; I ought to know the strength he likes by this time. And then we'll drink the health of the ladies—and so good night!"

Rackham carried the thing off with a flourish; some ten minutes later he went off down the drive, with an arm affectionately through that of Ventoul, and with a voice that was carolling an air that Angelica stood still to hear.

"Isn't he wonderful?" said Angelica softly, as she stood at the French windows, and looked after them.

"One of the jolliest evenings I ever remember to have spent, Horace," said Rackham boisterously, when they were out on the road. "I'm sorry now that I waited so long in London; I seem to have been missing quite a lot. This is the sort of existence I could go on leading for ever—if only I didn't see too much of you."

Horace Ventoul wrenched himself free from the other's arm, and faced him on the moonlit road. "Go back," he exclaimed hoarsely, "go back, and leave me to go to the inn alone. I'm sick of the sight of you."

"I can't possibly go back, my dear Horace, and tell them that I've left you to face the horrors of a country road alone," exclaimed Rackham. "What would they say to me? Besides—it's no use your getting sick of the sight of me, because you're going to see quite a lot of me, I can assure you. Will you never be reasonable?"

"What's your game? What do you intend to do down here?" demanded Ventoul, beginning to walk on again sulkily.

"My present intention is to show off the merits of dear Horace Ventoul as much as possible," replied Rackham airily. "I laud him to the skies—I tell everybody what a fine fellow he is; I positively rub in his merits to the girl. What more can you ask?"

"Yes—and show off your own merits in the meantime," exclaimed Ventoul, turning upon him savagely. "What the devil's the good of that to me?"

"My dear Horace—if Nature has seen fit to make you an inferior being to myself, why blame me?" asked Rackham. "You wouldn't have me play the dull dog, simply to allow you to shine by contrast—would you?"

"I'd have you get out of the way, and leave the field clear for me," said Ventoul.

"That I cannot do, my dear Horace, until I know what you intend to do when the field is clear," said Rackham. "Now, don't let's talk any more about it; we'll go down to the inn, and there, for the good of the house, we'll make more or less of a night of it. I only do that for your sake, Horace—because I suspect that you don't spend much there, and I want to give you something of a spurious reputation for generosity. There's a style about me, my dear Horace, that you don't possess; as your guest at the inn I shall do you credit."

The unwilling Ventoul was led triumphantly to the inn by Rackham, and marched in. In less than five minutes it seemed as though Rackham owned the place, and owned Ventoul as well. He noisily ordered refreshments, and insisted that Ventoul, even if he would not drink in the place, should sit up for awhile and keep him company.

"You're so devilish unsociable, my dear Horace," he said. "I come down here to this benighted spot for your benefit—and yet you want to get rid of me. Sit down, my dear fellow; I'm not going for an hour yet."

Meanwhile, that grateful little man, Joshua Flattery, who had been so suddenly lifted out of that poor game of odd-job waiting in London, and who already began to sniff romance in the very air of this place, had taken the advice of Oliver Rackham, and had gone to view the scenery by moonlight. He did not go very far, because he knew nothing of the country, and there were no street lamps or lighted shops to guide him. He merely went what he would have termed "a turn down the road," humming to himself cheerfully, and liking the utter peace and silence of it all. He came back to the gate at the end of the drive, utterly unsuspicious of the fact that some one lay in wait for him there—someone who had already searched the house to find him.

The person who lay in wait presented no more formidable appearance than that of Daniel Street, apparently also taking the night air. But Mr. Street had been bringing a rather sharp mind to bear on the situation during the past few hours, and was beginning to speculate concerning what could be the reason for the extraordinary business with which he was so suddenly and intimately concerned.

During the first few days that he had been at the house the man had been content to let events develop of themselves; he was comfortably housed, and well paid, and the matter did not greatly concern him. In all probability, he thought, Ventoul wanted to make an impression on the girl, and was choosing a rather expensive way of doing it. But with the advent of Oliver Rackham, and the obvious deadly feud between him and Ventoul, a new turn was given to events, and Daniel Street began to take a deeper interest in them.

Obviously he could not question those who, while ostensibly his guests, were yet in a position of authority over him. But there might be a possibility of getting something out of that extraordinary-looking seedy man-servant who had accompanied Rackham. So that the meeting at the gate was by no means accidental.

Joshua Flattery touched the brim of his bowler-hat to the master of the house, and would have passed on; but the master of the house detained him with a friendly word.

"You've been out to take the air?"

Flattery stopped, and touched the brim of his hat again. "Yes, sir," he answered, "and very nice air it is, too, sir. Mr. Rackham advised me to try it, sir—to go out and 'ave a look at wot 'e called the scenery—though there ain't much of it to be seen, sir, by this light."

"You don't know very much about the country, I take it?" suggested Street carelessly.

"Cockney born and bred, sir; scarcely ever 'ad so much

as a day in the country in my life," said Flattery, with a laugh. "But w'en Mr. Rackham says to me—'I'm going down to the country,' 'e says, 'an' I don't see w'y I shouldn't take you along with me'—well, I 'adn't the 'eart to resist it, sir."

"So you've not been very long with Mr. Rackham?" said Daniel Street.

"Bless you, sir—on'y a matter of a hour or two, as you might say, sir," answered the little man, glad enough to chat with this affable gentleman. "On'y Mr. Rackham 'as been very good to me, sir—very good indeed. Of course, 'e will 'ave 'is joke, an' 'e sets me larfin' many an' many a time. But 'e's a gent all through, sir—every inch of 'im. Picked me up quite casual, 'e did; found out that things wasn't goin' too well with me, 'an, 'aving known wot it was to be a bit down 'imself, made up 'is mind sudden like to 'elp me."

"So Mr. Rackham has suffered reverses of fortune—eh?" Daniel Street appeared to suppress a carefully contrived yawn, but he listened eagerly enough for the answer.

"Bless you, sir—w'en I first met Mr. Rackham, 'e was wot you might call broke to the world. A gentleman, mind you—but a mighty poor one. And then suddenly up 'e goes—jist like a rocket, sir; an' now 'e's going to stop up, if I know anythink of 'im."

"A master to be proud of—and I expect he'll find you a very faithful servant. And he goes so far in friendliness to you as to have his joke with you—does he?" That was merely a chance shot, because as yet Daniel Street knew nothing, and had discovered nothing.

Joshua Flattery, liking the master of the house more and more every minute, rubbed his hands together, and chuckled. "Yes, sir—I never come across anybody to make a joke of things like wot Mr. Rackham does. Why, now, sir—'ere's a little thing in point. W'en I was 'olding back, not quite sure whether I'd accept Mr. Rackham's offer, I says to 'im—jokin' like—'Is there money in it?' I says. 'Money?' 'e says, 'there's 'alf a million!' 'e says. An' of course I larfed, an' I said I'd come, sir."

Daniel Street stood still, literally stunned. The whole thing had broken upon him with the force of a flash of lightning; he wondered that he had been so blind before. Almost he laughed as he stood there, with Joshua Flattery still rubbing his hands, and still chuckling at that great joke.

"Very funny, indeed," he murmured. "And now—good night to you."

"Good night to you, sir," said Flattery cheerfully; and went off to the house.

Daniel Street slowly paced up the drive, thinking hard. The whole thing now was clear as daylight. This girl who was to be so carefully tended; the house specially taken; the fictitious master and mistress put into it; and then the coming of the first rogue, followed by the appearance of the second. The swaggering, roystering fellow, perhaps in his cups, had blurted out the business to this little man he had suddenly found it necessary to employ as a man-servant. Daniel Street had not taken his night walk in vain.

"And I'm to be paid at the rate of so many shillings a week, and to be bullied like a pickpocket if things go wrong—while I help these fellows to lay hands on half a million of money—am I?" he murmured to himself. "This is the best night's work I've done for many a long year; that babbling little fool has given me the key to the whole business. These fellows have discovered that the girl is coming into half a million of money—and they're both after it. That accounts for the quarrelling, and for the deadly rivalry; that accounts for one aristocratic gentleman with his manservant staying at the village inn, and the other one, with his apology for a man-servant, quartering himself here. Well, whichever of 'em gets it, or tries to, I think I shall be in at the death, when we come to divide the spoils. And if by any chance they cut each other's throats over the affair, then I stand a very good chance of not having to divide the spoils at all. Daniel, my boy—things are coming very much your way."

He half thought that he would tell his wife; but he rejected that idea instantly. She was not to be trusted in any such delicate matter as this—in fact, in any matter in which she might fear that he was once more going to place himself within touch of the Law. No—he would keep it to himself; now that he had the key to the whole business he would know how to work. He would know, too, how to tap sources of information that Rackham and Ventoul would find it difficult to reach. He went back to the house, and sat down there, and rolled a cigarette—taking the tobacco in little shreds from his paper packet.

Mrs. Street, waking from a short nap in the most comfortable drawing-room chair, looked up, to see him smiling softly to himself. They were alone, for Angelica had gone to bed.

"You seem happy, dear," said Mrs. Street.

"My dear Daisy," he answered solemnly, "the country suits me, I think. I've quite come to life again."

But Oliver Rackham, making night hideous along a quiet country road by shouting the chorus of a song, knew nothing of all these things, as he went swaying back to the house where Angelica slept—perhaps dreaming of him.

CHAPTER X

THE MIDNIGHT OIL

There followed a week during which Rackham and Ventoul, in a sense, marked time—a week in which also Daniel Street merely awaited events, with a new light thrown upon them for his guidance. Angelica dutifully read the newspapers or a novel every morning to Mrs. Daniel Street, while that lady, for her part, wondered a little why she did so, or how long this business of pretence was to last.

Yet Angelica may be said to have read almost with an eye upon the open window near to her, and with an ear ready for the sound of a footstep in the house, or the ringing of a bell. For Angelica was perturbed; never in all her life before had she found herself the centre of such happenings as now.

She was the one woman in the house. (Mrs. Street, of course, did not count, in the sense that Mrs. Street was undoubtedly happily wedded to Mr. Street, and had no thought for others.) And every day there strolled up to the house from outside Mr. Horace Ventoul; and every day there appeared before her from inside Mr. Oliver Rackham.

The methods of the two were different. Horace Ventoul claimed her sympathy by reason of the fact that he had wrapped himself in a little air of mystery—was, in fact, a man who had come out of the great world—and was willing to put up with the difficulties and inconveniences of this little place, in order that he might seek that seclusion and peace necessary to him and his work. There was fascination in that; it was wonderful to think of such a man coming down to the level of such a life.

On the other hand, Oliver Rackham had been her first friend; there was much in that. There was a little subtle bond of sympathy between them, because of that first night when they had met in London and had talked together —because of that other great and wonderful night when they had supped together. And now the fact that both these men had, by the merest chance, as she believed, come down to this place, stirred Angelica's romantic feelings as nothing had ever done.

Quite unknown to Angelica, however, there was another element in the amazing game that had to be reckoned with; and that element was Daniel Street. That gentleman was playing for his own hand; and it was necessary that he should cast about to find exactly who was most likely to be of use to him when that hand had at last to be played. He remembered, astutely enough, that the man who was paying the piper was Horace Ventoul, and, above all, that he was the man who had the arranging of all the details in his hands. Rackham was a mere outsider, who had apparently forced his way into the game, and was prepared to fight for his chances by rougher methods. Clearly, if any help were needed at all, Daniel Street would have to look, in that final grabbing of the spoils, to Ventoul rather than to Rackham.

Therefore, not knowing exactly what the position of

affairs might be, but recognising that the man who had paid the money had the first right to consideration, Daniel Street favored Ventoul. If it were possible for him to arrange that Angelica should meet either of the men, he arranged in favor of Horace Ventoul; and contrived, with the aid of his pliant wife, that Rackham should be set aside. So that Angelica, without knowing it, discovered that Mrs. Street subtly made arrangements to have convenient headaches at times when Ventoul had called at the house or was likely to call; while Daniel Street contrived to detain Rackham, on more than one occasion, when he might have been disposed to monopolise Angelica.

It resolved itself at last into a game of hide-and-seek. Rackham had a bad habit of sleeping late in the morning; Horace Ventoul was unusually alert at what Rackham would have regarded as an unearthly hour. Consequently, Horace Ventoul, arriving at the house with smiling apologies soon after breakfast, would find Angelica arranging flowers for the vases, or performing some other light duty, at the suggestion of Mrs. Street; and would contrive to have quite a long chat with her, knowing well that Oliver Rackham was above stairs and not yet dressed. And when Oliver Rackham finally descended, he would be told that Mr. Ventoul had called, and, as Mrs. Street was not in want of Angelica's services that morning, they had gone for a stroll together through the woods.

On one such occasion Rackham, on the mere chance of finding them, went off after them. It was a morning of repentance—a day when he had to remember that he had sat late the night before in Ventoul's room at the inn, and had drunk deep, with the mischievous desire to keep Ventoul out of bed. And yet he knew now, when he went through the fresh greenery of the woods in search of the man and the girl, that Ventoul had drunk nothing, and was cool and calm and clear-headed this morning—which Rackham was not.

When presently he came out into a little clearing in the woods, and saw them together, he stopped, watching them. Not exactly watching Ventoul, perhaps, except as a figure in the picture; he had eyes really only for the girl. For the first time he realised how wonderful she was, and how mean and sordid he seemed, standing there in the morning sunlight looking at her.

She was sitting on a bank, with her hands clasped round her knees; she was looking straight in front of her, with her chin slightly raised. At her feet Horace Ventoul was stretched, and in his hand was a book from which he was apparently reading. Rackham had come upon them unawares over the soft turf; he was within a few yards of them when he stopped to look at them. He heard Ventoul's rather high-pitched voice reading from the book.

" 'The man who has it in him to love a woman, without thought of anything save that he loves her purely and simply and truly, honors her and raises himself in loving her. And no matter whether it shall happen that they have been parted, or have trodden the road of life together, at the end of things the memory of that love shall be a sweet and pleasant thing—passing understanding.' "

"By the Lord!"—whispered Rackham to himself—"he's making love to her out of my mouth!"

"That's beautiful," breathed Angelica, without turning her head.

"And very true," murmured Ventoul. "At least I thought so at the time I wrote it—and I think so now—more than ever."

"You might read that bit again, old chap," said Rackham, stepping forward and coming within range of their vision. "You've got such a wonderful voice for reading things like that."

Ventoul petulantly closed the book, and got up. Angelica sat still, turning eyes that were smiling upon Rackham, and stretching out a hand to him.

"Mr. Ventoul has been reading some bits out of his famous book to me," said the girl. "It's wonderful how a man can think of those things; don't you think so?"

"Marvellous!" said Rackham. "And it staggers me to think that anyone can take them seriously." The man was in a bitter and dangerous mood—utterly reckless of what he said.

"Why—Mr. Rackham—I don't know what you mean," said Angelica. "That's not like you at all to talk like that. I think it's all beautiful."

"Tastes differ, Miss Brown, I'm afraid," said Rackham. "Why—I should think anyone could reel off that sort of stuff to any extent, if they tried."

"Why don't you try, my dear old Noll?" asked Ventoul, greatly daring. "I know it looks very easy to one who hasn't done it; but I'm glad at least that Miss Brown should appreciate it. Perhaps it is poor stuff—but when one has put one's heart into it, it is scarcely fair or just to sneer at it." He turned away, with an air of offended dignity that was amazing to Rackham, and that won instant pity from the girl.

"I didn't know you were so easily upset—especially over that book," said Rackham. "However, if Miss Brown likes it, it's nothing to do with me. I'm sorry I intruded; I came at an unlucky moment."

He turned and strode away. In truth he did not really understand himself; and he fought fiercely against the mere suggestion that it mattered to him a row of pins that Ventoul should apparently have caught this girl's fancy, and should have done it by such methods. The whole business was hateful and repulsive—just as he himself that morning was hateful and repulsive in his own eyes. And now, by a chance word, he had made it appear as though some feeble jealousy was stirring in him against the other man.

Angelica stood looking after him with slow tears gathering in her eyes. He had spoilt her morning—had dimmed the sky for her. When Ventoul ventured to suggest presently that he should read to her again, she half-petulantly stopped him.

"I don't want to hear any more, thank you—not now," she said. "I think I'd like to walk back; Mrs. Street may be wanting me."

They went back slowly together, and almost in silence. Ventoul was inwardly cursing the man who was for ever stepping into the plot to its undoing; he tried to decide on some plan for getting rid of Rackham—perhaps even of buying him off, after all.

But Rackham was to save him that trouble, and to cut the knot for himself. As he walked away he made up his mind what he would do, and proceeded forthwith to do it. He would go away.

"I'll find some honest work to do in the world; I won't dangle after a sentimental girl and a man like Ventoul, in the hope that some day I may get a little money out of them. God! there must be something in the world for me —something cleaner for me to touch than Horace Ventoul and all his works. I'll go."

It was a big resolution for him, but he meant to carry it out; nothing should stop him. He walked a long way, with determined steps, and with his purpose growing with every moment. He would get to London again; he would start his fight there, clearly and simply, and do whatever work came to hand. He felt better and cleaner already, just to have made up his mind about it.

He stopped at the thought of Joshua Flattery. He could not take that faithful follower with him, because he had not the least idea what he was going to do, even for himself. He must perforce leave him behind—a problem to be solved by others. After all, Daniel Street would be afraid to get rid of the man, because he would not know whether Rackham intended to return or not; and Ventoul would be equally afraid. Even in the midst of his high determinations, Oliver Rackham stopped to chuckle at the prospect of Flattery living on at the house, and no one quite knowing what to do with him.

Some perverse spirit in the man urged him to linger a little at the last, in the hope that he might see the girl. Not with any sentimental motive; he scorned the idea of such a thing. Only her bright eyes haunted him a little; her voice—just to hear it once again—would be a thing to remember. So that, with his small preparations made, for he was carrying practically nothing away with him, and very little money, he seized an opportunity, when Angelica was walking in the grounds, to meet her and speak with her. If she had but known, Rackham had been waiting quite a long time.

There had been a horrible dinner party, at which Rackham had appeared in his tweed suit, pleading that he had not had time to dress, and at which Ventoul had of course been present. Ventoul in quite brilliant form, for him—telling stories, and inventing anecdotes about men he had never met, but was supposed to know quite intimately—all for the delectation of Angelica. And one gloomy man at the table had watched and listened, and said nothing—because this was the end of it all for him.

"I'm going out into the world," thought Rackham to himself, with his eyes upon the girl. (She was seated at the other side of the table to-night, next to Ventoul, by some mischance or by design.) "I'm going to try and make an honest, decent man of myself—and I'm going to leave her. She can take care of herself; or, with her prospects, the raising of a finger will bring someone to take care of her—not a graceless dog like old Noll. Being the last time, I'll punish dear Horace's wine—and so go out into the world happier than I might otherwise have done. Funny to think"—this to himself, as he waved a hand to a servant to fill his glass—"that this is the last time that I shall see you, Angelica Susan Brown—the last time I shall ever look into those bright eyes of yours, or hear you laugh. Quite a lot to be giving up."

So it came about that he lingered irresolutely, until by chance he met her in the grounds. A little to his surprise, she came quickly towards him, and spoke eagerly at once.

"Mr. Rackham—I haven't had a chance of speaking to you all day; and there's something I wanted to say."

He tried to steady his voice; that glass had been filled more times than he had reckoned. Why hadn't he gone away, as he had intended, directly dinner was over? "Go on, please," he said.

"I didn't mean to drive you away this morning, Mr. Rackham—I didn't, indeed," said Angelica, trying to search his eyes, while he obstinately kept them downcast. "I wouldn't like to treat a—a friend like that. You've been so good to me——"

"Have I?" he interposed a little wearily. "I wonder! If, in any thought you have of me, you feel that I've been good to you, dismiss it from your mind. I came into your life by chance; I may go out of it again in just that way—by chance. And that wouldn't hurt anyone very much."

"It would hurt me," she said, almost in a whisper.

"I don't think so," he answered slowly. "I'm no friend for anyone to have—and the time may come when you may feel that I've been a poor friend to you. I'm one of those men that must go through the world forever meaning to do great things, and good things, and decent things —and yet never doing them. Now and then some better inspiration comes, and whatever is good in me rises up. And then, because I'm afraid of it—I drown it."

"I won't believe that of you," she said quickly. "It isn't true."

"Oh—it's true enough," he answered. "Nevertheless, you have been something of an inspiration to me—something compelling me. But even that won't last—nothing lasts with me. I came out here to-night because I wanted to say a word about that business of this morning on my own account; but I see you understand already. And so we part—friends."

"Part?" she faltered.

'Oh—for to-night," he answered carelessly. "You needn't be afraid; you won't get rid of me so easily as all that."

"I don't want to get rid of you at all," said the girl.

"That's good of you," he said, without looking at her. "And, Miss Brown"—he seemed to find a difficulty with his words—"to-night I should be glad if you would remember something you once said to me."

"What was it?" she asked in a whisper.

"Once—almost in fun—you said something about saying a little prayer for me—quite for myself."

"Do you need it so much—to-night?" she asked.

"To-night, perhaps—more than ever," he answered.

Some half-hour later he was in the grounds again, with his final preparations made, and ready to start. It was a still and windless night; through the long, lighted windows of the drawing-room he could see the Streets, sitting in their separate chairs, and Ventoul seated near the piano. Angelica was playing; her voice floated out to the lonely man as though she sang to him alone. And when presently he strode out through the gates, and went on his way, he walked as one goes blindly; for there was a mist in his eyes.

In that mad impulse of flight he had thought of nothing except the mere getting away. So that it happened that when, after a considerable walk, he came to the station, he was informed by a surprised porter, who was locking up for the night, that the last train to London was gone.

"That's a devilish silly arrangement," said Rackham, staring at the man blankly.

"We don't 'ave no call for trains this time o' night, sir," said the man, a little resentfully. "Folks down these parts don't travel late."

"Late! You've got such a funny idea of what late means," said Rackham. "And what the deuce is going to become of me, at nine o'clock at night, in the middle of Nowhere?"

To return to the house was out of the question; that big decision had been made, and he would not give way now. He had started out into the world, there to do great things; he would not return over a mere matter of a train. He inquired the way to the next town of any size, and finding that it was a matter of some ten or eleven miles, determined to walk. It was, of course, impossible for him to put up at the one inn in the village at which Ventoul was staying; that would be to give the game away to Ventoul at once. He would go on to this next town, and in the morning would take the train for London. Thus Oliver Rackham marched out into the world, in characteristic fashion, to begin his great fight—rather congratulating himself, if the truth be told, on the fact that he was striding out towards the battle, as it were, instead of merely going, in a commonplace way, by train.

He thought of many things as he walked on—of Angelica, seated in the lighted room and singing—Angelica, whom he was never to see again, save perhaps by accident; of Ventoul, who now surely had the field to himself, and would be already scheming for the spending of that half million of money; of poor Joshua Flattery, left behind in a situation that was no situation at all. Try as he would, Oliver Rackham could not fix his mind on any future that had anything definite about it; all his thoughts were behind him, in that house he had left.

It was near to midnight when he reached the town that was his destination. He found a modest little hotel, and rang the people up, and got some supper and a room; he told himself that the hotel was a remarkably comfortable one. He made no inquiries about trains; there would be time enough for that in the morning. Besides, his long walk had tired him; he wanted a long night's sleep.

The sun was high when finally in the morning he woke, and turned over lazily, and realised where he was. It was a very comfortable room indeed, and the service in the little old-fashioned hotel, when presently he rang his bell, proved to be excellent. This was the sort of place at which a man might stop, on summer days like this, and have a good time.

While he dressed, he wondered what they were doing at that house at Pentney Hill. Inquiries would have been made by this time—or perhaps they thought he was sleeping late. Ventoul, arriving there as usual, would be puzzled at his disappearance. Questions would be asked, and vaguely answered. Ventoul, if he thought about it at all, would picture Oliver Rackham in London; whereas here he was, within less than a dozen miles—ready to pounce down upon Ventoul again, if such a proceeding became necessary.

That thought was an arresting one. It might be necessary for someone to pounce down upon Ventoul, and see that he ran straight in this business; it might be necessary for that helpless girl Angelica to have someone near at hand. Had he done quite the right thing in running away, as he had the previous night?

Besides, there were other reasons. London was not a place to which one would willingly turn one's face in this gorgeous summer weather; the little tree-bordered High Street of this little country town, as viewed from his bedroom window, was much more attractive. There was a very old church in this town, if Rackham remembered rightly—a church of great antiquity. He would have a look at that after his late breakfast; it would be nice to go and sit in the old place, and dream of all the dead and gone people who had built it, and worshipped in it, and been buried near it.

All this, of course, is only another way of saying that Oliver Rackham went no farther. Now and then London loomed before him, as a place in which, in some distant time, great things were to be done, and a certain Oliver Rackham was to be rehabilitated; but that time was not to-day. The little hotel was comfortable, and there was still money in Rackham's pockets—and the old town was interesting. It was pleasant to be waited on; pleasant to wake in the morning, and to go down to the coffee-room, and to look out over the old broad High Street while one ate one's breakfast. Pleasantest of all, perhaps, to dine there in the evening, and to take a stroll afterwards among the shadows about the old church.

And then the day came when Oliver Rackham woke up, and found himself, as he expressed it, "between the devil and the deep sea." He had made a miscalculation over a mere matter of a sovereign; he had not sufficient money to take him to London, even in the cheapest way.

This was disastrous; this should never have happened at all. Why had he lounged through a few summer days in this pleasant place, while the battle was waiting to be fought, and while London, with all its possibilities, was actually calling him. Now he was trapped; he was driven by Fate to return to that place to which he had vowed never to return.

With the feeling that the money he had left was not sufficient to keep him going for long, and that within a dozen miles of him was help and succor, Oliver Rackham troubled his mind no more with thoughts of finance. He would do the thing well, in the little time remaining to him; he would save just sufficient to take him back by the local train to Pentney Hill; the rest was a matter for Horace Ventoul. And he had meant never to appeal to that gentleman again!

That part of his programme he carried out to the letter. When finally he left the hotel, after his few days' sojourn there, a respectful proprietor bowed him away from the premises, with the pious hope in his mind that this man would come again; and waiters and chambermaids blessed his shadow as he departed. That was late in the evening (for Oliver Rackham had made the very most of it) and he caught the last train back to Pentney Hill.

He walked that considerable distance to the inn in the little village, and stalked into it at last, with a feeling that he was glad to come back. He asked airily for his friend Mr. Ventoul; but that gentleman had not yet returned.

"Then I'll wait for him," said Rackham calmly, "in his sitting-room. It's all right, thanks; I know the way."

He went up the stairs, and opened the door of that room, and went in. The respectable man-servant Wood was seated in the easiest chair by the window, reading a newspaper; he dropped the paper behind him, and sprang up as Rackham entered.

"Now—why did you do that?" asked Rackham, with a smile. "I'm sure you looked very comfortable, and I'm equally sure that anyone who knows you knows that it's quite impossible for you to mix with the vulgar herd in the bar-parlor below. Where's your master?"

"He's down at Mr. Street's place, sir—dining there, as usual, sir," answered the man.

"As usual," commented Rackham. "You didn't expect to see me—did you?"

"I was given to understand, sir, that you'd gone away," said Wood.

"And heaved a sigh of relief at the information, I'll be bound," retorted Rackham. "But I've come back, you see; and I intend to stop. Now you can go away—and take your newspaper with you. I want to be alone."

The man took up the newspaper, keeping a furtive eye upon Rackham, and backed out of the room. Rackham rang the bell, and ordered refreshments and the best cigar the house could afford; and then settled himself down, to await the return of Ventoul. He wondered how the game had been progressing during those days when he had not been there to watch its varying moves. For almost the first time he was in a false position, in that he had voluntarily put himself outside it all.

The man-servant Wood, being in deadly terror of this man who seemed to come and go as he liked, and whose conduct was not at all on Wood-like lines, discreetly went to bed, leaving his master to face the situation. So that when, in due course, Horace Ventoul walked along the moonlit roads to the inn, unsuspicious of any visitor, he was forced to face Oliver Rackham alone.

Ventoul came in jubilant; Rackham, listening, could hear him coming up the stairs two steps at a time. And when at last Ventoul opened the door and came in, Rackham merely glanced round at him idly, and waved a hand.

"I've come back, you see," said Rackham.

Ventoul stopped, staring at him; then slowly closed the door. "Where have you been?" he asked, all his jubilant manner gone.

"That doesn't matter," retorted Rackham. "You should know me by this time, my dear Horace; I suddenly got sick of the whole business, and especially of you. I went out into the world—and the world didn't want me; so I've come back again. Do say you're glad to see me, Horace!"

"I was never glad to see you yet—and I don't suppose I ever shall be," said the other. "You've been sponging on me for some time, and I suppose you've come back to try and sponge again—eh?"

Oliver Rackham got to his feet—slowly uncoiling the length of him, as it were—and stood before Ventoul. "Have you by any chance been impressing the lady with any further readings from your immortal work?" he asked.

"Oh—I know what you mean," said Ventoul. "You

think you've got a right to draw on me, on account of that, for as long as you live, I suppose."

"I can hold it over you, my dear Horace," said Rackham calmly, "and I mean to make the most of it. Now, little author and little lover, sit down and tell me the news. How are you progressing?"

"There's nothing to tell you," said Ventoul, taking out a cigarette, and lighting it, and frowning over the process. "You're outside the whole business; it's in my hands now."

"That's what you think, dear Horace; but then you were ever prone to jump to conclusions. It should surely occur to you that the mere fact of my being here again proves that I am very much in the business. Besides, your attitude when you came in just now," went on Rackham slyly, "seemed to show me that you are progressing very well."

Ventoul's natural vanity came to the surface. "Well—and what if I am?" he said quickly. "What if I've found it rather an easy task to impress a little ignorant girl, who knows precious little of the world? What if, while you have been running about, here, there, and everywhere, I've contrived to make the proverbial hay while the sun shone? What of that?"

"You're never going to tell me, little Horace, that she's in love with you?"

"Oh, yes—she's in love with me right enough," said Ventoul. "It's been a slow business—but then a girl of that sort isn't sure of herself, and doesn't actually rush into a man's arms."

"I should think not," said Rackham slowly. "Come,

my dear Horace, why don't you let your poetic nature have vent, and pour out in fiery words all that you really feel? Don't mind me. I like it, and shall prove a good audience. Sit down, little man, and let's know all about it."

Ventoul seated himself carefully in a chair, and adjusted his tie, and spoke languidly. "I've been in a mood once or twice to shake the girl," he said petulantly. "Fancy her putting on airs and graces with me—this girl, who was nothing and nobody until we discovered her."

"Perfectly shocking!" exclaimed Rackham, with mock solemnity.

"One day eager enough and willing enough to talk to me—another day without a word to say for herself, and avoiding me as much as possible."

"You're inexperienced, my dear Horace; that shows love, if ever anything did," said Rackham.

"And then—just when I thought that I was getting on rather well—would come in with some absurd question about you. Where was Mr. Rackham?—and had I heard from him? and was he coming back? I can tell you, Noll, I got pretty sick of it."

"Naturally," retorted Rackham easily. "And how do you stand now?"

"To-night there appears to be a very excellent understanding between us," said Ventoul complacently. "I got the Streets out of the way, and I talked seriously to her——"

"And you're such an easy and fluent talker—aren't you?" suggested Rackham.

"Drop it!" exclaimed Ventoul, turning on him viciously. "That's just where I fail—just where I break down. The girl's all right—and the money's all right; but she's such a stand-offish little beggar that I can't make the running with her, do what I will. She's shy, and she's proud, and she holds me at arm's length. Besides"—Ventoul gazed down at the point of his shoe, and moved it restlessly—"there's something else."

Rackham said nothing; he had not the least notion what was coming. He smoked, and watched the other man, and waited.

"You see, Noll—she's the sort of girl that has never had any romance in her life," Ventoul went on, "and therefore, when it does appear anywhere near her, she stretches out both hands for it—she's hungry for it. She expects me, for instance, who am supposed to have written that beastly book——"

"Don't call the thing names; it's been mighty useful to you," broke in Rackham.

"She expects me to speak differently from other men. I've got to make love on different lines; I mustn't do it in any commonplace way."

Oliver Rackham was shaking with laughter. "That's your own fault, my dear Horace," he said. "You've set yourself such a high standard; it's difficult to live up to it. It's quite a pity you ever let her see that book; you might have taken bits out of it, and sent them on to her."

"It's nothing to laugh about," said Ventoul savagely. "No man likes to feel a fool before a girl. There I sat to-night, while she looked at me; and I knew that she was expecting me to say all sorts of things that she could turn over in her silly little mind, and think wonderful."

"And you couldn't do it?" said Rackham, after a pause.

"But she hasn't got a silly little mind, my dear Horace; she's quite a brainy little person. The mere fact that she appreciated that book shows that she's brainy."

Ventoul softly drummed his heels on the floor for a moment or two, and stared moodily at the carpet. "Then she's got another fatuous idea in her head," he said at last. "She says she wishes I would write to her—write something like some of those beautiful phrases in that infernal book."

"Ah—that touches you on the raw, Horace!" exclaimed Ventoul. "There, I grant you, she has got you in a tight corner. Was ever lover in such a situation? There she is—absolutely pining to be addressed as never maiden was addressed yet—by a man whose trade it is; and the man can't do it. What's going to happen to you, Horace?"

Ventoul got up, and moved restlessly about the room for a moment; walked to the window, and looked out into the dark village street. At last he turned round, and in the tone of a man made desperate addressed his companion.

"Look here, Rackham—I've made up my mind to see this thing through now," he said. "The girl's not half bad; she could be made presentable. She's not far short of being what I should call a lady. And then, of course, there's this huge fortune behind her. In other words, I've made up my mind to do the square thing, and to marry her."

"It's well you've made up your mind to that," said Rackham, with a sudden little quick intake of his breath, and a hard light in his eyes.

"Only it happens that I fall short," went on Ventoul, "in that absurd business of touching the romantic. Well —you wrote the book that gave her that idea of me; it occurs to me that you can write something that shall keep up that idea."

There was silence in the room for a moment or two; Rackham, seated on the edge of the table, was staring down at the other man with a bewildered expression on his face. For the life of him he did not understand what thought was in the mind of Ventoul.

"You want money—don't you?" asked Ventoul, in a low tone. "I never knew you when you didn't want money. Now, if you do this thing for me—write these absurd letters to this girl—I'm prepared to pay for them. I suppose you'd call it literary work—wouldn't you?"

"Do you seriously suggest that I"—Oliver Rackham touched himself on the breast, and spoke slowly—"that I am to write love letters to this girl that are supposed to come from you?"

"Why not? She wouldn't know the truth—and you seem to have the silly trick of doing it. It's your trade, I suppose."

Rackham got down from the table, and paced up and down the room. "No—no—my dear Horace," he said at last. "There are limits even to what I will do. To write to the fair Angelica, and to cram my letters with sentiments that are supposed to be yours, but which you are incapable of expressing . . . thank you—I think not."

"Very well. Then you leave me to arrange the business in my own way—by fair means or foul?" asked Ventoul, in a low voice. "I've been trying to live up to my supposed reputation; I've been trying to play the game decently, and even romantically. I offer you money to help me in that—and you won't do it."

"No—I won't," said Rackham.

"Very well, my friend; then here's my last word," said Ventoul slowly. "I can afford to laugh at your threats and your bombasts; I can afford to snap my fingers at them. You've got out of the business of your own accord—you kept away all these days, taking no notice of the girl or of anyone else; you're outside it all. You're outside me, for the matter of that—for I'll never pay you another half-penny as long as you live. You can go off, as you've done before—and starve. The cards are in my hands—and if I choose to play them not too cleanly, or with one concealed, don't blame me."

"What do you mean by 'not too cleanly'?" demanded Rackham, walking across the room to where the other stood.

"That's nothing to do with you; that's my affair," retorted Ventoul. "I'm in a better position over this thing than I was before you went away, and I've got my chance."

"Not while I'm here you haven't," said Rackham, his temper rising. "I'm going to stay here—I'm going to see fair play."

"How much money have you?" demanded Ventoul, with a laugh.

"I'll wring what I want out of you—if I have to put you to the torture for it, you whelp!" exclaimed Rackham.

"You won't get a penny," said Ventoul. "I'm top dog this time. Come now; will you do what I ask—just the writing of a few letters to a romantic girl—something she'll never know about? And when those letters have filled her head and her heart, I'm going to marry her."

There was a long pause, while Rackham furtively slipped his hands into his pockets, and remembered what coins were there. He thought of all the chances: of having to go away now, and leave her; of that covert threat of Ventoul's about how he might play the cards. Above all, there came to him the subtle temptation, the strength of which he did not then fully realise—the temptation to write—and to her. Even while he stood there thinking about it, he found himself forming phrases that should delight her, and that she should linger over.

"What are the terms—and conditions?" he asked at last, without looking at Ventoul.

"She's got an idea that she wouldn't like to have letters sent to her just through the post; someone might see, and might comment upon it; besides, it's too commonplace. There's a hollow tree at the end of the grounds by the fountain—do you know it?"

"Yes, I know it," answered Rackham. He remembered to have seen her there once on a sunny morning, seated on the edge of the fountain.

"Well—I've promised that that shall be our letter-box; a letter shall be left there for her. Those letters you can write; you know the sort of stuff a girl like that wants and expects; and you can put them there."

"What about the writing? Hadn't you better copy them out?" suggested Rackham.

"Not I; I'm not going to take to that sort of labor," said Ventoul. "She's never seen your writing—has she?"

"Never."

"Then it's quite safe. You can add forgery to your other crimes, Noll, and sign my name."

"How much are you going to pay?" whispered Rackham. "You drive me to this bargain—because I can't starve, and because I must keep a watch on her, and on you."

"A fair amount would be, I think, a sovereign a letter."

"You're a generous man; why, it's hack work," said Oliver Rackham, laughing. "Well—I'll do it. Am I to write what I like?"

"Knowing the situation, it should not be difficult; I leave it entirely to you," said Ventoul. "As I have said, there's a very good understanding between us; and you may be quite affectionate. You can grow warmer and more passionate as the days go on."

"I'll take now, then, for the first letter in advance," said Rackham. And then, as he pocketed the money: "Didn't I tell you, my dear Horace, that you wouldn't be able to get on without me?"

He went back to the house; it is scarcely too much to say that he began to compose that first letter to Angelica as he walked. And yet, when he thought it over, some of the flowery phrases he had first designed fell away from him; he thought of what he should say with a graver face.

Daniel Street had not gone to bed; he received Rackham without surprise and without enthusiasm. It was very late, and Rackham went at once to his room. He did not know that, as he mounted the stairs, a door above him was opened softly (for the ringing of the bell had been heard) and Angelica peeped over the stairhead. Then, with a smiling face, she went softly back into her room.

After a time Rackham drew a sheet of paper towards him, and headed it with the address of the inn in the village. And then he wrote two words as a beginning:

"My dearest——"

And then, in the strangest way, dropped his pen, and laid his arms on the table, and hid his face on them.

CHAPTER XI

THE POST-BOX

"MY DEAREST,

"*Dearest—because there is no one in all the world so near my heart; mine—because I know that in your heart of hearts you are that, and will be always. Out of what world did you come—or did God let you come—into my life? And yet I think it must have been from the beginning—for all my life seems to have been filled with memories of you.. Surely there never was a time when I did not know you; I must have loved you while I waited in the silent world to come into this. All the little winds that ever have blown, since the first air woke and stirred, have whispered it; every little river that ever has run its course has murmured of it, as a tale that was old, and yet was ever new.*

"*I love you! There—it is written—and as I write it the echo of it, beginning like faint music, goes sounding on, as it must sound through all my life and yours—as it must sound for me, long after the grave takes me for my last sleep; and even there I shall dream of you. You have been something so wonderful in my life; you have stirred old beliefs and hopes in me that never were stirred before; you have made my spirit stretch, as from a long slumber, and wake refreshed and strong. For that I bless you.*

"*Love me a little, my sweet. I will not ask you yet with my lips; but write to me sometimes—tell me what is in your heart.   Yours in life and love.*"

That was the letter which Oliver Rackham wrote that night while the house slept. It had taken him a long time to begin it; it took but a short time to write it. The words flowed from his pen hurriedly enough—racing after each other, just as his thoughts raced. And then, when the sheet was filled, he got up, and went away from it; and looked back at it almost like a man in terror.

"I've never written anything yet that I didn't mean," he whispered, "and—God help me!—I mean that. I didn't understand till to-night; I didn't know what it all meant. Now I know that she must have danced her way into my heart that first night I met her; and she's lain there coiled up ever since—and I didn't know it!"

He came back to the letter, and picked it up, and glanced at it; suddenly made as if to tear it. Then he laid it down again, and stood for a long time looking down at it, although the words were blurred and he did not read them.

"And I've got to put his beastly name to it," he said slowly. "I've got to let her think that he writes to her like that—pours out the soul and the heart of him to her. Bah!—what does it matter? What am I but the husk of what a man should be—a thing driven by the wind this way and that—a poor devil without a friend!"

He sat down, and scrawled under the letter the name—"*Horace Ventoul.*" Then he threw down the pen, and stood moodily staring at that signature.

"I suppose it isn't true that I haven't a friend; I think she likes me—I'm sure she does. She likes as one might like a dog—something that would fetch and carry at her bidding. Besides, I once did her a service—or she thinks

I did; I've given her a glimpse of life. Why—I've even introduced her to a lover—such as he is. There—play the game, my boy, no matter what sort of game it is. You've lied and bluffed and cheated all your life—or most of it, at least; you can surely go on doing that a little longer without whining about it."

He put the letter into an envelope, and thrust the thing in his pocket. Then, on an impulse, he went out of the house by a side door, and made his way to that hollow tree that was to serve a new and romantic purpose.

"Lovers are supposed to be proverbially impatient," he murmured to himself, "and so our dear Horace will, of course, have written at once—this very night. And he will have walked straight down from the inn, and will have posted his message; at least, that's what she pictures him doing—whereas the villain is probably fast asleep, not dreaming of anyone except himself. And here am I out in the darkness, doing this devil's work."

He found the tree, and slipped the letter into the opening. Then he went back to the house, letting himself in quietly. Scarcely thinking about the matter, he made his way to the dining-room, and struck a light, and took out the decanter and a glass. In the very act of taking out the stopper he paused, and set the decanter down.

"No—not to-night," he said softly. "This is a sacred and wonderful night—something that happens once to a man, and never again. I'm a cleaner thing to-night; I've got a soul somewhere knocking about inside me. To-night I'll keep it fairly clean."

He put the things away, and went to bed. For the life of him he could not help thinking now over some of the phrases he had written—wishing he had added this, or taken out that; wondering a little what she would think about it, when she came to read it. But, as he had expressed it, it didn't matter; and in that mood he presently got to bed, and slept.

He woke early—while as yet the house was not stirring. It was a delicious morning—soft and warm and sunny. The song of the birds seemed to call to him; the mood of the night before was with him still. This was not a morning to stay in the house; he must get up, and go out.

Someone else was stirring too. As Oliver Rackham gained the hall, and was fumbling with the fastenings of the door, he heard a step behind him on the stairs, and looked back over his shoulder. It was Angelica.

She had paused at the turning of the wide staircase, with one hand upon the rail, and was looking down at him. He remembered long afterwards what she looked like then—remembered the look on her face—the slightly parted lips—the color coming and going in her cheeks—her bright eyes a little wide and startled. She stood where the sunlight, coming through the staircase window, fell upon her; she was radiant—she was Love and Sunshine and Life personified.

"Oh!" said Angelica softly; and began to move slowly down the remaining stairs.

"You're up early," said Rackham, with his eyes upon her.

"It's such a lovely morning; I couldn't bear to stop in bed," she answered.

All this, you must understand, in whispers. Then she came down the stairs, and helped him to fumble with the bolts and locks of the big hall door; and he fumbled the more, with her bright face so close to his, and her hair almost brushing him. But at last they got the door open, and went out together into the sunlight.

And then, of course, the difficulties began. Common politeness demanded that he should walk with her, and should talk about the beauty of the morning, and things of that sort. Yet she had obviously come down with but one purpose in her mind—to get to the hollow tree by the fountain; indeed, she had dressed hurriedly and slipped downstairs with that idea in her mind, and that only. So that they began a game of cross-purposes—Oliver Rackham knowing perfectly well why she had been hurrying secretly out of the house, and Angelica, of course, never suspecting for a moment that he knew anything about the business.

Rackham would have been glad for her to get the letter and to read it; and yet, because it was signed with that hateful name, he wanted to keep her away from it. Moreover, he could not very well say—"Now I know that you want to get to the hollow tree, and to take out the letter you believe is waiting for you; run away and get it, and read it at your leisure." Neither could he say—"I shall walk about with you in the grounds here until it is time to go in to breakfast—because that is the proper and amiable thing to do."

Therefore they strolled about for quite a long time—always making by roundabout routes for the fountain. And at last they actually got to it, and Angelica, with a sigh, seated herself on the edge of the fountain, and glanced casually at the hollow tree.

"It's a beautiful morning," said Angelica, after a very long pause.

"I cannot ever remember seeing a finer one," said Rackham, standing leaning against the tree, and watching her. "How lucky that I was tempted out of doors at the same time you were—isn't it?"

"Very lucky indeed," said Angelica, with another little sigh. "We must have thought about it just at the same moment—mustn't we?"

"Yes—I expect so," he said. "By the way—how have you been getting on these past few days?"

"Oh—just the same as usual," said Angelica, with a little quick blush at the remembrance that she had forgotten this morning that he had been away at all. "You went very suddenly."

"I was called away—unexpectedly," he said. "I came back—just as unexpectedly."

"Did you go to London?" she asked suddenly.

"No," he replied.

Angelica got up and moved away a few paces; Rackham strolled beside her. At the distance of a yard or two she glanced back over her shoulder at the tree; Rackham stopped, and looked at her squarely, with a whimsical smile on his face.

"What's the matter, Mr. Rackham?" she faltered.

"Go back and get your letter," he said quietly.

"Letter?" she whispered, with an involuntary glance at the tree.

"I believe there's a letter waiting for you," he said quietly. "My dear—you needn't be afraid of me; I've got nothing to do with it. Go and get your letter."

"How—how did you know?" asked Angelica.

"Horace and I are as brothers; we have no secrets from each other," said Rackham solemnly. "We talked last night, and I know quite enough about everything. Your letter is waiting."

Still she made no movement to get it; she stood looking at the man, and her eyes were troubled. "There's no harm in it," she pleaded.

"As though you needed to tell me that!" he exclaimed lightly. "I think it's all rather pretty and romantic. Horace hasn't told me any secrets; I only know about the hiding-place for the letters—that's all."

Still she stood there, looking at him, and hesitating what to say. At last—"No one has ever been in love with me before," she faltered.

"That does make a great difference, doesn't it?" he answered gravely. "Hadn't you better see what the letter says?"

"You're not displeased with me?" One little hand was touching his arm now; her eyes were very close to his. It was a little difficult for him to steady his voice.

"Why should I be displeased with you?" he answered. "All that you do is good and wonderful."

Her face cleared, and she ran back to the tree. He heard, in the still morning air, the quick ripping of the envelope; but he did not look back at her. When presently she joined him again he stole a glance at her face; her chin was up, and her lips were parted, and her eyes were like stars.

"Well?" he asked.

"It is beautiful," she whispered. "You see—when

things are printed in a book it seems just an ordinary matter—something that someone has thought out carefully—and perhaps altered a great deal. But when anyone writes . . . I didn't think it possible that anyone could ever write such a letter to me. It makes everything so—so different."

They walked on side by side for a moment or two in silence. If only he could have questioned her as to what she had thought of this or of that in the letter; if only he could have talked to her as the writer of it was surely entitled to talk!

"I suppose you're very much in love with him?" he asked quietly at last.

"I—I think so," she said. "I don't mind talking to you about it; you've always been my friend, and you've understood me so perfectly. And these last few days have been wonderful."

"I suppose so," he answered.

"You see, Mr. Rackham," she went on eagerly, "in the old life everything was so different. I lived for myself only—thought only of myself. I had my little time-table of pupils, and I worked hard, and I thought I was happy. Nobody troubled very much about me, and I didn't trouble very much about anybody else. There was no one to talk to me wonderfully, as someone has talked to me and read to me lately; there was no one to be fond of me, and to admire me, and to look forward very much to seeing me. And then, suddenly to come down here—and to meet a man who is great in his own world—a man that people talk about and write about; it was just as though I had been plunged straight into a new existence altogether."

"I think I understand that," said Rackham slowly. "And so our friend writes as beautifully to you as he writes to the public—eh?"

"It seems to be more beautiful still," said Angelica. "I almost feel I want to show it to you—but of course I can't do that. I almost feel as though I want to show it to everybody—just to let people understand that this one man holds me—poor little Angelica Brown—high above everyone in the world. Don't you understand, Mr. Rackham, that this is a truly marvellous thing to have happened?"

"Yes—I understand that," said Rackham again, without looking at her. "And it's good to know that you're happy. Now we'd better go in to breakfast, I think."

They were actually at the door of the house when Angelica turned to him quickly with an appeal. "You won't tell anyone?" she said.

"Why—of course I won't," he replied.

Mr. Daniel Street had a letter this morning—one which he read over and over again through half-closed eyes; one which he thought about a great deal. And as he read it he glanced at Angelica, who, for her part, was utterly absorbed. For Angelica held her wonderful letter on her lap, just under the tablecloth; from time to time she glanced at it, looking up guiltily when anyone spoke to her.

Mrs. Street addressed her husband. "Anything important, dear?" she asked.

Daniel Street took a final look at the letter, and then folded it deliberately, and put it in his pocket. "A little matter of business, Daisy," he replied.

Mrs. Street was in a talkative mood. "Nobody ever

seems to get letters in this house—at least, not often," she said, shaking her head. "Not that I ever expect to hear from anybody; no one has any cause to write to me particularly. But you, now, Miss Brown—I should have thought you'd have had quite a lot through the post."

"No—no—I don't get letters—through the post," stammered Angelica. "You see—I didn't have many people—friends, I mean—in London that would be likely to write to me."

She stole a quick glance at Rackham, but he was not looking at her. She softly crumpled the letter up in her hands, and held it so until breakfast was over and she could escape. Then she fled to her room, and read the thing over and over again until she had it by heart. She was wondering what sort of reply she could send to it—was tormented with the thought that she must write something almost as beautiful in return. If he should be disappointed in what she should write; if he should feel that it was mean and commonplace and ordinary! Oh—she must be more than careful!

Meanwhile Daniel Street was pacing up and down a garden path, reading and re-reading the letter he had received. It was a mere scrawl on a sheet of cheap notepaper enclosed in a cheaper envelope; and it bore the address of that little public-house in a court off Chancery Lane.

"*My Dear Dan,—Thanks for the postal order for half a crown—although I did hope you might have made it five shillings. I have begun to enquire about the name mentioned in your letter—though not having money makes it awkward for anybody to find out what they otherwise might do. But I have been to the place you suggested, and the name is down there all right; the place is an Agency for missing persons, and all that sort of thing—but I can't get anything out of them unless I pay a preliminary fee; with that I can get a copy of the will and all information. I don't even know how much the property is that the person you name is entitled to; but the name is all right—Angelica Susan Brown. Also the age seems to fit in. If you could send me some more money I could find out something more for you—or perhaps you might be coming to London yourself, and we could go into it together. Glad to know you are so comfortable. Yours,*

"JAMES PEEL."

This was the reply to a discreet and cautious note, sent by Daniel Street to one of those who, like himself, had been a hanger-on in shady legal circles, and had frequented that little private bar in the court off Chancery Lane. Daniel Street had been afraid to say too much; but he was satisfied even with this vague reply. He chafed at the thought that he could not at present get to London; once there, he would have known exactly how to set about his inquiries. However, so far, so good; the matter could wait.

Shyness kept Angelica close to Mrs. Street that morning; never was obedient companion more eager to serve her employer. There was this to be done, and that to be attended to; she had been neglectful of late, and had not performed her duties as thoroughly as she might have done. So that Horace Ventoul, calling at about noon, was informed by means of a message that Miss Brown was extremely busy, and could not possibly see him then. And

Miss Brown, bending over a self-imposed task, watched Ventoul turn away and stroll off with Oliver Rackham.

"What's the game?" demanded Ventoul, when they were well away from the house.

"I don't understand," said Rackham, who had heard the message delivered. "What game?"

"She's too busy to see me," said Ventoul. "I gave that Street woman clear instructions that the girl was never to be detained at any time if I happened to call."

"My dear Horace—you have no soul and no sentiments," said Rackham. "The letter signed with your name last night, and received by the lady this morning, was of the sort that should keep her away from you until she has had time to digest it and to frame a suitable reply. Did you think she was going to rush into your arms at once?"

Horace Ventoul stood still, staring blankly at the other man. "What trick have you been playing?" he demanded. "What have you written to her?"

"I couldn't tell you for the world," answered the other. "It was late—and I was tired. However, it was quite a good love letter, as love letters go—and she was delighted. Don't suggest that I don't know my business. I pitched it strongly, my dear Horace; I don't think you'll have cause to complain about the result."

"I wish I'd never left the matter in your hands at all," exclaimed Ventoul.

"My dear Horace," murmured Rackham, with a hand on the other man's shoulder, "you wouldn't have stood a ghost of a chance without me. My letter is the most wonderful she has ever received; she told me so. There never has been a letter like it written in the world; I think she is only troubled about what sort of reply she shall make to it. Avoiding you this morning is only a pretence; the business, as far as you're concerned, is done—and you have won your case. Take my word for that."

"Well—you'd be a fool if you played tricks on me now," said Ventoul, after they had walked on a little way. "I wouldn't have trusted you at all, but for that nonsense the girl had got into her head—that I should write to her. I want to hurry this part of the business; I want to get to the practical part of it. To tell you the truth, Noll, I'm getting bored to death in this dead-and-alive hole; I want to get back to London—to something more exciting. Look here; you know more about the sentimental side of things than I pretend to do; do you think this girl can be carried off her feet, as it were—made to marry me—romantically —in a hurry? I'm tired of this expensive game."

"You put the thing so delicately and so charmingly that one can quite easily understand you," replied Rackham. "I should say that, in her present mood, Miss Brown could be quite easily swept off her feet. The only difficulty is that you're such a dull dog that one has to tell you everything, and teach you how to set about doing it all. You're about the poorest specimen of a lover I've ever come across. What do you purpose doing? Running away with her, or getting a special license—or what?"

"I might run away with her—providing myself with a special license beforehand," said Ventoul, after a pause. "I suppose she'll send some sort of reply to that letter of yours?" he added.

"If I know anything about her she is probably writing it now," answered Rackham. "That is the sort of letter, my dear Horace, that takes a long time to write; that sort of girl doesn't give away her feelings in a hurry. You've been lucky enough, with my assistance, to catch her in the right mood; don't worry yourself, little man."

They returned to the house later on for lunch. Daniel Street, fortified with the remembrance of the note he had received, was watchful of all that was happening, and was, above all, watchful of Horace Ventoul and of the fashion in which he greeted Angelica. For Angelica just glanced at him timidly for a moment as she took his hand, and then, with a heightened color, lowered her head and turned away. Rackham she greeted more ordinarily, with a charming smile as of comradeship.

Angelica carried her precious letter with her; phrases from it were singing through her head while she sat there watching the man she believed had written it. She wondered a little why he did not talk; was hurt sometimes, though she scarcely knew it, when he spoke abruptly to Mrs. Street or to Rackham. But then she was sure, as every woman even a little in love is sure, that there were two sides to the man, and that she had seen the one that was hidden from everyone else. She was content with that, and hugged the thought of it to herself.

Rackham remained at the luncheon table with Daniel Street after the others had gone. Street had rolled a cigarette as usual, and Rackham was smoking a cigar; Ventoul rarely smoked at all, except late at night. Therefore quite naturally he walked out of the room with Mrs. Street and Angelica—Mrs. Street, with a murmured excuse, disappearing at once.

"You had my letter?" asked Ventoul.

She looked at him fully for the first time; her eyes should have told him everything. "I've read it—and read it—and read it again," she whispered. "And I want to read it just once more—and then I'll write to you."

"What will you say to me?" he asked, getting possession of her hand, and moving nearer to her.

She laughed, and drew away from him to the length of her arm; came back to him coquettishly, and answered—"Just what you asked me to say," she whispered. "All that is in my heart!"

She turned and ran up the stairs, glancing back at him for a moment before she disappeared. Ventoul stood looking after her with a little puzzled frown on his face. He wished he had had the courage to say more to her—to demand some more definite answer.

"I suppose that sort of thing would please Noll," he muttered to himself. "But how long does she mean to play with me, I wonder!"

Angelica, in her room, was strangely enough finding difficulties in the way of her reply. It had seemed at first that it would be quite easy to say all that was in her heart —that is, it had seemed quite easy when she stood in the morning sunlight and read the letter for the first time. But now there was a difference; she had seen the man again—and the man and the letter somehow or other had no connection. Yet that was absurd, of course; she laughed at the thought that Horace Ventoul was not all that her girlish fancy had pictured him. All great men were like that—shy and diffident. Even his roughness to poor Mrs. Street might be excused on those grounds.

Yet even with the letter written at last, she felt she

could not take it to the place of hiding. She must wait, and put off the time—not to hurt him or make him anxious—but just out of womanly perversity. She would creep out a little later and post it in the tree.

Under all the circumstances it must be admitted that it was hard on Horace Ventoul. In no sense a lover, the man was chafing over the delay; this stupid business of waiting irritated him beyond measure. Moreover, Angelica remained obstinately with Mrs. Street (something to that lady's dismay), and was not to be drawn out into the grounds.

Horace Ventoul went back to the inn at last to dress for dinner; and then it was that Angelica slipped out into the grounds, and posted her letter. She was minded, after she had done it, to undo it; once she actually took the letter out of its hiding-place—only to put it back again a minute later. And then, lest she should be tempted afresh, ran back to the house.

Horace Ventoul, coming by another gate into the grounds, so that he might pass the fountain, slipped his hand into the tree, and found the letter. With a half-impatient exclamation he drew it out, and then, hearing footsteps, slipped it into his pocket. Looking up, he saw Rackham smiling at him.

"Hullo!" exclaimed Ventoul, with a suspicious glance at him.

"Hullo!" responded Rackham genially. And then, with a hand outstretched—"Hand over, little man."

"What do you mean?" asked Ventoul, putting a hand instinctively to the pocket that held the letter.

"I want that letter," said Rackham. "Come—no nonsense. If you don't hurry up—by the Lord!—I'll turn you upside down and shake it out of you."

"It's my letter," spluttered Ventoul, "addressed to me. I must know what she says."

"You shall know what she says," replied Rackham calmly. "But there may be things in it that you wouldn't understand or appreciate. I wrote the original, and I'm going to see the reply."

Slowly and sulkily Horace Ventoul took out the letter, and handed it to him. Rackham calmly ripped it open, and spread out the sheet, and read it; while Ventoul stood a pace or two away, frowning, and shifting about on his feet, and watching him.

"Well, what does she say?" demanded Ventoul.

"Don't be in such a hurry; I haven't had time to read it yet," answered Rackham.

"*My dear,*

"*(I am afraid to say 'dearest,' although you are that to me, of course) I find it more difficult to write than I believed it would be; there are so many things I want to say to you—you who bring Love to me for the first time—and I don't know how to say them. They are all folded away in my heart; I think they have been there, waiting for you, ever since, as a tiny child, I dreamed in the firelight of impossible things. I have read your letter over and over again—I wonder sometimes how you can think such beautiful thoughts; I am proud and glad that I should be the one to whom you can write them.*

"*And I love you! There—I have written that, too, and so have sealed everything. Lock it away in your heart, please, and guard it; it is the most precious thing I have ever written or said or given to anyone.*

"And write to me again; I want you to do that for a little while, before we meet and say to each other all that now we are writing. There—I have kept my promise, and have told you what is in my heart! Your own,

"ANGELICA."

"Well?" demanded Ventoul, as Rackham, with a smile on his face, placidly folded the letter and placed it in the envelope.

"Things you wouldn't understand, and might even be disposed to scoff at," said Rackham. "Suffice it that she loves you—or thinks she does; you are to write to her again before you talk to her with your lips. It's quite a pretty game—isn't it?"

"Give me the letter!" exclaimed Ventoul savagely. "I'm not going to be played with like this."

"You shall have the envelope, little man, as a solace and a comfort, and in order that you may show it to her if she thinks you haven't got the letter," said Rackham, taking out the letter, and putting it into his pocket, and tossing the envelope to Ventoul. "Don't forget that I'm managing your love affairs, and don't interfere with things you don't understand. Tell her it's a beautiful letter, and that you'll write to her again. I'll manage that part for you—to-night?"

Ventoul, with a muttered curse, stooped and picked up the envelope; looked at it for a moment or two disdainfully; and then thrust it into his pocket. He walked on towards the house a few steps, and then turned and looked back at Rackham.

"How do I know that you're not fooling me?" he asked. "How do I know that both you and the girl are not in the same plot against me?"

"You wrong the lady in thinking that," said Rackham. "I'm capable of anything, I know—or you think I am; but Angelica is not that sort at all. You've put this matter in my hands, and I'm going to manage it in my own way. Be thankful for little mercies, my dear Horace, and do as you are told."

CHAPTER XII

ANGELICA SAYS "YES"

HORACE VENTOUL, fortified with the meagre information Rackham had consented to dole out to him, sat next to Angelica at dinner, and wondered what he should say to her. That business of sitting next to her had been arranged by Mrs. Street, at Ventoul's demand; but then, what was the use of it, when Oliver Rackham at the other side of the table monopolized the conversation, and drew everyone into his net of talk?

Poor Angelica—expectant of great things, and perhaps even of tender whisperings now and then—got but little. She found herself glancing from time to time at Horace Ventoul; and once again those strange little subtle doubts went like tiny threads through her mind. He had written so wonderfully—he had even contrived to speak one or two fine things, although she had forgotten what they were; they had merely impressed her at the moment. But then, she had been in the mood to be impressed by anything that this man, who had sought her out above all women, might care to say to her.

Rackham, glancing from one to the other, and watching the game idly and yet with interest, saw exactly where Ventoul failed. This girl demanded everything; she who knew nothing of life was avaricious, and expected more than another might have done. On the other hand, Ventoul pretended badly; and Angelica was not asking for pretence. She demanded the real thing, and she believed that it had been given her; now she was beginning to have a little doubt as to its value. So that, while she thought she loved the man for that side of his character she alone had seen, the other side of his character, shown alike to herself and others generally, repelled her.

With dinner ended, and the ladies gone from the room, Ventoul was for setting aside any pretence of the gentlemen lingering over their wine and cigars, and for joining the ladies at once. Within a matter of a minute or two he got up from his chair, and tossed aside the cigarette he had lighted.

"We don't want to sit here staring at each other," he said roughly.

"Sit down, my dear Horace; don't be in such a devil of a hurry," said Rackham, as he puffed at his cigar. "Our dear friend Daniel Street will smoke another cigarette, and I will have another glass of wine. Restrain your wild impatience, my dear Horace; it doesn't look decent to rush out after the ladies like that."

"There is certainly no hurry," said Daniel Street surprisingly, as he pushed the wine towards Rackham.

Horace Ventoul stared at him. "Don't you interfere," he said to Street. "Remember that you're here to do as you're told."

"There's no necessity to remind me of that," retorted Street. "Only I think we ought to keep up appearances, at all events."

Ventoul gasped, and sat down. He looked from one to the other covertly, while he drummed with his fingers on the table; but Daniel Street, with an inscrutable face, was watching the cigarette he was rolling, while Rackham was smoking, with his eyes on the ceiling. A little chill feeling of uneasiness stole over Ventoul; he trusted no one at this time.

Presently Rackham got up, and yawned, and stretched himself, and went to the door. "I think we can join them now," he said, with a grin.

Exasperatingly enough he linked his arm in that of Horace Ventoul as they walked into the drawing-room. Horace Ventoul did an unwise thing as the door was being opened; he whispered a direction sharply to Rackham.

"We don't want any of your music to-night."

That was quite sufficient for Oliver Rackham; his eyes hardened a little, and his lips set in a closer line. When presently Horace Ventoul walked across to the girl, and whispered, and she laid down the work she was doing and got to her feet, Rackham, humming carelessly to himself, strolled to the piano. As Ventoul and the girl set foot over the ledge of the French windows to go into the grounds, Rackham struck the keys, and began the first notes of one of the "Songs without Words." Although apparently he was absorbed in thought, yet he saw the quick turn of Angelica's head, and the sudden fashion in which she took her hand from Ventoul's arm, and stepped back into the room. She stood there listening while Rackham played.

For quite a long time Rackham played that game— gliding from one thing into another, and still apparently absorbed with the music and with his own thoughts. Mrs. Street sat, as usual, dabbing furtively at her eyes with her handkerchief; Angelica had slid into a seat, and was listening and watching, fascinated. Ventoul stood against the window, with his teeth set hard, and one foot impatiently beating on the carpet.

Presently Ventoul could stand it no longer; he strolled, apparently aimlessly, across the room, and got close to the piano. There, on the pretence of examining a photograph standing upon it, he bent down, and whispered to Rackham—

"Will you stop it?"

"Go to the devil, little man!" murmured Oliver Rackham, with his hands gliding over the keys and his rapt eyes on the ceiling.

Nor were Ventoul's troubles over for that evening. When presently the music ceased, and Mrs. Street (who had dried her eyes, and had been brought to laughter by some merry thing that Rackham had played finally) had murmured her thanks, and Angelica had looked them, Ventoul was moving confidently towards the girl, when Daniel Street suddenly and surprisingly got to his feet, and intercepted him.

"I'm going to ask Miss Brown to take a turn with me in the grounds," he said, without a movement of his face. "This room is hot and oppressive; I should like to get into the air."

"I'll be delighted, Mr. Street," said Angelica, a little surprised. "Won't Mrs. Street come, too?"

"Mrs. Street doesn't care for the air," said Daniel Street; and his wife, who had half risen, sank into her seat again as the man and the girl passed out through the French windows.

Ventoul was at Rackham's side in a moment; for this was a common danger. "What the devil does it mean?" he whispered fiercely. "You saw his behavior at dinner; you see it now. Has he heard anything?"

"How should I know?" said Rackham. "It's curious for Daniel to take the bit in his teeth like this. It looks as if you'd better hurry up a bit with your wooing, friend Horace, if we are to see anything of that money."

All this was said in whispers, for Mrs. Street was obviously perturbed. This flouting of those responsible for placing Daniel and herself in the house was to her inexplicable; she could not understand it in the least. She heaved a sigh of relief when presently, after a gloomy silence in the room, they heard Angelica's voice outside, and she and Street stepped in again.

"I've just told Mr. Street that I'm quite sure Mrs. Street ought to be persuaded to come out, if only for five minutes," said Angelica. "It's a wonderful evening; won't you all come out?"

A look from Daniel Street conveyed the necessary permission to his wife; they all went out into the grounds together. After that, of course, it was an easy matter for Angelica and Ventoul to separate themselves from the others, and to wander off alone; and then the business of walking in the grounds for the others became merely tedious. Daniel Street and his wife made a pretence of it for a few minutes, and then went back into the room again; Rackham went off to another room to smoke. Nor did he stir from there until, in due course, the time came for Horace Ventoul to take his departure.

"Are you going to walk down with me, Noll?" asked

Ventoul, as they all stood together for a moment in the hall. It was not a suggestion; it was a command. Probably the man had something to say to him, and Rackham therefore accepted.

"I'll walk a little way," he said.

He stepped out into the darkness, leaving the other man to follow.

Ventoul made a pretence of saying "Good night" to Street and his wife, and hinting his thanks to them for again inviting him to the house; then he took the girl's hand, and whispered to her impressively.

"Good night. I'll write to you again, as you wish. But when will you let me talk to you?"

"Oh—I don't know; I haven't thought about that," she said hurriedly. And then, pushing past him, called out into the darkness—"Good night, Mr. Rackham. I'm going to bed, and shan't see you again to-night."

"Good night," the voice called back from the darkness.

She waited a moment, looking out in the hope that he would return; then, a little disappointedly, came back into the house, with a nod and a smile to Ventoul. After a moment's hesitation Ventoul went out.

Rackham had reached the road before the other man overtook him, and to do that Ventoul had to hurry. "You might have waited a moment, I should think," said Ventoul, out of breath.

Rackham slackened his pace. "I don't like watching partings between lovers," he said.

"Lovers, indeed!" cried Ventoul. "That girl's an icicle; I can't get near her. This kind of thing may go on for months—with just letters being sent, and replies received; I'm like a man working in the dark. By the way, I want you to write to her to-night."

"I'm not going to do it," said Rackham quietly.

"What do you mean?"

"Precisely what I say, my dear Horace," said the other. "I've done with the whole silly business. I've gone as far as I mean to go; I've laid the foundations for you—it's for you to build. And if you take my advice you'll do it quickly."

Ventoul looked round at him. "You're thinking of that man Street?" he said.

"I am. Daniel Street knows something, or guesses something—and Daniel Street was once in the law, and did not hesitate to break it when he saw the chance of making money. You've got to be quick, little Horace, I can assure you."

They walked on in silence for some time. Rackham, for his part, had his head in the clouds, and had almost forgotten that anyone was walking beside him; but presently the voice of Ventoul recalled him.

"You'll write one more letter—and I'll double the price."

"I've said that I won't—and I mean that I won't. Don't refer to the matter again. If you've nothing further to say to me, and you're not afraid of the dark, I'll go home."

"All right," said Ventoul sharply. "But as you've done with the business you'd better let me have that letter that she wrote."

"No," said Rackham slowly: "I shall keep that. It wouldn't be the least earthly bit of good to you, because you don't know what my letter said, and therefore you wouldn't understand her reply to it. Thank your lucky stars that she says she loves you. Good night!"

Ventoul did not reply, and the two parted. Rackham, sauntering slowly back to the house, thought to himself of many things—and thought of them a little bitterly.

"Does she love him? Does she love anyone? Or is she in love with love itself, and life, and all the joyous things they promise? If it could ever have happened that she could have looked twice at me—what a destiny for her! I should have dragged her down, and spoilt her life, and broken her dreams, and bruised her spirit. If she marries Ventoul she'll be fairly safe, because his vanity will keep him from ever letting her find him out. And yet—Noll the fool, who never took life seriously yet, and still has found it a mighty serious matter—if it had happened that she had looked twice at you, or even only once. . . ."

He had said that he would not write to her, and he meant to keep his word. After all, that might bring things to a crisis. Nevertheless, when he got to his room he pulled a sheet of paper towards him, and sat down, and began to write. But when he had written for quite a long time he suddenly threw down the pen, and twisted the paper up fiercely in his hands, and set it to the flame of the candle. He let it burn out to the last tiny scrap between his fingers; then caught at the charred thing, and rubbed it up in his hands, and tossed it from him.

"Ashes!" he whispered—"dust and ashes! And in that only like all that I've ever done, or tried to do!"

Angelica, in the full hope and expectation that after all Ventoul might have come back very late, or very early, with a letter for her, slipped out into the grounds before breakfast. Perversely enough she almost hoped that Rackham would be there; if there should be a letter in the tree she would like to talk to him about it.

Rackham was not there; as a matter of fact at that moment he was fast asleep. But someone else was there—someone who came creeping round the side of the house towards the drive like a guilty thing. Coming almost face to face with Angelica, the guilty-looking one stopped, and faltered, and revealed himself as Joshua Flattery.

"Mornin', miss," said the little man.

"Good morning," said Angelica, feeling equally guilty. "You're up very early."

Joshua glanced back at the house, and looked mysteriously all round about him, and laid a finger on his lips. Then he walked a little way in one direction, and peered round the corner of the house—and then a little farther in another direction, and peered down the drive, shading his eyes with his hand. And then he came back to Angelica.

"Whatever is the matter?" asked Angelica.

"Matter of fact, miss—I'm runnin' away," said Joshua, in a whisper. He held up as he spoke that very cheap suit-case, which had been his only article of luggage on his arrival, and which he had been endeavoring to conceal behind him. "I've left a note for Mr. Rackham, miss, so that 'e won't think anything's 'appened to me."

"But why are you running away?" asked Angelica. "Don't you like Mr. Rackham?"

Joshua Flattery hurriedly squeezed his fingers into his eyes, and turned away his head. "I'd lay down, an' let 'im darnce on me, miss," he exclaimed, in a choking voice; "I'd let him kick me all the way to London town, an' never ask 'im to stop. Never 'ad a friend before, miss—if I can take the liberty o' callin' Mr. Rackham a friend. Picked me up w'en I 'adn't got anythink to bless meself with—'e did!" By way of a change Joshua rubbed the sleeve of his frock-coat into his eyes, and sniffed.

"Then why are you running away?" asked Angelica.

"Because I'm a burden on 'im—because I'm a useless, 'elpless, old man that ain't no good to anybody—'cept w'en it comes to 'anding refreshments or waitin' generally," exclaimed Joshua, now almost sobbing. "Because it never struck me 'e 'adn't got too much money of 'is own—an' because I'm going back to London to be a man, an' to earn a man's wages. That's w'y, miss."

"But have you any money?" asked Angelica gently.

"'E give me 'alf a sovereign yesterday," said Joshua, diving into a pocket, and producing the precious coin. "'E will 'ave 'is joke, miss; said 'e 'adn't come by it honest, but 'e'd made a sovereign unexpected, and I should 'ave 'alf of it."

"Please," said Angelica (and the little man wondered why there were tears in her eyes), "please wait a moment!"

She left Joshua Flattery standing there, and fled back into the house. In a minute or two she came flying out again, and suddenly seized the hand in which, in his dazed condition, he still held the little gold coin, and pressed something into it. Looking down, he saw two half sovereigns instead of one.

"I couldn't do it, miss—I couldn't indeed," said Joshua hurriedly.

"Yes—you must," she whispered. "Press it quite close

against the other one—the one he gave you—and don't ever tell anyone where you got it from."

"But why should you do it, miss?" asked Joshua Flattery.

She closed his hand over the coins, and drew him suddenly towards her. "Because," she whispered, with a glance round at the house, "because I think I love him a little—as you do. And that's something again that you must never tell anybody. Now go—and God bless you!"

The little man went away through the grounds, and disappeared into the road; Angelica went with lagging feet towards the tree. There was nothing there, of course; and almost it did not seem to matter. She went back to the house, and sat down with the Streets—remembering her duty so far as to hope that Mrs. Street had slept well.

"Mrs. Street always sleeps well," said Daniel, answering for her. "It is a very blessed thing for anyone to be able to sleep—without dreaming—as my Daisy does."

"It seems to take a few of your troubles away," said Mrs. Street, with a sigh.

Rackham came in late, with apologies. "I sat up late last night," he said to the three of them generally. "Stupid of me; there was no reason for it."

"What were you doing, Mr. Rackham?" asked Angelica.

"That's the stupidest part of it all," he answered. "I was trying to write."

"And you found it very difficult, I suppose," suggested Angelica, with a smile.

"Very difficult indeed—in fact, impossible," answered Rackham, looking at her. "I burnt all I had written."

Thinking that it might be possible that Ventoul had, after all, left a letter for her in the tree—perhaps romantically stealing in while they breakfasted, and placing it there —Angelica went again to the fountain. Again she found nothing; she was turning away when she saw Rackham coming towards her. She blushed guiltily when she saw the whimsical smile on his face; while he, for his part, was in a mood to regret that he had not written a letter after all, if only just for the pleasure of seeing her receive it.

"No post this morning?" he asked.

"I'm not going to tell you," she answered, with a laugh. "You've no right to pry into my affairs—especially——"

"Especially when they are love affairs—eh?" broke in Rackham. "You were ready enough to talk about them yesterday."

"And this morning I want to talk about something else," she said quickly. "There's no letter—and therefore nothing to talk about—at least, in that direction. I saw that man of yours before breakfast," she added.

A puzzled frown came over Rackham's face. "I've found a letter from him," he said; "he's gone away."

"I know; I saw him go," said Angelica. "And I thought it very splendid of him—very wonderful."

"He's quite mistaken, of course," said Oliver Rackham. "I'd have stuck to him as long as he cared to stick to me. I'd taken quite a fancy to the little chap."

"And he'd taken quite a fancy to you," said Angelica. "He told me so; said he wouldn't mind if you danced on him, or kicked him all the way to London."

"He's got rather a weird taste in amusement, hasn't

he?" said Rackham, laughing. "Well—I hope he'll get on all right; when I go back to London I must try and find him. And now, Miss Brown," he went on, "since we may not talk of love affairs, or letters, or even of my man, since he is gone, what shall we talk about?"

"I didn't say you mustn't talk about your man," said Angelica. "I wanted to talk about him; I wanted to tell you how splendid I thought it was that you should take an old fellow like that, and be so good to him. I wanted to tell you——"

"Miss Angelica Brown—we will *not* talk about my man," exclaimed Rackham hurriedly. "Another subject, please."

"Then will you talk about yourself?" suggested Angelica.

"That's a poor subject," he said. They were seated together on the stone edge of the fountain; everything about them was very still and peaceful. Rackham sat staring at the ground, with his arms resting on his knees; Angelica, half turned towards him, was watching his lined face earnestly.

"I don't think so," said the girl. "I'm very much interested in you, and I want to know all about you. Your friend Horace Ventoul has told me all about himself, almost from the very beginning."

"Horace Ventoul would do that," retorted Rackham slowly, "because, you see, he's fond of himself; but I'm not fond of myself."

"Why shouldn't you be?" asked Angelica.

"Because, my dear Miss Brown," he said, turning his head, and looking at her for the first time," "there's nothing in me to be fond of. I've done all sorts of things that are poor and pitiful; I wake sometimes in the grey light of the morning, and see myself for what I am. Please let us talk of something else."

"You said I might choose the subject, and I've chosen you," said Angelica. "You once let me tell you all about myself—and you listened very patiently. Now I want to know all about you. How did you begin?"

"You're a most persistent person," said Rackham, looking at her with a smile. "Well—I began, if you must know, rather nicely. I have a vision of myself which may be altogether a wrong one—a vision of myself in a garden one long hot summer—as a child. There was a woman in the garden, and while she was there I never remember that it was anything but summer, with the sun always shining. It was after she had gone that the winters began."

"Go on," said Angelica softly.

"She was my mother—and I know now that she died very young. I woke in the grey morning only quite recently, with the feeling that I lay against her breast, and that she was carrying me up a wide staircase, singing to me. It was the end of a long day, spent all in sunshine, and I was tired—just happily tired, as a child may be that is ready for bed, and lies deliciously in loved arms. Shall we talk of something else?"

"Not unless this hurts you," murmured Angelica.

"It was after she died that things didn't go well with me. I'm not making excuses; I'm only telling you what happened. I was a bit of a reckless boy at school—always in trouble, and always with heaps of friends among my fellows. I remember that I never went to any home for

"SOMETHING IN YOUR FACE TELLS ME, MR. RACKHAM, THAT THERE'S A LOT MORE IN YOUR LIFE THAN YOU'VE TOLD ME."

Page 249.

the holidays, unless it was to someone else's; I didn't understand what the word meant. And when finally I left school, with not too good a character, I fear, I was passed on to an uncle, who gave me to understand that he had been paying my bills out of an estate to which I was entitled when I came of age. He wasn't a nice uncle, and I hated him."

"And what did you do then?" asked Angelica.

"I went to the 'Varsity—and after that I knocked about the world for a year or two; then I came to London. And in London I played that mad, reckless game of throwing money about—just for the sport of seeing how fast it could go. And I was suddenly pulled up short by the discovery that there was no more money to throw about, and that my debts were appalling."

"Didn't your uncle help you?"

"He was that sort of uncle," said Rackham slowly, "that had prophesied from the beginning what my inevitable end would be, and now rubbed his hands with satisfaction to find that he had been right. And now, Miss Brown"—he got to his feet slowly—"so far as my poor self is concerned —the rest is silence."

"You don't want to tell me any more?" asked Angelica.

"I can't tell you any more," he said. "Are you going back to the house?"

"Wait a moment," she said, standing up, and coming close to him. "Something in your face and in your eyes tells me, Mr. Rackham, that there's a lot more in your life than you've told me—things you wouldn't, perhaps, like me to know. Yet if it would comfort you to tell me anything——"

"If I could tell anyone I would tell you," he said earnestly.

"You spoke to me of your mother," said Angelica gently. "Has there been no other woman in your life who has ever helped you?"

"Yes—one."

"Who was she?" asked Angelica quickly.

"Her name is Angelica Brown," answered Rackham solemnly.

"No—no; I wasn't speaking of myself," said the girl impatiently. "Has there never been anyone who loved you—anyone with whom you've been in love?"

"There has never been anyone who loved me," he answered.

"Or anyone with whom you have been in love?" She was looking at him out of those deep eyes of hers fearlessly, and her lips were parted. "Are you sure?"

"I think I can say that I am absolutely sure," said Oliver Rackham. "And now—shall we talk of something else?"

Rackham did not put in an appearance at dinner that night; he had left word that he was going for a long tramp in the country, and would dine at an inn and return later. Ventoul rather welcomed the news when he heard it; he would have Angelica to himself, with no possibility of any distraction in the shape of music or other things. He got away from the dinner-table within a few minutes after Mrs. Street and the girl had gone; he went into the drawing-room, to find Mrs. Street alone.

"Where's Miss Brown?" demanded Ventoul.

"She's gone into the grounds," stammered Mrs. Street. "She didn't say which way——"

Ventoul went out quickly through the French windows. He had something of a hunt to find Angelica; he found her at last, something to his satisfaction, near that absurd tree in which he was supposed to post letters, and from which he was also supposed to receive them.

Angelica had been seated on the stone edge of the fountain; she got up quickly when she saw him coming, and stood waiting.

"My dear," he said, "why did you run away like that? I've been looking for you. There's something I want to say to you."

"Yes?" said Angelica faintly.

"I've tried to write it—and you've tried to answer it," said Ventoul, speaking with confidence. "But I can't say in writing all that I—I want to say. I'm very much in love with you, Angelica; I want you to marry me. You know all we've talked about; I'm sure you understand that it was all leading up to this."

"Yes," said Angelica again.

"I love you very much—and very dearly. Will you marry me?"

"Yes," said Angelica. Then, as he stepped forward, and suddenly put his arms about her, she wrenched herself free; and, looking at him with a startled face, cried out a strange thing.

"No—no—you mustn't do that," she said. "At least—I mean—not here!"

And, before he could stop her, fled from him into the house.

CHAPTER XIII

A CHANCERY PUZZLE

Mr. Daniel Street, for ever on the look-out from those furtive eyes of his, had noticed that business of Horace Ventoul monopolizing the girl whenever he had the chance, and had indeed, as has been shown, originally assisted it. But now, with his new knowledge of what Ventoul's motive really was, Daniel Street was playing for his own hand, although he did not exactly know what cards to use. At present he was in the condition of a man who can only stand aside, and watch and wait.

Strolling out early the following morning, with the design to intercept the postman and get the house letters, he found, when they were handed to him at the gate, that there was one addressed to himself. He opened it and read it before walking back to the house, and found that it was from his former shady correspondent, James Peel.

"*My dear Dan,*

"*Could you make it convenient to run up to town? I've been working very hard on your account, and I am just now at a sort of loose end; I can't get any further. Too long to write it all down here, but can explain when I see you. It's the rummiest affair I've ever struck in my life, and I've seen some rum ones. If you come up you'll find me any day at the old spot.* "*Yours always,*
"*JAMES PEEL.*"

"Jimmy is the sort of man that would make a muddle of anything," said Street to himself. "I expect I shall be able to straighten it out."

He decided to go that day; and, lest objections might be raised by Horace Ventoul, started off before that gentleman could, under ordinary circumstances, reach the house. Indeed, so careful was he, that he made a detour, so as to avoid the inn in the village where Ventoul was staying; he feared lest that gentleman should catch sight of him from the windows. Having money in his pocket, he travelled to London comfortably, and, finding that it was just about lunch time on his arrival, went to a restaurant, and spent some part of Mr. Horace Ventoul's money in regaling himself well.

After that he drove to Chancery Lane, telling himself confidently that he would very quickly put this matter right, and show James Peel what a wholly inadequate person he was in such a matter. Dismissing his cab, he turned into that little court out of Chancery Lane; pushed open the familiar door; and was once again in that little bar that had been his office and almost his home for so many dreary years.

It was just the same—save only that James Peel had taken his vacant place against the wall, although James Peel's shoulders did not quite reach the mark left there by those of Daniel Street. James Peel was that little man in the faded check suit who had been so unceremoniously dismissed by Street on the day of our first meeting with him.

"Well—this is lucky," said Peel, coming away from the wall, and stretching out a hand to his old friend. "Something seemed to tell me to-day that I should find you here—or rather that you'd walk in, in quite the old style. Doin' yourself well, ain't you, Dan, my boy?" he added, with a glance at the other's clothes. "Quite the country gent. What's it to be?"

He turned expectantly to the bar, and peered under the screen in search of the barmaid. That young lady condescending to put in an appearance also commented upon the coming of Daniel Street, and had a little banter with that gentleman concerning his improved looks. Mr. James Peel not producing any money, Daniel Street threw down half a crown, and the necessary order was given.

"Now," said Street, when the barmaid had retired, "let's hear all about it."

"It's a rum go," said Mr. Peel, rubbing his nose with a grimy forefinger, "and it looks to me, Dan, as if you were a day after the fair."

"What do you mean by that?" demanded Street, setting down his glass, and staring at the other man.

"Now—don't get impatient; I'm going to tell you all about it," said Mr. Peel soothingly. "I went to work as you suggested in certain quarters, and I found out that inquiries had been made for a Miss Angelica Susan Brown"—he lowered his voice, and looked round the bar suspiciously—"and that the fortune was co-lossal!"

"Oh—you heard that—did you?" said Street.

"Further inquiries showed that it was just over half a million. Oho!—thinks I—this is what Dan has suddenly bolted into the country for—is it? Off I goes again to see what else I can find out—digging here, there, and everywhere, and always coming up against brick walls. And at last, Dan"—James Peel laid a forefinger impressively on Daniel Street's breast—"at last I came up against one that was a regular facer!"

"A facer? What do you mean?" asked the other slowly.

"The fortune was all right—the girl was all right—but it was gone."

"Gone? Why the devil don't you be more explicit?" demanded Street angrily.

"The fortune was all right—but it had been claimed," said Mr. Peel, greatly enjoying the other's wonderment. "A Miss Angelica Susan Brown had been found—had got her money—and there was an end of it. I've got it somewhere here as clear as daylight."

While Daniel Street stood feebly staring at him, James Peel dived into various pockets, and at last produced a scrap of folded paper. This he spread out flat on the edge of the bar, and then handed it, with an air of triumph, to the other.

"There you are; read that," he said. "I cut that out of one of the legal papers in the reading-room across the way when nobody was looking. Read it."

Daniel Street read the scrap, and read it again. It merely stated that the Court of Chancery had appointed certain persons to be the guardians of the Miss Angelica Susan Brown who had recently proved her claim to the fortune that had been so long in the hands of the Court.

"There's a mistake," said Street at last, slowly. "There must be a mistake."

"I think not," said Peel, with a short laugh. "Those

people don't make mistakes; they hold on a bit too tight to money to give it up to the first one that comes and holds out a hand for it. It's you that's made the mistake, Dan."

And then quite suddenly, without making any verbal reply, Daniel Street leaned against the bar, and began to laugh. He had never been known to do such a thing before, and he found it difficult now, because he could only emit a high cackle of laughter that shook him from head to foot, and which he seemed to find it impossible to control. When at last he did get himself into some order, he wiped the tears from his eyes, and shook his head feebly at the other man.

"It's so funny!" he exclaimed. "It's the funniest thing I've ever heard of. I can't tell you anything about it, Jimmy; it'd take too long. But, oh!—to think of that girl—nothing too good for her, and houses and people bought on her account and to keep up the game—and then —puff!—all gone in a moment. We'll have another, Jimmy; I feel weak."

"I should like to know something about it," said Mr. Peel a little resentfully, when the glasses had been refilled. "I've had a lot of work and trouble——"

"And you shall be paid for it, Jimmy," said Street. "It means for me that I've got to come back to London; and I'm not sure that I'm altogether sorry. I've had a bit of a rest—and it's done the wife good, I think. At the same time," he added grimly, "as I've been put in possession of a cheque-book, I think I'll contrive to clear my account at the local bank before they get rid of me. It'll be something to start on, Jimmy."

He left James Peel finally the happier by the gift of a

sovereign—a gift which seemed to promise unending liquid nourishment to that gentleman—and set off to return to Pentney Hill. Although he knew that the game was ended —or nearly ended—so far as he was concerned, he yet more than once astonished his fellow passengers by breaking out into another ghastly fit of laughter, that shook him from head to foot, on his journey home. And it was with difficulty that he composed his features when he reached the house and entered it.

He let that evening pass without saying anything of his amazing discovery; he forced himself to remember that he must snatch what spoils he could before his retreat. Therefore he sat, as usual, in the drawing-room, smoking his thin paper cigarette, and listening to Rackham playing, and watching Ventoul seated beside the girl. He, who knew that the little comedy was to end in a tragedy and a fiasco, watched them all out of his half-closed eyes, and wondered exactly what move the figures would take when that bolt from the blue fell among them.

But—master though he was of the situation—he was to be outflanked by no less a person than Mr. Horace Ventoul. Horace Ventoul had passed through another evening when Rackham had carried all before him, and when Angelica's eyes had alternately danced with laughter or filled with tears as the man jested or played his infernal music. And Horace Ventoul had that trump card up his sleeve, and had determined to fling it down before them all.

Characteristically, Ventoul waited until the last moment, when as usual he was setting out for the inn. Then, as he stood with the others in the hall, at the moment when

Angelica shyly held out her hand to him he drew her almost roughly towards him, and kissed her suddenly on the lips. With a little exclamation she stepped back, glancing from one to the other nervously.

"Oh—it's all right," said Ventoul, with a glance at Rackham. "It's just as well that everybody should know it; we've nothing to hide. Mrs. Street"—he had taken the centre of the circle, and he spoke aggressively—"I think you ought to know that Miss Brown and I are engaged to be married."

Before Mrs. Street could reply, a surprising sound burst from Daniel Street; it was really like a sort of small explosion. He turned it into a spluttering cough, and murmured an apology; while Mrs. Street, for her part, murmured congratulations.

"I'm sure it's most romantic," said Mrs. Street—"you coming down like this, Mr. Ventoul, and meeting Miss Brown. Not but what I've seen it coming for quite a long time," she added slyly, "though of course it wasn't for me to say anything about it. And if good wishes are any good to anybody, I'm sure you have all the best——"

"Yes—yes—that's all right," broke in Ventoul hurriedly. "I thought it only fair to mention it; we hope to get married very soon. It has been a bit romantic, as you say," he added, with a dry laugh, "and for that, of course, we're very grateful to you. And now I think I'll say 'good night.' Are you walking a bit with me, Noll?"

"Not to-night," said Rackham shortly.

So Ventoul went off alone, carelessly whistling an air as he walked, and feeling that he had got over the business rather well. Angelica, with a very hurried "good night" to each of them, slipped away, and Rackham went off into the dining-room, and lit a light, and sat down to smoke.

After a few minutes he got up, and went across to the sideboard, and poured out some whiskey and soda. Holding up the glass, he laughed softly to himself after a moment or two, and drank.

"Here's to you, little lady!" he whispered. "You've made your choice—and I expect you'll be fairly happy—and you'll certainly be very rich. And a poor devil that loved you as he had never loved anything on earth before will go out of your life, and won't be heard of again. Well—so best!"

The door was opened at that moment, and Daniel Street came in. He nodded at Rackham; and then, surprisingly enough, came across the room and took up a glass. "I think I'll join you," he said.

"By all means," said Rackham. "I'm in a convivial mood to-night, and I'm willing to put up with even your companionship. Help yourself—and sit down."

Daniel Street helped himself, and slowly rolled a cigarette—picking out the little shreds of tobacco from his paper packet meagrely and with care. When he had got the thing alight, he said, without looking up at Rackham—

"That was a pretty business to-night, Mr. Rackham."

"Do you think so?" asked Rackham. "Of course, if you think so it's all right. It doesn't seem to occur to you that it's put an end to your part of the game. I mean that Mrs. Street loses her companion—and you and Mrs. Street lose your situations."

"In the long run I don't think that'll make very much difference," said Daniel Street, carefully smoothing down the paper at one end of his cigarette that had come loose. "If it comes to that, I think we are all going to lose our situations."

Oliver Rackham had not been listening to him; he only grasped that final phrase after a moment or two. Then he set down his glass, and stared at the man with a frowning face. "What the devil do you mean?" he asked.

Street sipped his mixture slowly, and rolled it round his tongue, and swallowed it. "I mean," he said, "that all this myth about half a million of money is exploded."

Rackham even forgot his glass. He left it, and came round the table so that he could face the other man; leaned upon the table, and spoke sharply.

"Myth? What have you heard? What do you know?"

"I heard, by the merest chance," said Street slowly, "that in this business of bringing this girl down here, and giving her a position that was no position—and all the rest of it; I heard that there was a matter of half a million of money. Is that right?"

"Yes—that's right. I see you've fathomed the business. It was a plot to get hold of the girl; and in that Ventoul has succeeded. I've been in it, too; we've all been in it."

"And the whole business, from beginning to end, has been all wrong," said Daniel Street, raising his head, and opening his eyes, and looking fully at Rackham. "The taking of the house—and the persuading the girl to come here—and the carefully planned love-making . . . all thrown away."

There was a silence, although Rackham seemed to echo those last two words voicelessly with his lips. Then

Street got slowly to his feet, and brought down his hand softly on the table, and looked again at Rackham.

"You've got the wrong girl!" he exclaimed, in a whisper.

"Good Lord!" The answer was a whisper on Rackham's part; and so for a moment or two they stood staring at each other. Then Street straightened himself, and spoke in his usual cold voice.

"I don't know yet what the mistake has been," he said. "I simply know that I have been to London to-day to make inquiries, and I have seen an extract from a legal paper which shows me that the real Angelica Susan Brown has proved her title to the fortune, and has got it. Guardians have been appointed by the Court, and the whole matter is ended."

"It's impossible!" exclaimed Rackham. "There couldn't be two with exactly that name, and under exactly those circumstances. There's some gigantic blunder."

"The Court of Chancery doesn't blunder in that way," said Street. "It makes hideous mistakes in other directions, but it has a way of hanging on pretty tightly to money. I tell you you've got the wrong girl."

Rackham began to walk about the room. Once or twice he stopped before the imperturbable figure, and held out a hand, and made a movement as if to speak; but evidently recognized that the argument he was about to bring forward was futile, and so walked on again. He went to the sideboard, and picked up his glass, and looked at it stupidly; then set it down, and came hurriedly across to Daniel Street.

"But do you realize, man, what this means to her?" he broke out suddenly. "Do you realize that she doesn't know that it's been a great game; she thinks that this man has genuinely fallen in love with her—a poor little companion in a country house at fifty pounds a year—and is marrying her just for the love of her. What do you think she'll say when she knows that I've tricked her—lied to her—and brought her down here, to deliver her into the hands of a man like that? God in heaven!—can't you see all that?"

"Why don't you ask me why *I* don't complain? why don't you ask what *my* feelings are?" asked Street.

"You went into the matter with your eyes open; you saw this thing from the beginning. You were ready enough to be employed comfortably down here; the finding out about the money was an accident. You've been in the plot—just as I have—and just as Ventoul has."

"I wonder what Mr. Horace Ventoul is going to do now about his engagement?" asked Daniel Street slowly. "It would be interesting to know—wouldn't it?"

"You callous devil!" exclaimed Rackham, pacing about the room. "What do you care about what happens to her, or what she does—or anything?"

"You didn't care very much when you arranged to bring her down here—did you?" said Street. "I'm sorry for the girl, of course; but, as she doesn't know anything about the fortune she was supposed to have, I don't see that it matters very much."

"No—you wouldn't see that," retorted Rackham. "You wouldn't understand what she'd be likely to feel when she knows that those she has counted upon as friends—the first friends she has ever had in all her starved little life—that those people have lied and pretended to her, because they thought she had half a million of money and they could dip their hands into it."

"But meanwhile, my friend—what is Ventoul going to do?" suggested Street, sucking at his cigarette. "That seems to be the whole question."

"You mustn't tell him; he mustn't know," said Rackham quickly. "Let him find out afterwards—when he has married her. Come, Street—you couldn't be brute enough to smash up that business."

"He's not in love with her," said the other.

"That's not the point; she's in love with him. That's quite another matter. He's got to stand to his word—or he shall reckon with me."

Daniel Street did some hard thinking. After all, the game was up, so far as he was concerned, and he would be left stranded. There was one consolation: he still possessed that cheque-book, and there was a fairly substantial sum standing in his name at the local bank. He must have another day at least in which to get hold of that money; his wisest course was to hold his tongue for the present. Since Rackham put the matter in this sentimental and romantic way, Daniel Street felt that he might as well fall in with the other's mood.

"I think you're right," he said, with a nod. "There's not much doubt she's in love with him, and, after all, he's got money. She'll be better off with him and an income than finding herself thrown on the world again to earn her living. You're right; I'll hold my tongue."

"Good!" exclaimed Rackham with satisfaction. "And, after all, there's another side to the medal: Ventoul might just as well be made to do the decent thing; it's quite virtuous on our part, Street, to make him do that—and all for love; I hadn't thought of that side of the business."

"You won't get anything out of it," said Street, after a pause.

Rackham was silent for a moment or two; when he answered it was in a changed voice. "I'm not altogether sorry," he said, without looking at the other man. "Perhaps it's just as well. I shall come out of it with cleaner hands than I anticipated. Meanwhile, I'm grateful to you for your promise."

"Don't mention it," said Street, as he rose to his feet. "After all, it serves my purpose better; I shall get a little grace before being turned out of this place. And now I suppose we'd better get to bed."

He went out of the room, leaving Rackham standing there. Oliver Rackham stood for a long time deep in thought; presently he voiced his thoughts.

"Oh—my dear—I wonder if he'll be good to you when he knows the truth?"

CHAPTER XIV

ANGELICA WAKES UP

Daniel Street, more watchful and alert than ever, saw with satisfaction that everything was apparently going on its usual course on the following day. Horace Ventoul came over as usual—entering with a new confidence, and taking possession of Angelica immediately. Rackham kept out of the way, and did not put in an appearance until noon.

As a matter of fact Rackham rather dreaded to meet the girl's eyes. He believed that Street, for his own sake, would be silent; but he dreaded lest any accident should explode the whole business, and so put an end to everything. He seemed to be walking on the thinnest possible crust of earth, which might give way at any moment.

That most respectable of country gentlemen, Mr. Daniel Street, strolled to the bank in the afternoon, and had a chat with the cashier about crops and the weather, and other matters; finally asked casually what his balance was. Being informed, he looked surprised and somewhat perplexed.

"I thought it was more than that," he said, although of course he knew perfectly well what it was to a penny. "However—I have some dividends coming in, in a day or two. I've got rather a lot to pay at the moment; I shall have to run it close."

Laughing genially with the cashier concerning his present impoverished condition, he drew out the whole sum, with the exception of some three or four pounds; had another joke with the cashier, and strolled out. He paid a visit to the house of the local fly-driver, and ordered a carriage to meet him at a certain spot, about a quarter of a mile from his own house, at a surprisingly early hour the following morning.

"I've got to be in London very early," he said, "or I shan't be able to get back at night. I want to drive to the junction, and catch the first express. You'll be on time, won't you?"

The man assured him that he would be there to the minute, and Daniel Street thanked him, and strolled away. Everything was now complete.

Horace Ventoul, coming as usual to dinner that night, proved to be in a mocking humor. Finding that Oliver Rackham was by no means his genial self, and that he made no attempt, as usual, to monopolize the conversation, Horace took the opportunity of talking as much as possible, and, above all, talking at Rackham. Perhaps he shrewdly suspected what torture he was inflicting whenever he made any allusion to the girl, although he did not, of course, have the faintest suspicion of what was in Rackham's mind, and in the mind also of Daniel Street.

"You're dull to-night, old Noll," he said, not for the first time. "What's the matter with you? I never saw you gloomy before."

"I wanted to give you an opportunity of playing the agreeable rattle to-night," said Rackham. "A happy man like yourself ought to be able to chatter like the proverbial magpie."

"Ah—I believe that's what makes you gloomy," said Ventoul. "You're envious."

"Very; I frankly admit it," said Rackham calmly.

"Perhaps a little jealous," suggested the other. "But then, you see, old Noll, it isn't likely that anyone will take the trouble to fall in love with you—is it?"

Angelica bent forward quickly, and whispered protestingly to Ventoul; but he waved her aside.

"It's scarcely likely—as you suggest," answered Rackham, looking at him squarely. "She would be making a mighty poor bargain—wouldn't she?"

"I should think so, indeed," retorted Ventoul. And then, warned by something he saw in Rackham's eyes, he desisted from further persecution, and turned his attention to other matters. In due course the dinner ended, and Ventoul, without any attempt at explanation or apology, walked out with the ladies.

Daniel Street turned to Rackham. "The girl has told my wife that she and Ventoul are to be married almost at once," he said slowly.

"Thank God for that!" murmured Rackham piously.

Oliver Rackham went for a long walk that night in a drizzling rain. The weather mattered nothing to him; there were certain things that had to be fought out—certain problems that would have to be solved. And the great problem was: Should he tell her?

Should he tell her, and send her back to the safe, clean things of life—to the little room near the stars, and the hard drudgery of each day that she had never counted drudgery at all? Or should he be silent, and wait, in the hope that after all Ventoul would be good to her, and would love her a little, if only just because she loved him? Hard problems to solve, especially with such a man as Oliver Rackham to solve them alone.

He came back very late, and almost wet through, having as usual made up his mind to let matters alone. After all, in accepting Horace Ventoul Angelica had taken the matter into her own hands, and must work out her destiny. In any case, Rackham was powerless in the matter, he told himself.

He went to bed, and slept soundly. Daniel Street, on the other hand, did not go to bed, and did not sleep soundly. He had sat up later than usual, and had gone to his room only some five minutes before Rackham's return; he heard that gentleman come in. At that time Daniel Street was silently packing his own and his wife's clothes, and was making his final preparations.

At a very early hour in the morning he stood beside the bed whereon his wife lay sleeping. She looked rather pretty asleep, he told himself; and the man heaved a little sigh at the thought that once again he must take her out into the world, and once again begin the old precarious business of picking up a scratch livelihood.

"She deserves something better," he murmured to himself, with a little shrug of the shoulders, as he stood looking down at her. "If I could go back over the years! ... She was the prettiest bride I ever saw, and I was the happiest man. Who'd have thought it possible then, when I walked down that church, with her hand on my arm, that I could have made her shed the bitterest tears ever a woman shed in her life? Who would have thought that she would have had to wait, shabby and lonely, outside the gates of that prison for me?"

He turned away, and after a time came back to the bed again, and laid a hand gently on her shoulder. "Daisy!" he said, in a whisper.

She took some shaking before being finally roused from slumber; and then she sat up, a little crumpled and a little frightened—looking just like a large overgrown baby, wakened suddenly and surprisingly.

"What is it, Dan?" she asked.

The man remembered then that that was just what she had said once before, when, under similar circumstances and at a similar hour, he had awakened her to tell her that he contemplated what was to prove a wholly ineffectual flight. Perhaps the memory of that was with the woman now, for she clutched at him, and stared at him with round frightened eyes.

"There's nothing the matter; I want you to get up and dress," he said. "We've got to go at once; I've packed all your things."

Poor Mrs. Street, in the very act of putting a plump leg over the side of the bed, began to cry. Not with any violence, but just hopelessly and helplessly. This was the thing that she had been expecting from the first—the thing she never forgot, save in sleep. Dan was in trouble again, and the old weary business was to be begun afresh.

"Now, my dear Daisy—don't be silly," he remonstrated in a whisper.

"It's all very well to say that, Dan—but it doesn't help much," murmured Mrs. Street, going on mechanically with her dressing. "Didn't I beg and pray of you not to come down here—not to mix yourself up again with anything that was shady? We were living hard, and living poor; but we managed to scrape along. If only you'd listened to me, this wouldn't have happened."

"Will you listen to me for a moment, my dear, and not talk so much?" he pleaded. "The game here is ended—done with; we've got to clear out. I've made all arrangements, and we shall go to London comfortably, and have a little money to make a start on. I've been spoiling the Egyptians a little—but that doesn't matter. The money is due to me, if it comes to that, for all the trouble I've had—to say nothing of giving up my business."

"But we were so happy and comfortable at dinner to-night," pleaded Mrs. Street. "And Angelica and Mr. Ventoul just going to get married. I was really beginning to feel, Dan, that we could settle down and be quiet—I was, indeed."

"Don't talk so loudly," whispered the man. "I tell you the game is up; the very purpose for which this house was taken, and we were engaged to live in it, is a purpose no longer; it has ceased to exist. Within twenty-four hours everybody here will be scattered in all directions; and I can assure you I'm not going to be the last to leave."

"But what about the girl?" said Mrs. Street. "I've got quite fond of Angelica, Dan."

"I can't tell you everything now," said Street impatiently, with a glance at his watch. "Suffice it that this girl was supposed to be somebody entirely different; and although it's not her fault in the least, she has turned out to be a fraud. In other words, this man Ventoul was going to marry her for the sake of a big fortune she was supposed to have; and there's no fortune at all. That's the whole story in a nutshell."

"Then I'm not going to leave her," exclaimed Mrs. Street, beginning in a great hurry to take her clothes off. "I'm not going to run away and leave her in the hands of these men; I won't do it."

In this extremity there was but one way in which to deal with Mrs. Street. "Look here," whispered her husband, "this has been a gigantic fraud from beginning to end—and I've been mixed up with one before. Do you want to see me in the hands of the police?"

Mrs. Street's lips began to quiver; her eyes were wide and terrified. "No—no, Dan—I didn't mean that. Of course I'll stick to you—didn't I vow and declare it, goodness knows how many years ago? I won't say another word, Dan—though goodness knows I do wish you'd taken my advice, and listened to what I said before we left London. I always knew no good could come of it."

She was dressed at last, and, with many injunctions as to the necessity for silence, Daniel Street got her out of the house. He carried their luggage, and they crept away from the place in utter silence, save that Mrs. Street, behind a vail that flapped in the breeze and seemed to be fastened nowhere at all, wept bitterly at this ending of all her hopes. So they came to the carriage that was waiting at the spot indicated on the previous day by Daniel Street, with the driver sitting in the open doorway smoking a pipe.

He got up in a hurry when he saw them, and knocked the ashes from his pipe. Mrs. Street stumbled into the vehicle blindly, and Daniel followed her; they set off at once for that cross-country drive that should take them on their way to London.

Rackham had slept soundly, as has been said; and for once he rose in time for breakfast. Angelica had been out in the grounds for an hour at least; he found her seated in her place at the table alone. No suspicion of what had happened entered his mind; he greeted her brightly at once.

"Good morning, Miss Brown," he said. "We both seem to be early this morning."

"Good morning," she said, holding out a hand to him. "I think Mr. and Mrs. Street must be asleep; I haven't heard a sound from them. I suppose it won't matter if we begin breakfast—will it?"

"I should think not," he answered, laughing. "We shall have everything cold if we don't. Perhaps we'd better send some of the dishes back to be kept hot."

Angelica gave the servant the necessary instructions; and presently Rackham and the girl were left alone together at their meal. Once or twice Rackham, glancing up, found that the girl was looking at him; and although she instantly turned her eyes on her plate, the mere fact of being caught like that was disconcerting. Presently she spoke, but without looking at him.

"We haven't had any of our lovely talks lately, Mr. Rackham," she said. "I used to like talking to you; there's never been anybody in all the world that I felt I could say the things to that I said to you."

"I'm glad to hear you say that," he answered, with a heart that ached at the thought of what she might come to think of him in the time to come. "But of course I understand that now you are—engaged—someone else has the first claim on your time and on your attention. You must find a lot to talk to Horace about, I'm sure."

She did not answer; she was crumbling her bread, and looking down at it. Suddenly she looked up—not to answer his question, but to speak of something quite different.

"I had a funny dream about you last night," she said. "It was a wonderfully clear dream, and I can see it all now as plainly as possible."

"What was it?" he asked lightly. "You've no right to be dreaming about me, you know."

"I thought we were both in London, and that I was back again in my old lodging. Somehow it wasn't quite the same; it seemed poorer and meaner than it used to be—and I was shabby. Also it seemed to me that I wasn't as hopeful as I used to be—I was more afraid of things. And in my dream I looked out of the window towards that lamp-post on the other side of the way—you remember the lamp-post you leaned against for over an hour one night, waiting to see me?"

"I remember it perfectly," he replied.

"There was someone leaning against the lamp-post," went on Angelica, "and it seemed to me in my dream that I must go down and see who it was. I went out of the house and across the road—and it was you."

"You were only dreaming of what had once happened," said Rackham.

"But that wasn't the bad part of it," said Angelica slowly. "You looked thin and ill—and you were quite ragged. Wasn't that horrible?"

"Very horrible," the man answered, as lightly as he could. "But dreams never mean anything, you know; so I wouldn't worry about it, if I were you."

The meal came to an end, and Angelica looked with an anxious face at the clock on the mantelpiece. "I think someone ought to go and see about Mr. and Mrs. Street," she said. "They can't know what the time is."

"I'll go up and knock at the door," said Rackham.

He went upstairs, and knocked at the door; a moment later he knocked again more sharply. Then, with a sudden set look in his face, he turned the handle, and walked into the room.

He realized with stunning force what had happened. The room was in confusion; wardrobes and drawers stood open; there was every sign of flight. He stood there, leaning against the door, and looking round in a bewildered way. He realized that the game was ended; that with this everything must become known at once. He came out of the room, closing the door carefully behind him, and walked slowly downstairs. His first instinct was to gain time.

He found Angelica awaiting him. She noticed at once the drawn look on his face; she made a quick movement towards him. "Is anything the matter?" she asked.

"No—nothing; I'm not quite up to the mark this morning," he answered, with a laugh. "Mrs. Street says they'll be down—presently," he went on lamely. "I can see Ventoul coming," he said, looking out of the window; "hadn't you better go and meet him?"

She turned and went out of the house, waving a hand to Ventoul as he advanced. Rackham, watching them, saw them meet, and then turn and walk slowly away. For his part, he stood swaying like a drunken man, holding to the table; he was wondering what he was to do.

"The brute! The lying brute!" he whispered. "To desert a girl like this—to clear out of the place, and leave her to face the music. What in Heaven's name am I to do? Ventoul must know—it can't be kept from him; and I know perfectly well what he'll do then. He's not the sort to mince matters, and I can't go on lying to cover up the retreat of the Streets; it isn't possible."

He went up again to the room, in the faint hope that some note might have been left behind, suggesting that this going away was only a temporary matter. In his own mind he knew, of course, that there was no earthly hope that that could be so; but he was clutching at straws.

He found nothing there; he came down again, to discover the servant waiting for him, with a puzzled air, in the dining-room. She naturally wanted to know what she was to do about the spoiling breakfast.

"There won't be any more breakfast wanted," said Rackham petulantly. "I've just been up to see Mrs. Street."

The girl, evidently perplexed, went away, and Rackham once more faced this new problem alone. About an hour later the servant again appeared—this time with a very scared face.

"If you please, sir, I took the liberty of going up and knocking at Mrs. Street's door, to ask if I could take them up any breakfast—and they've gone!"

"Yes—I know; but they're coming back," said Rackham distractedly. "It's all right; you needn't stare at me like that. I haven't murdered them, or made away with them. They're coming back, I tell you."

A little later he saw, with a sinking heart, Horace Ventoul and Angelica coming slowly towards the house. It is probable then that he would have taken flight himself had there been a chance for him to do so; but the sorry music had to be faced. He walked out of the house, and, controlling his voice as much as possible to a light tone, hailed Ventoul.

"Good morning, Horace," he called. "Can I have a word with you for a moment? I won't detain him a moment, Miss Brown," he added to the girl.

Ventoul left her side, and walked to where Rackham was standing. Rackham slipped a hand through his arm, and drew him away a little. Something in his face, as Ventoul looked at him, caused that gentleman to ask a question quickly.

"What's the matter?"

"Rather a bad business, Horace," said Rackham, in a low tone. "The Streets have bolted."

"What?" Ventoul shook himself free of the other man's hand, and stood staring at him. "Bolted?"

"They didn't appear at breakfast, and I went up to their room. They've packed up everything, and gone," answered Rackham. "What are we going to do now?"

"Does Angelica know? Have you told her anything?" asked Ventoul quickly.

"Of course not; she believes they're still in their room," answered Rackham. "But she's got to know it soon; even the servants have found it out."

"But what's the object?" asked Ventoul irritably.

"The man was comfortable enough, and well paid. I can't make it out."

Still Rackham did not tell him; still he fought for delay, however short it might be. "He always was a bit of a slippery customer, according to your account," he said at last.

Ventoul stood deep in thought; Angelica had gone into the house. Both men knew, as they watched her go, that at any moment now the discovery might come, and she might demand explanations.

"I shall go down to the village," said Ventoul at last, "and see if I can hear anything of them. Don't let her know about it, if you can avoid it; invent some excuse— say they've been called away, and are coming back. You understand?"

"Perfectly," answered Rackham. "But don't be surprised, when you come back, if you find that she knows all about it."

Horace Ventoul went off at once to the village, leaving Rackham to return to the house and face Angelica.

Angelica met him on the very steps of the house. "Mr. Rackham," she said at once, "do you know that Mr. and Mrs. Street have not come down yet?" she asked, in an awed voice. "Do you think anything can be the matter with them?"

"I should think not," answered Rackham. "I wouldn't worry about it, if I were you, Miss Brown."

"But I do worry," retorted Angelica. "I think I shall go up myself, and see what's wrong."

"I wouldn't do that——" he began; but she turned, and ran up the stairs at once.

He waited miserably in the hall until she came down again. She walked straight up to him; and now her air was one of consternation. "They're not there," she said. "What does it mean?"

"They—they've gone away," said Rackham, without looking at her.

"Gone away? But they didn't say a word about it to me—not a single word," whispered Angelica. "And why did you come down and pretend that they were in their room? What's all this mystery, Mr. Rackham?"

She was one fiery note of interrogation, and it was obvious that she must be answered. "I can't explain it all clearly, Miss Brown," he said, "but I believe they're coming back."

"Believe? Don't you know?" she demanded.

"Ventoul's gone down to the village to make inquiries; he's as much puzzled as I am," said Rackham. "It'll be all right, I tell you; we shall know something when Ventoul gets back."

She looked at him searchingly for a moment or two. "There's something you know—something you're keeping back from me," she said. "Or why did you go upstairs, and pretend that you had spoken to them—and then come down, and—and lie to me?"

He winced under the word, but said nothing. What could he say? Angelica went on mercilessly.

"Perhaps I'm wrong," she said stiffly. "Perhaps they were in their room then, and have gone since."

"They were not in their room," he answered her.

"Well—I can't understand it," she said helplessly. "You

were their friend, and have been staying in their house; did they say nothing to you about it?"

"Not a word," he replied.

The pair of them moved aimlessly about the house—looking at each other furtively when they encountered, but saying nothing. Once or twice Oliver Rackham made up his mind that he would tell the whole miserable story to the girl, and so have done with it; but each time he looked at her he lacked the courage. And at last Ventoul, after an absence that had seemed interminable, was seen coming across the grounds. Angelica flew out at once to meet him.

"They've gone?" she cried, before she reached him.

"I wonder who told you that?" he snapped out.

"No one told me; I found out for myself," she replied. "Horace—what does it all mean?—what have you found out?"

"Lots of things," he answered irritably. "Now, my dear girl—for goodness' sake, let me alone for a minute; you shall know all about it afterwards. I must see Noll."

"But why have they gone away?" she persisted, clinging to him. "What has happened?"

"You shall know everything presently," he answered, thrusting her aside, and walking on rapidly towards the house.

She followed dejectedly, and saw him speak to Rackham; then saw the two men disappear into the dining-room and close the door. She sat down, with a blank look on her face, in the drawing-room, wondering what it all meant.

And Horace Ventoul paced up and down the room, with his hands locked behind his back, and his lips working; Rackham impatiently waited for him to speak. This he did at last, in a series of short, savage sentences.

"Street went down to the bank yesterday, and absolutely cleaned out the account standing in his name—except for a pound or two for the sake of appearances. I inquired at the railway station; but nothing had been seen of them there. Then I went to the house where the man that drives the fly lives—and there the whole mystery was solved, so far as their flight is concerned, at least."

"What did you find out?" asked Rackham.

"The man Street hired a fly to meet him at the cross roads near this place at five o'clock this morning; told them he wanted to catch the express from the junction. They've cleared out, bag and baggage, and taken all the money they could lay their hands on. What the devil does it all mean? Can you explain it?"

"I—I think I can," said Rackham slowly. "Street has found out something, and has decided to clutch whatever he can lay his hands on, and leave the sinking ship."

"Sinking ship?" Horace Ventoul stared at him with a puzzled face. "What are you talking about? The only thing Street discovered, in some mysterious way, was that there was money in this thing; why should he bolt with just the little he could lay his hands on?"

"Suppose it happened that he found out that there was no money in it? What then?" asked Rackham slowly.

"I don't understand you in the least," said Ventoul. "How could he possibly discover that? We know that there is money in it——"

"I know that there is not," said Oliver Rackham slowly.

Ventoul came round the table, agape; clutched Rackham's arm, and shook him roughly. "What do you mean? What are you talking about?"

"Street went to London two days ago; he got wind of this idea of a great fortune, and he evidently wanted to find out for himself. Well"—Rackham spread out his hands, and spoke despairingly—"he discovered that the great fortune was a myth—that it was all gone, so far as this girl was concerned."

"Street's a fool!" cried Ventoul roughly. "He's heard some cock-and-bull story, and believes it to be true. By Jove, Rackham"—he passed a hand over his forehead, and laughed—"you gave me rather a shock. Why, man, I've seen the papers and the advertisements; I know all about it. The fortune's safe enough, and so are we. It means we must start some other scheme; that's all. The Streets don't matter."

"No other scheme is possible," said Rackham slowly. "The game is ended."

There was that in his tone that caused Ventoul to turn swiftly and stare at him afresh. "You know something—or you think you do," he said. "Let's have it."

"There's been some blunder that I don't understand," said Oliver Rackham. "Daniel Street went to London, and ferreted out this matter; it seems that the fortune was claimed from the Court of Chancery by a Miss Angelica Susan Brown a week or two back; and that the Court, having satisfied themselves that she was the real identical person, have appointed guardians for her, and have arranged the whole business. Our Angelica Susan Brown is someone else, and has no fortune at all."

Horace Ventoul stood there leaning against the table, and staring at Rackham; his brain was in a whirl. "Then she must have lied to you at the beginning," he cried at last violently. "You've made some hideous blunder, and I've had to pay for it."

"She's not the sort to lie to anyone," exclaimed Rackham, with a momentary flash of his old temper. "You'd better ask her yourself; that's the shortest way out of it."

Ventoul hesitated a moment; then, with an exclamation, strode to the door, and pulled it open, and went out. Rackham, going hurriedly after him, heard him shouting in the hall—

"Angelica! Angelica!"

She came hurriedly out of the drawing-room, and faced them. "Oh—have you heard anything about Mr. and Mrs. Street?" she asked, looking from one to the other. "I want to know——"

"Never mind about them!" broke in Ventoul curtly. "I want you to tell me what your name is?"

She stared at him as though she thought that he had suddenly gone mad. "My—my name?" she faltered.

"Yes. Your full complete name; what is it?"

"I thought you knew; besides, what does it matter now?" she faltered. "Angelica Susan Brown—only I never use the Susan."

"Were you christened with those names?" he demanded.

Angelica looked from one man to the other; hesitated a moment, and then replied. She faltered out the poor little confession quite as though it were something she was ashamed of; in spite of her terror and surprise, she was blushing.

"No," she said. "I was christened Susan—and I hated it. Mother used to call me 'Angel'; and when I took up the music teaching I made it 'Angelica.' But what does it matter now?"

CHAPTER XV

"FOR THIS WAS LOVE!"

THE thing was so unutterably simple, now that they understood, that it left them dumbfounded at the ease with which the mistake had been made. It was simply a coincidence—a matter of a little bit of girlish vanity. And round this Susan Brown had been built up a plot to rob her of that which she was never to possess. The bricks of all that great edifice that had been so carefully built seemed to be there about their feet as they stood in the hall of the house staring at the girl. It was a matter in which words failed.

Angelica was the first to break the ghastly silence; she broke it with a repetition of that question that had remained unanswered. "But what does it matter now?"

"Matter?" Horace Ventoul was beside himself with rage and humiliation; he made a movement towards her, with both fists raised in the air, as though he would have struck her. Rackham seized one wrist, and forced it to his side, and dragged the man away.

"Matter?" shrieked Ventoul, struggling vainly with the stronger man. "Don't you understand what you've done? You've robbed me right and left; you've put us all into a position that we never ought——"

"That will do!" exclaimed Rackham, giving a sudden jerk to the arm he held. "You'll do no good by that sort of thing. If the matter has to be told at all, and explanations made, we'll do it quietly."

"But what has happened?" asked Angelica, shrinking back against the wall, and looking from one man to the other fearfully. "What does it all mean? What have I done?"

Oliver Rackham opened the door of the drawing-room, and signed to her to go in. Ventoul, with a shrug of his shoulders, marched towards the hall door; a hand on his shoulder turned him about.

"You've got to face it out," said Rackham, with a jerk of his head towards the drawing-room. "I'll carry you in, if you don't go quietly."

Ventoul looked at him with a lowering expression for a moment; then marched into the drawing-room, and flung himself upon a couch. "You can tell her," he said to Rackham. "I can correct you if you drop into any sentimentalities or inaccuracies. Fire away!"

Poor Angelica stood there, glancing from one to the other, absolutely at a loss, of course, to form any conjecture as to what it all meant. Hovering in her mind was a confused jumble of thoughts—about the Streets and their disappearance—and that amazing demand for her baptismal name—and the extraordinary attitude of her lover. And now here was that lover stretched out insolently on a couch—frowning and ugly—and taking not the faintest notice of her, save to throw her an occasional disdainful look.

"Get on with it," said Ventoul, after the silence between the three had seemed to threaten never to end. "What are you waiting for?"

Rackham stiffened, and half made a movement towards him; then looked at the girl helplessly, and waved a hand towards a chair. "Won't you sit down—please?" he murmured.

"No—thank you; I'd rather stand," said Angelica quickly.

"It's an awkward thing to explain, Miss Brown," said Rackham, shifting about from one foot to the other, "but I'll do my best to make it clear and straightforward—so that you can understand. I daresay you remember the first time I ever met you—by the merest chance—at that little dancing academy in Hamlyn Street?"

"Perfectly, Mr. Rackham," said Angelica, with her bright eyes fixed intently upon him.

"I heard your name by chance—and I had heard it before," he went on. "A certain Miss Angelica Susan Brown was entitled to a huge fortune—more than half a million of money—and people were looking for her. When I heard your name, I felt, of course, that you were the young lady that was wanted."

"Why should you have thought that?" she asked, in a whisper.

"Why?" Ventoul half raised himself on the couch, and stared at her with an ugly laugh distorting his lips. "Because of some silly, sentimental talk—something about your always having expected a fortune through your father. That was why; that and the name did it."

"That was only the talk of a child," said Angelica gently—"the silly, sentimental talk, as you call it, between a mother who hoped the best for me and a child who dreamed dreams. But what has that to do with me now?"

"Ventoul and I talked over the matter together," went on Rackham, in a harder tone. "He had heard of the fortune; I had met you. A plan occurred to us to get hold of you"—he made it sound as brutal as he could—"and to try and get hold of part of the fortune as well."

"To get hold of me?" She looked from one to the other; she spoke in a whisper. "I'm afraid I don't yet understand."

"It was thought that if we got to know you—and got your fortune for you—and helped you, and all that sort of thing—we might come in for a share of it," said Rackham. "Can't you understand?"

"I'm trying hard to understand," she said, looking at him fixedly.

"We brought you down here—and Ventoul came down here, just so that he might meet you. The Streets were put in this house, just so that you might be companion to Mrs. Street—and so that Ventoul might meet you easily."

Ventoul twisted about again on the couch, and finally sat up. "And that is why, Miss Susan Brown," he said, "I have come over here day after day, to read to you and to talk to you—and to make love to you. Are you getting any nearer to it now?"

"Because you thought I had more than half a million of money—you wanted to marry me for that," said Angelica unsteadily. "You brought me away from London— just that you might—might get hold of me? Was that it?"

"She's beginning to understand at last," said Ventoul.

"It's all been a blunder from beginning to end," said

Rackham, after another pause, during which it seemed as though the girl's bright eyes burnt through him. "We didn't know that you were not the real Miss Brown for whom everyone was looking; that name you had assumed was the cause of all the mistakes we have made."

"So that, if you could have got hold of the other—the real Angelica Susan Brown—you would have robbed her?" said Angelica quietly.

"Of course we should," exclaimed Ventoul, getting up and moving towards the girl. "It was Street who found it all out; he's laid hands on all the money I gave him to carry on this affair, and has bolted. And now it comes to this; the game is at an end, and this house will be shut up. It's your blunder, and our dear friend Oliver Rackham's blunder, too; I've lost enough over it, and I've done with it."

He was making for the door, but Rackham stood there, blocking the way. Ventoul glanced from one to the other, and at last, with a sudden movement of his hands, said, with a little laugh—"Well, what more is there to be said?"

Angelica spoke directly to Rackham. "You haven't told me," she said, "why you did this thing."

"He's told you all that's necessary; it was that absurd name that was the cause of all the trouble," said Ventoul shortly.

"You haven't told me," said Angelica again, ignoring Ventoul, "why you did this thing."

"I've told you all I can," answered Rackham, in a low voice.

"You found me in London—and I think you found me

happy, and a little in love with life," she said, with an ominous quiver in her voice. "God help me!—I had asked nothing of anyone of any kind, except just to be allowed to live, and work hard, and get a little fun out of things. I trusted you; I told you more about myself than I had ever told anyone before. I liked you—and I believed in you. What had I ever done to you that you should plot against me as you have done?"

As Rackham stood silent Horace Ventoul blundered in again. "Can't you understand that the whole thing was a mistake?" he asked roughly.

She set him aside with a little movement of her hand. "Be quiet, please," she said; "I'm not speaking to you. I don't yet understand what it all means—but I believe Mr. Rackham will tell me. No one could invent such a thing as this against one helpless girl; it's impossible."

"She still believes in you, Noll," said Ventoul, with a sneer.

"I believed in *you*—until to-day," she flashed out at him.

"I never thought about it," said Rackham to her; "it never seemed to me to matter—at first. You were just somebody coming into a great fortune—and I hadn't a penny in the world——"

"So you were to dip into my fortune, too?" she exclaimed quickly. "You were not merely helping Mr. Ventoul because he had asked you to?"

Ventoul answered for him. "Oh—Noll was in it all right," he said. "Noll wanted money—came to me when he was starving, and begged me to help him—didn't you, Noll?"

"It doesn't matter much what you say," said Rackham bitterly.

"I can't yet quite understand it all," said Angelica, after another long pause. "That you"—she looked at Ventoul —"you could come out of your world, where you were famous—and could stoop to do this thing. That you, who could write such things as you have written, could have done such a thing as this. I shall never believe in anybody again as long as I live."

"Stop a bit," said Ventoul, with a covert smile at Rackham; "there's something I should like to explain. You've always talked a lot of nonsense about the beautiful things in my book—and the wonderful phrases I have written. Perhaps you'll get a better grasp of the whole thing from beginning to end if I tell you I never wrote a line of it."

"You—never—wrote—it?" she breathed. "Oh—won't one of you tell me something that is truth; I have heard nothing at all that I can grasp yet."

"My dear girl—our brilliant genius is Oliver Rackham," said Ventoul, with a wave of his hand towards the other man. "He was the man who wrote the book you admire so much; I simply put my name to it."

"But why?" asked Angelica.

"Poor old Noll was not in a position to publish the thing himself—were you, Noll?" asked Ventoul, with a grin. "Why don't you tell the lady where you were, and how it all happened. Speak out, Noll!"

Rackham looked all about him for a moment, as though seeking some chance of escape; he spoke at last like a man in a dream. "I told you that I had lost all I had, and that I wasn't worth a penny; that was why I first went into this affair," he said at last. "When I met you first I had just come out of prison."

She did not answer; she was looking at him steadily, and waiting for what else he had to say.

"It was while I was in prison that he got hold of my book," said Rackham, with a jerk of his head towards Ventoul, "and had it published. He put his own name to it—and I couldn't do anything."

"In prison!" she breathed, never for a moment taking her eyes from him.

"So that you see, my dear Miss Brown," said Ventoul, "old Noll has been helping all the time. He wrote the book; and it was the book that first captured your fancy. Then, when it came to the love letters——"

"You didn't do that?" she cried swiftly to Rackham.

"Oh—didn't he, though!" cried Ventoul. "He can reel that sort of thing off by the yard when he wants to."

"Yes—I wrote that letter," said Rackham hoarsely.

She flamed out at them both then as she had not done before. "And you could lie and cheat even in that!" she cried. "You could write to me like that, and make me believe that he"—she flung out an arm towards Ventoul—"that he had written it! You could let me talk about it—and let me write a reply to it—saying what was in my heart! You could tear the soul out of me—just to dip your hands into money that you thought belonged to me!"

Gazing straight at Rackham, she pulled out from her pocket that precious letter, and suddenly tore it into fragments, and flung them at him; and then as suddenly subsided on to a seat and burst into tears. Ventoul, with a shrug of the shoulders, moved towards the door.

"Well—now you know all about it," he said. "I did my best—and if it had turned out all right I should undoubtedly have married you. No one can say I've been to blame over the matter; I've just been misled, as everyone else has been. The game's up, and I, for my part, am going back to London, to see if I can get hold of that fellow Street and get some of my money back."

He stopped for a moment, with his hand on the door, as though wondering if there was anything he had left unsaid; then, with a shrug of the shoulders, pulled open the door, and went out, slamming it after him. Angelica sat in the same attitude, sobbing unrestrainedly.

After a moment or two Rackham moved uneasily, and then went across to where she sat. "If I might say a word——" he began.

She sprang up quickly, and faced him. "What can you have to say to me?" she asked, with a little sob in her throat. "It's all over—all done with, Mr. Rackham."

"What will you do?" he asked gently.

"I shall go back to London—and I shall begin all over again," she said, in a strangled voice. "What does it matter?"

"I don't suppose that after to-day I shall ever see you again," he said slowly. "But I can't let you go without saying one thing; I think I should cut my throat if I felt I had let you go without telling you."

The deadly earnestness of the man arrested her; she stood still, looking at him. "What is it?" she asked.

"In the old, mad days, before ever I met you, I sank as

low as a man could sink—I robbed and cheated; I was shut away like a wild beast from my fellow men," he said. "Before God—you were the first clean wholesome thing I'd ever met—and you came into my life as something wonderful."

"Why couldn't you have let me alone?" she whispered, with a little catch in her voice.

"I didn't understand then," he said. "When I first heard of you, before ever I thought I should meet you—or rather when first I heard of the other girl to whom the fortune belonged—I was shabby and forlorn; I was sleeping in the streets. I was ready to prey on anyone that had money; and you didn't matter then. It was only afterwards that I found out what was in my heart."

"Something so great and fine," she answered him bitterly, "that you could write that letter to me, at the bidding of another man. Perhaps he paid you to do it?"

"Yes—he paid me to do it," Rackham answered. "And yet, when I wrote it, I wrote what was in my heart; I wrote what I knew was true. I didn't think of him; all that I set down there I meant—every word of it."

"I can't believe it—I won't believe it," she answered.

"It's true," he said earnestly.

"And yet you discussed it with him—perhaps arranged what you should say—with him," she said angrily.

"He never saw the letter—he never had your reply," answered Rackham. "Mine to you was something wrung out of my heart; it was only meant for you. And yours was something so beautiful that I couldn't have let anyone else see it."

"Don't!" she whispered, hiding her face in her hands.

"It's all over now—and you know all about me," he went on. "But that morning, when you stood in the sunlight by the fountain, and asked me if anyone had ever loved me in all my life, and looked into my eyes, I could have taken you in my arms, and told you what I tell you now—when it's too late. I could have told you that I loved you as I had never loved anyone before."

"It isn't true," she said sadly.

"It is so true that the memory of you, when presently I go out of your life, will be with me as the one sweet and pleasant thing that has ever touched me. I have done you a great wrong; I would lay down my wasted life to-day if I could atone for that, or if I could put you back again in the little room under the stars, and see you living the old life. I never meant to harm you; I never thought about it until it was all too late. Won't you believe that?"

Angelica, between her strangled sobs, murmured an answer to him. "No—I can't believe it," she said.

He went out of the room then, and left her. After a time, when her sobs had died down, and she had dried her eyes, she went upstairs to her room. Everything seemed changed; there was a dreadful, deadly silence about the place that seemed to speak of the ruin of it. Even the servants, suspecting that something was wrong, crept about like ghosts, and spoke in whispers. Angelica, kneeling beside her small trunk, began to pack her possessions. A knock at the door startled her, she kept her face well over her trunk as she called out brightly to whoever it was that had knocked to come in.

The door was opened, and the maid-servant who had

first made the discovery of the flight of the Streets came in. She closed the door, and spoke in a mysterious whisper.

"If you please, miss, I just looked in to see if there was anythink I could do—or anythink you'd like to say to me."

"I don't think there's anything you can do—thank you," said Angelica quickly. "I'm going away, you know; I'm going to London."

"Are you indeed, miss?" said the girl. "We was all of us upset at the idea of master and mistress goin' off like that—an' I said to cook——"

"Will you please arrange for somebody to get the fly for me; I've got to go to the station," broke in Angelica hastily. "I don't know what time the train goes, but I expect the flyman will know. And I'm very sorry to be going away from you all, Jane—because we've been very comfortable here—haven't we?"

"There's always bin a bit of a mystery about it to me," answered the girl. "An' now to be suddenly given your wages, and told to be off, without so much as givin' you time to turn round . . . well—as I says to cook—I don't 'alf like it. Nothing 'appened to the master or mistress, I suppose, miss?"

"Good gracious—no," answered Angelica, with a laugh, and with her head buried in the box. "They've had to go to London suddenly; they've decided to give up the house. Now, please run away, and see about the fly for me, or I shan't get to London at all."

So it came about that Angelica, having packed her trunk, packed up the canary with his brown-paper cover round the cage—catching her breath swiftly as she remembered with what high hopes she had packed him up before —and sat down to wait until the fly should arrive. When, in due course, it rolled up to the door, and the servants had carried out her trunk, she stood with the bird-cage in her hand for a moment, waiting, slim and erect, to get in. And just then Horace Ventoul sauntered round a corner of the house, and came up to the door. The servants had retired, and, save for the flyman holding the door of his vehicle, they were alone.

"Well—you haven't lost much time, Angelica," said Ventoul. "I thought we might have some trouble in getting rid of you. Glad to see you're sensible."

Angelica handed the bird-cage to the driver, who deposited it carefully inside. Then she stood quietly buttoning her gloves, and smoothing out the creases in quite the old way; she said not a word.

"I don't bear you any ill-will," said Ventoul, in a low voice, "and if at any time you should care to look me up I'll be glad to see you. Mitre Chambers, Westminster, will always find me."

Angelica got the last button fastened, and the last crease smoothed out; she raised her head and looked at the driver. "I want you to drive me to the station, and see that I don't miss my train," she said.

"I suppose you won't object to saying 'good-bye' to a friend?" suggested Ventoul, holding out a hand a little doubtfully.

Angelica got into the vehicle, and the man who was holding the door, after a moment's hesitation, closed it, and climbed to his box. People's private difficulties were nothing whatever to do with him; he touched the horse with the whip, and drove away, leaving Horace Ventoul staring after the vehicle.

Ventoul went back into the house. He had paid the wondering servants (who could not in the least understand how the question of their wages came to be a matter with which he had to deal), and he now turned sulkily into the dining-room; he was simply killing time until he could get the house locked up, and so rid himself of his responsibility in regard to it. And in the dining-room was Oliver Rackham.

"Well, this is a pretty good ending to it all—isn't it?" said Ventoul savagely. "I wish I could have hurt that little baggage a bit more; I don't think she's got any feelings. She was as cool and calm when she went away as though nothing at all had happened; and wouldn't even speak to me. I wonder how she'll get on in London."

"God knows!" whispered Rackham. "One thing is certain: she won't whine about it, and she won't ask a soul for help. And now"—he heaved a sigh, and looked in an uncertain way about the room—"now I think I'll go."

"And what are you going to do?" demanded Ventoul. "What's your next move?"

"I don't know," said Rackham. "I must get to London; I must make a start at something, I suppose. I'm always making a start at something, if it comes to that."

"Have you got any money?" asked Ventoul, rattling his own in his pocket with the air of a man who at least is superior in that respect.

Rackham shook his head. "A shilling or two," he said, with a strange little laugh. "I'm used to that. I shall walk."

Ventoul burst into a roar of laughter. "Walk?" he cried. "I should like to see you doing it."

Rackham had moved across to the sideboard, and was pouring out some spirits. He paused in the act of doing so to look over his shoulder at the other man.

"Don't you laugh at me," he said. "I'm in no mood to be laughed at, I can assure you. If anyone laughs at me it shall be myself; do you understand that?"

Carrying his glass in his hand he came across the room, and looked at Ventoul with a strange light in his eyes. "This is the last time I drink in your company, my dear Horace," he said; "let that be a consolation to you. It was kind and thoughtful of you to remember to tell her what I was, and what my record had been; for that I am grateful. And now I should like, as it is for the last time, and as the whole mad business is utterly hopeless, and as neither of us will ever see her again—I should like to tell you something else."

He drained his glass, and suddenly flung it from him with a crash into the fireplace; and spoke with a sudden fire of passion that astonished Ventoul.

"You had every weapon at your command—and you spent your money in all directions—and you bought people —myself included—to lie to her and cheat her. And she never loved you for a moment—not for a moment."

"She would have done; she'd have married me," said Ventoul sulkily.

"She never loved you," cried Rackham in triumph.

"She loved me—just as I loved her; she loved this worthless dog you call jail-bird; and she's gone away with that in her heart." There was a catch in his voice, and he turned away his head. "That's something to remember, even though I am never to see her again."

He strode out of the room, and took up his hat and stick; and so went out of the house. Ventoul, glancing through the window, saw him going away at a great rate through the grounds towards the high road which should take him to London.

And Angelica, arriving in that London towards which Oliver Rackham was tending, drove in some trepidation to that little street wherein, not so long before, she had had a lodging near to the stars. She rang the bell; and when the door opened there was the little plump landlady, looking just the same as ever, and with an amazed smile of welcome on her face.

"I suppose," said Angelica, trembling, "I suppose it isn't possible for me to have my old room—is it?"

"Well, of all the wonderful things!" exclaimed the landlady, holding up her hands, and appealing to the cabman and the cab and anything else within hearing to observe this miracle. "If it didn't 'appen on'y yesterday that the lodger that took it (an' not at all the sort of person I care for, my dear) didn't up an' say she was goin' elsewhere, an' leave it on my 'ands, so to speak. Come in, my dear; it's absolutely waitin' for you."

Angelica's luggage was carried up the stairs, and Angelica followed with the canary. A little wearily she took off his brown-paper wrapper, and hung him up on his old nail in the window. She got rid of the garrulous landlady at last, and stood looking round the old room for quite a long time in silence.

Then suddenly she flung herself full length on the little bed, and hid her face in the pillow, and sobbed as though her heart would break.

CHAPTER XVI

JOSHUA FLATTERY READS THE STARS

NEARLY twelve months had gone by—with a hard and bitter winter sandwiched in between the summer that was past and the summer that had now fairly begun. And Joshua Flattery, glad to find the summer here again, and yet with grateful memories of a winter that had meant for him almost continual employment (for the winter was ever Joshua's best time), came out one night to take the air.

Life had gone on for Joshua Flattery in the old jog-trot fashion, with nothing exciting about it. Joshua resented that a little, because the little man was incurably romantic. He had never ceased to think of those wonderful happenings that had begun at the statue erected to a certain great engineer, and had ended with his running away secretly from the house at Pentney Hill, with two half sovereigns pressed closely together, in accordance with directions, in his pocket.

He thought of it now as he walked along the Embankment, unconsciously enjoying the beauty of the night. He would have been glad to call it all back again—the tall stranger on the stone seat—and all the other strange figures that had grouped themselves about him. Joshua sighed at the thought that it was all over.

And, just as he sighed, came again to the statue. He had a look at it, as at a familiar friend; then glanced mechanically at someone sitting on the stone seat, with his hat drawn forward over his eyes. Joshua Flattery stopped, with his heart beating a little more quickly; and yet it surely could not be possible——

"I'll ask him the time," thought Joshua; and took a step forward. The man raised his head, and thrust back his hat, and stared at Flattery; then with an exclamation got to his feet. It was Oliver Rackham. All in a moment Joshua Flattery forgot himself; and in the most unaccountable way found himself shaking hands with great heartiness with Rackham. And Rackham was laughing.

"What—you still haunt this place—do you?" said Rackham.

"First time I've bin 'ere, sir, I give you my word, since last time we met, and you persuaded me to go off with you to that place down in the country, sir. Lor'—what a time we did 'ave there—didn't we?"

"Wonderful!" said Rackham slowly. "I come here sometimes, because it reminds me of things," he went on, seating himself again, and touching the seat beside him to indicate that Joshua should sit down. "And it does a man good sometimes to be reminded of things, Joshua."

"It does that, sir," said the little man, with an emphatic nod. "And 'ow's the world been usin' you, sir, if one may make so bold as just to ask? Not come down to nothing at all again, sir, I 'ope?"

"I've come down to nothing at all over and over again," answered Rackham; and Joshua, glancing at him, saw that this was a thinner, more gaunt Rackham than he had known, with a little touch of premature grey at his temples.

"'Ave you, indeed, sir?" asked the waiter, with much sympathy.

"It's a funny thing, Joshua," went on Rackham, after a pause, "but I've come out of it all—and I'm getting on." He laughed with the glee of a schoolboy, and rubbed his hands together, and laughed again. "Isn't that funny?"

"Not a bit, sir," said Joshua. "I said once that anythin' might 'appen to a gentleman like you; you was up one day, an' you was down the next; yet always comin' out on top. Nothink you ever did would surprise me."

"After you ran away from me, Joshua—and I've forgiven you for that long ago, my friend, because I know why you did it"—he dropped a hand on Joshua's knee for a moment—"I had to begin the world all over again. Somebody had taken hold of me, without knowing it, and had given me a shake. I found I couldn't go back to what I had been before. And that was funny—wasn't it?"

"'Ow did you begin, sir, if I might make so bold?" asked Joshua softly.

"I began by starving—which is always the best way; when you're lean and hungry you've got time to think, and think hard. I came down again, Joshua, to sleeping in the streets; but I didn't mind that, because each day I was working. I went back to a trade I had dabbled in before; I started writing."

Joshua Flattery's eyes were round with admiration. "Did you indeed, sir? Now, fancy takin' to anythin' like that, sir, when there was so much more you could 'ave earned money at. But, there—I suppose you could do anythink almost, sir."

"Many and many a time I almost turned back—almost went again down the easy road of lying, cheating, shiftlessness. And always something pulled up at the right moment."

There was silence for a long time; Joshua knew that this was not a moment for interruption on his part. When at last Rackham spoke it was almost as if to himself.

"I knew that somewhere in the world was someone that loved me—and had believed in me. It was to be my fate never to see her—never even to touch her hand; but I knew that she loved me. I wasn't working just so that I might some day or other crawl to her, and say that I had done this, and done that, and been a good boy; I wasn't striving after that at all. It was because I knew she loved me that I simply had to do something to make myself understand that she loved a man—and not the thing that I had been. That was funny again, Joshua," he went on, looking round, "because she won't ever know it—won't ever know what she's done."

Joshua sighed. "Seems a pity—don't it, sir?" he said. "An' so this writin' business 'as prospered—eh?"

"It will prosper some day," said Rackham. "At the present moment it keeps me in food, and keeps a roof, such as it is, over my head. But I was a long time getting to a roof, Joshua, I can assure you. I used to write in all sorts of places—free libraries, and coffee-houses, and all manner of places. And when at last I did get a room, it was all right; I was a made man. You must come and see me, Joshua; I shall be glad to see a friendly face again. Don't be too proud to come and see me; I don't suppose I make as much money as you do yet, little waiter-man. But I live in hope."

Joshua Flattery laughed. "Ah—you always would 'ave your joke, sir," he said, shaking his head. "Do you remember the last time as ever we sat 'ere, sir? Do you remember w'en you wanted me to go down into the country, an' I asked you if there was any money in it? 'Money in it!' says you—'there's 'alf a million!' you says."

Oliver Rackham stiffened slowly in his seat; nodded slowly. "I remember," he said. "I wish I could forget."

Josehua Flattery, feeling that he had blundered, sat very still for a time. At last he said, in a voice scarcely above a whisper, "She don't ever come to them 'ops now, sir. I 'aven't set eyes on 'er since that mornin' in the country w'en she—w'en she said good-bye to me, sir."

"You saw her then?" asked Rackham. "But, of course, I remember she told me that she had seen you."

"You an' me, sir, 'ave always been what I might call fair an' open with each other, sir," said Joshua hesitatingly, after a little pause. "I think I ought to tell you, sir, that that mornin' she asked me 'ow much money I'd got—to carry me on my way. An' I told 'er that you'd given me 'alf a sovereign the day before—makin' a joke of it like, sir."

"Well?"

"And she gave me another one, sir—an' w'en I asked 'er why I should take it—not 'alf likin' to, you see, sir—she said somethin' about I was to press it close to the one you'd given me—because—because she loved you a little, sir—same as I did."

Rackham got up quickly, and moved away a pace or two; then came back again. "Why did you tell me that?" he asked, almost harshly; and then added, "There—there—it doesn't matter. You'll come and see me, Joshua—won't you?"

"I should be proud an' 'appy, sir," said the little waiter. "It'll be somethink else to think about, sir. If I go on like this 'ere, I shall be gettin' above me station—shan't I?"

He laughed heartily at that great jest, and repeated it, with much chuckling. The two men parted, after Rackham had given Joshua Flattery a card on which he had scrawled the address; and Joshua went home, highly pleased and excited at his interview.

It happened two or three evenings later that Joshua Flattery, having no professional engagement, stopped at the address that had been given him, and with a beating heart knocked at the door, and having been directed to the very top of the house, climbed the stairs with hesitating steps, and with a strong inclination to turn round and run away again. He came, however, to a door, and, very literally shaking his head at the great liberty he was taking, knocked upon it softly. A voice he knew roared to him from within the room to "Come in"—and Joshua turned the handle, and, hat in hand, walked in.

Oliver Rackham was seated at a table, writing as if for dear life. He glanced up as Joshua entered, and frowned a little—waved an impatient hand as a signal to the little man to sit down and be quiet. Joshua slid into the chair, and murmured an apology.

"Of course, if I'm intruding, sir——"

"Be quiet! Be quiet!" exclaimed Rackham fiercely. "I'll talk to you in a minute."

More than ever convinced that he should never have come at all, the little man sat dejectedly dangling his hat, and scarcely daring to breathe. It had, of course, been quite wrong of him to take advantage of an invitation so casually given. It was all very well to meet a gentleman in public, as it were, on the Embankment, where one might be supposed to meet anybody; but to intrude upon his privacy like this was abominable. If he had had the courage, Joshua would have opened the door and made a bolt for it; indeed, more than once he looked furtively at the handle of the door.

The furious writing was finished at last, and an envelope was seized, and an address written upon it. In the very act of pinning the sheets together and folding them up, Rackham barked out—"What's the time?"

Tremblingly Joshua Flattery drew out a plain old silver watch, and consulted it. "Five minutes to eight, sir," he said.

"Are you sure?" demanded Rackham.

"It's never gone wrong yet, sir," said Joshua in reply, a little reproachfully.

"I'm just in time," exclaimed Rackham, stamping the letter almost with violence. "Wait here till I come back."

He raced out of the room, without even taking a hat; and Joshua, more unhappy than ever, sat perfectly still on his chair, making great resolves never again to intrude on gentlemen in this fashion. In a minute or two Rackham came back, whistling, and closed the door, and turned with a smiling face to the other man.

"I caught the post," he said. "That means five bob,

little waiterman," he went on whimsically, "and in these days of stress and strife five bob is a fortune."

"You always would have your joke, sir," murmured Joshua feebly. "And I'm sure I wouldn't 'ave come in for the world if I'd known."

"Jolly glad to see you," said Rackham. "Don't sit on that devilish uncomfortable chair—and do put your hat down. I never liked that hat; it doesn't suit you. I think you'll like to know, Joshua," he went on in another tone, "that I'm prospering. I'm only doing it by shillings —but it's all right. I've been able to get tobacco—and that's a lot—isn't it?"

"And all of it done just by writin'!" exclaimed Joshua, with uplifted hands. "Much as ever I can do to make out my bills so that anybody understands 'em; an' even then you'll get gents impatient—an' pointin' to somethink I can 'ardly read myself, an' askin' what it is. Sure you're not offended, sir, at me takin' the liberty——"

"Haven't I told you that I'm very glad to see you?" said Rackham. "With the exception of a landlady who doesn't like me because I don't pay much, I scarcely see a soul from one week's end to the other. Besides, you were always such a queer nice little fellow that I like you. Do you smoke?"

"Never acquired the 'abit, sir—not bein' very strong in the stummick line," said Joshua.

Very humbly and very gratefully, after a time, Joshua took his departure—only putting on his hat when he was actually outside in the street. "Not to be done again," he said firmly to himself. "You always 'ave remembered your station, Josh, my lad; don't forget it again. 'E's a gent—an' you're a waiter; an' if it did 'appen at one time that 'e talked poetry to you, an' made 'imself affable, an' even showed you a bit of life—don't take advantage of it!"

Keeping that self-imposed advice well in mind, Joshua Flattery went there no more. He had his duties to perform; he had his memories for such leisure as he got. He could always boast to himself, as he frequently did in private, that he knew this great man, who actually wrote and was paid for doing it—the man who had carried him through surprising and astonishing adventures—the man who had, in fact, caused him to live at all, in the romantic sense of the word.

He had drifted back to that forlorn Academy of Dancing in Hamlyn Street, Tottenham Court Road. Always he looked a little wistfully for that slim, erect figure; yet he never saw her. Until one night, when the dancing was over, and the last of the dancers had drifted away, Joshua Flattery, coming out with his brown-paper parcel under his arm, felt a touch upon that arm, and turning, stared into a face he knew.

It was Angelica. She smiled at him a little wistfully; he noticed, in the first quick glance at her, that it was the same Angelica he had known at the first—with the neat but shabby frock, and the thin shoes, and the gloves without a crease in them. The little man took off his bowler-hat, and put it on again—and fairly gasped out his welcome to her.

"Well, miss—if this don't beat all!" he said. "To 'ave you comin' back to us like this—just ready to step in an' 'ave a friendly darnce——"

"I didn't come to dance," said Angelica quickly. "I

just waited, because I thought you might be here—and I felt I should be glad just to speak to you again. We were good friends once, Flattery—weren't we?"

"You're good enough to say so, miss," said Joshua. "An' 'ow 'ave things been goin' with you, miss, if I might make so bold?"

"Shall we walk on?" asked Angelica. "I've got a little time to spare."

Vainly endeavoring to conceal his brown-paper parcel, Joshua walked on, with the girl beside him. As they came to the broader street, she slipped her hand within his arm, and answered his question.

"I've been getting on very well, thank you," she said.

She did not tell him of all that she had gone through—of the blank hopelessness of having to begin all over again where she had left off. Of heart-breaking snubs, and much weary tramping of streets—and a cheerless winter, wherein she had had to fight every step of that hard way that means grinding poverty; she did not tell him anything of that. Instead, she led him to talk about himself and what he was doing. And then, last of all, asked that question that had been in her mind all the time—that question the demand for an answer to which had brought her to the little dancing-hall that night—and on other nights before, if Joshua had but known it.

"I suppose you haven't seen anything of any of our friends from Pentney Hill?" she asked, in as careless a tone as she could assume.

Joshua Flattery was growing wise. Joshua had blundered so often in his life, and especially in his relations with these wonderful people who had opened the world to him, as it were, that he was determined not to blunder again, if he could avoid it. He remembered that Oliver Rackham had said that never again could he see the woman who had loved him; never again could he even touch her hand. There must have been something about the little waiter that was in reality a fine, true sympathy for such a business as this. For now he lied to the girl with a calm face, while his thoughts were busy with the problem before him.

"Never set eyes on one of 'em, miss," he said. "I've 'ad so many things to attend to, one way an' another, that I 'aven't 'ad time. A good time we 'ad down there, miss —didn't we?"

"Yes," said Angelica. And then, after a pause, "You ran away from Mr. Rackham—didn't you?"

"I did, miss—an' I think I was a bit sorry afterwards," said Joshua, looking at her covertly. "'E was good to me, was Mr. Rackham; though 'e would 'ave 'is joke, miss. Wonder what's become of 'im?"

"I wonder?" said Angelica softly.

The poor bewildered Joshua Flattery was wondering what he should do. If he lost her now he might never see her again; if he told her anything about Oliver Rackham, she might spoil everything by going to see that gentleman; and Rackham had suggested, unless Joshua's reasoning was entirely at fault, that he could never see this girl again. Joshua walked along with his head in a whirl, scarcely knowing what he did or said.

"Are you goin' 'ome, miss?" he asked at last a little helplessly.

"Not yet," said Angelica. "I've been sitting in stuffy

rooms all day; I felt I wanted air. I'll walk a little way with you, if I may."

It is a most unaccountable thing; but at that very moment Joshua Flattery had an inspiration that almost made him drop his brown-paper parcel. He clutched it, and said quite briskly, "Why—I should be proud, miss. A little walk won't do me no 'arm, miss."

Joshua Flattery, talking of everything and anything, went in one set direction. Angelica, glad to listen to him, and to hear talk of those days that seemed so far away, did not notice in what direction they were going; until presently, coming down a quiet street, they found themselves on the Embankment.

"Favorite walk of mine, miss," said Joshua. "I like to come 'ere sometimes when the day's work is over—or the night's work, as it is with me, miss—an' I feel calm an' cool—an' think of things."

"What things do you think about?" asked Angelica gently.

"I think about the things that 'ave 'appened to me, one time an' another, miss," said Joshua. "Why—it was just about here, miss, that I first met Mr. Rackham."

That tighter hold upon his arm told Joshua that he was right; he went on more surely with his task. "You met him here?" she asked wonderingly.

"Broke to the world, miss," murmured the old waiter. "But I says to 'im then—I says—'You're the sort o' gent that might do anything,' I says. 'You've got it in you,' I says, 'an' some day,' I says, or words to that effect—'some day you'll do it. You've 'ad your downs, an' you've 'ad your ups,' I says to Mr. Rackham—'an' you might do anythink,' I says.

"You were very fond of him, Flattery," said Angelica.

"I was very fond of 'im, miss," replied Joshua.

They were coming near to that corner where the statue stood. Was that a figure lounging on the seat, or was it only Flattery's imagination? He walked slowly past with the girl, giving a quick backward glance as he did so. God be praised!—it was Rackham.

"And now," said Joshua, after they had walked a little way, and had turned to come back, "what about yourself, miss?"

"About me?" asked Angelica, bewildered.

"Yes, miss—about you," said the old man. "If I can read them stars shinin' up there, miss, it ain't all goin' to be loneliness an' 'ard work for you all the rest of your life. The stars tell me something different to that, miss."

"Then the stars don't know their business," said Angelica quietly. "It's always to be hard work and loneliness—except when I meet an old friend like you to-night."

They had got to the statue again. And now Joshua Flattery, with an adroit movement, as though he would bid the girl good night, turned so that Rackham should see him and should see the girl also. Rackham got quickly to his feet, and took a step towards them; and Angelica saw him. While the two faced each other, the little waiter stepped quickly aside, and walked away.

"Noll!" she faltered. (After all, it was the name that had been in her mind through all the dreary months; she said it quite naturally now.)

"Where have you come from?" he asked.

"Joshua Flattery brought me," she whispered. "I didn't mean to come and find you; I didn't mean to see you again." And then, in a sudden compassion, as she moved nearer to him, "Why—how thin you are!".

"I have been down into the depths," he answered, "and I have had to fight my way back again. But I have learned things down in the depths—and I have tried to be something a little nearer to what you would have me be. And what of yourself?"

She laughed. She had not laughed for a long time as she laughed then; it was like music. "Oh—I'm back in the old life again," she answered. "It seems as if I had never left it. But how are you living?"

"I'm working," he said slowly. "I've been working rather hard—writing."

"Oh—I'm glad," she answered. And then suddenly, in the old, impulsive way, "And it's good—splendid to see you again. I've wanted to see you—wanted to tell you that I never meant what I said on that last day—you remember?"

"I remember it all," he said. "But it will be better for us both to forget."

"It won't be better," she whispered. "Indeed—I do believe what you said to me—I do believe what you wrote to me. In my heart I've always believed it."

"It's good of you to say that," he told her. "I shall carry it with me as a blessed memory—in fact, I have carried it with me as a blessed memory—because I believed it all the time. I couldn't have done anything if I hadn't believed it, dear."

She crept close to him, and looked into his eyes. "I asked you once if any woman had ever loved you," she whispered. "Can you answer that now?"

"I've been a thief and a rogue; I've been in prison," he said brokenly.

"And have come out of it all—to love me," she whispered.

Joshua Flattery, coming back discreetly, and looking past the statue at the moment, saw them in each other's arms. There was no one about, for it was very late, and only the stars were blinking overhead. They did not see him; he crept away on tip-toe.

THE END

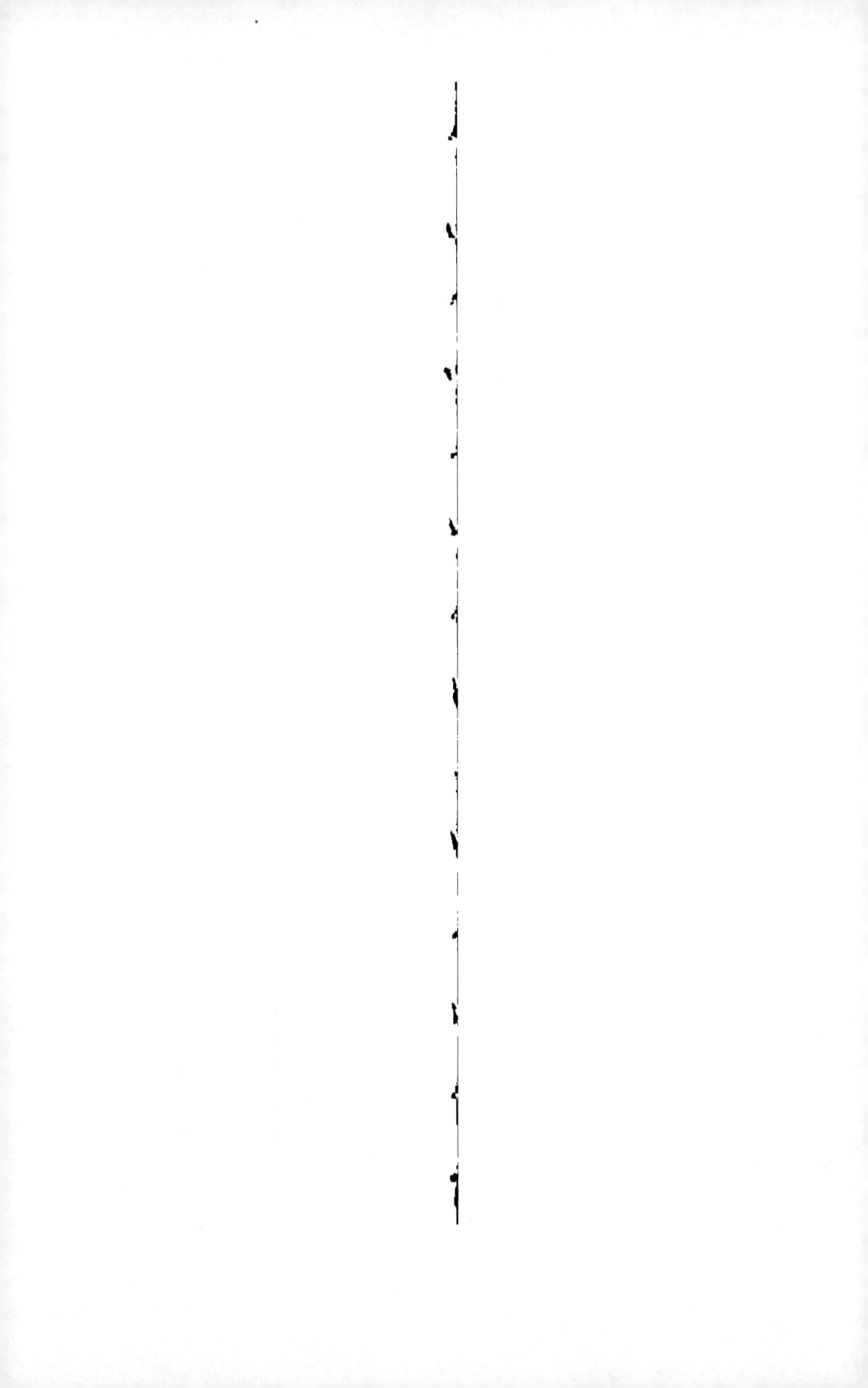

Milton Keynes UK
Ingram Content Group UK Ltd.
UKHW021944121124
451129UK00007B/205